Pussy Transmission

WOL-VRIEY

Burning Bulb
PUBLISHING

Other Books By Wol-vriey:

The Bizarro Story of I

Meat Suitcase

Chainsaw Cop Corpse

Vegan Zombie Apocalypse

Boston Posh (Bud Malone #1)

Vegan Vampire Vaginas

Vagina Mundi

Melanie Nemesis Catchpole

Bizarro 101: A Basic Primer

Boston Corpse (Bud Malone #2)

Dr. Orgasm

Boston Lust (Bud Malone #3)

Novellas and Short Stories By Wol-vriey

Big Trouble in Little Ass
A novella featured in
Westward Hoes

Forever Ago Sunshine
A short story featured in
The Big Book of Bizarro

Pussy Transmission

WOL-VRIEY

Pussy Transmission
By **Wol-vriey**

Burning Bulb Publishing
P.O. Box 4721
Bridgeport, WV 26330-4721
United States of America
www.BurningBulbPublishing.com

Cover illustrated by Gary Lee Vincent with the following licensed image from Shutterstock.com: 50902708 © Paintings.
Author Photo: Lolade Akinsowon © 2014.

First Edition.

Paperback Edition ISBN: 978-0692627488

Printed in the United States of America

PROLOGUE: THE ODD GALLERY

Jake

Zanesville, Ohio

The room was well-lit. It was long and wide, with arched shuttered windows running along its length, and two skylights—clearly designed to show off its treasures to best effect in daylight. Now, at two in the morning, its lighting was artificial, from fluorescent sconces recessed in its walls.

The room contained objects from long ago, most of them art. There were ranks of sculptures on pedestals, several framed paintings, and some musical equipment, including two theremins. There were also stacks of old VHS tapes lovingly wrapped against time's ravages.

The room's contents—worthless to most people—were priceless to collectors with a fancy for the arcane obscure.

Jake Neville, treasure hunter/art thief, was here at the request of one such individual.

After entering the room through a window, Jake—blonde and stocky, his handsome face hidden behind a ski mask—walked the aisle between its arrayed objects, searching the room's paintings for one in particular.

A portrait of Mary Sherman. No one either exceptional or spectacular, Ms. Sherman's sole claim to fame was that hers was reputedly the last portrait the artist who owned this house had ever done. Her painting marked the artist's exit from public life.

In a still unsolved mystery, Mary had vanished at the time of her portrait's completion, and had never been seen since. Neither had her likeness. The finished painting was never displayed in public.

Now, twenty years later, the very rich Jose Estrada had hired Jake and his girlfriend Raven (who was currently back in their motel, in bed with the flu) to steal the painting of Mary Sherman for him.

"Sentimental value," he'd told the pair.

Jake smiled now. *Sentimental value to you, old man; a hundred grand to me and my baby.*

Pausing a moment, he retrieved Mary Sherman's photo from a shirt pocket and studied it again. She was an okay-looking late-teen brunette with wild eyes like a party freak or rock groupie.

Jake put the picture away again. Mary's image refreshed in his mind, he resumed searching the room, considering the displayed objects with an expert eye.

For easy viewing above the sculptures, tapes, and obscure electronic equipment, the paintings in the room were all hung between the windows. Jake examined them quickly.

Several paintings were Warhol-style pop-art, like 'Pussy,' the one of a naked redhead holding a pink kitten in her crotch amidst swirls of psychedelic green, blue, and orange. There was another of a huge similarly pink cat seated atop a green, yellow, and red train, with the golden letters 'PT' emblazoned across the background.

Other oilwork was Daliesque. 'Ultrabitch 2000,' for instance, depicted a bald and goat-horned woman with leopard forelegs for arms. Her forelimbs were folded over her large lactating breasts (from which milk ran down her belly) and clasped a little headless man in their paws. Another painting depicted a nude man covered all over with fingers. Two life-size portraits were of fat women with slices missing from their bodies so the sky (which had solemn faces in its clouds) could be seen behind them.

Weird as hell, Jake thought with some unease. *It doesn't look like this lady painted anything normal in her life.*

Then he noticed a painting of Princess Diana, exquisitely done in shades of yellow, brown, and black. "Finally something *normal*," he muttered. Wondering at the portrait's value (if it was worth stealing), Jake walked up close to the wall to study it, then instantly reeled back in disgust and disbelief. *What? She painted the Princess of Wales's portrait with excrement? How inappropriate can you get?*

Walking forward, he noticed another 'poop portrait,' this one of Chairman Mao Zedong. *Okay, this lady has no political leanings, or maybe she just has beef with authority figures.*

He considered. *And . . . this clearly isn't her main gallery. Mary's portrait isn't in here. So where is it?*

He paused before a sculpture on a wooden pedestal. A young woman in a skirt suit. Two feet high, its detail was so perfect that she looked shrunken rather than carved and hand-painted. He stared at the sculpture for a long time, trying to work out what the oddity was about it—why it fit in here. He finally realized that both the woman's legs were actually fingers, her knees knuckles.

A cold breeze lifted some curtains and blew through the room. Jake shivered from both the breeze and a sudden, deeper fear. He touched the gun in his pocket, seeking reassurance in the weapon's cold verity.

Running disturbed fingers through his hair, he studied the carving. The depicted woman looked surprised, like she'd been startled and frozen. *Just like I could be if I'm not careful in here.*

Stop it! he cautioned himself. *Don't let the rumors spook you. She's not a—*

His thoughts cut off, truncated by his noticing something else. White bones between a nearby stack of VHS tapes and a patched-up Moog Modular system.

He walked closer. Peered into the gap. Gasped.

Lying along the wall was a complete human skeleton. Worse, it had fresh-looking blood on it.

Jake retreated from the gory sight, in his haste almost knocking the female sculpture off her pedestal. He caught it in time, balanced it again, then stood motionless, letting his racing heart calm.

Okay, that's it—I'm properly spooked. Where the hell are the rest of her paintings?

At the room's far end on his right stood an open door. Gun in hand, Jake quickly crossed to it and peered through.

He heaved a sigh of relief. *Ah, behold the artist's studio!* This room, half the size of the other, was filled with paintings—weird portraits and landscapes of various sizes—both hung and leaning against the wall, and also mounted on supports. Two canvases stood half-completed on easels.

A farther room seemed to contain yet more paintings.

He entered the first room and stood in its middle. Turning in a circle, he examined the canvas faces.

"What are you doing in here?" a harsh female voice suddenly demanded from behind him.

3

He spun around, training his gun at her.

A naked middle-aged blonde stood facing him. Beautiful, and with a good body. Lean and pale, however, like she'd not been out in sunlight for ages. Her breasts rode high for her age, with cold-stiffened nipples.

She ignored the gun Jake pointed at her. Cold and hard, her beautiful gray eyes met his without flinching. "I said—what the hell are you doing in my studio?"

In her right hand she held a paintbrush, in her left, a palette. Jake realized she'd been working, had left the room maybe just before he'd entered it. *Damn! This is just what I don't need now!.*

He composed himself. "Just stay calm, lady, and nobody gets hurt," he said gruffly. "The one thing you don't want to do now is start yelling for help."

"Help?" She glared coldly at Jake, then walked past him to an uncompleted painting of a woman floating over a fish. She put the palette down by it. She stroked the white portions of canvas a moment with long thin fingers, then turned back to regard the ski-masked man facing her. "You're another art thief, aren't you? Well, I dislike thieves. You're going to pay for this."

He considered his options. Even without the gun, he was much larger than her; there was no way she could overpower him.

It bothered him, however, that she seemed unperturbed by his weapon. She still held her paintbrush, but what use was that?

I can't be scared of an unarmed, naked woman. There was no questioning it, though. He was. VERY scared. He stared at her paintings, imagining that they were trying to warn him of something. And the paintings' very oddness threatened to unnerve him. *Like that one! She has eyes for nipples, goddammit! What the . . .*

He drew his reserves of courage around him like a cloak. "Okay, lady, I'm here for Mary Sherman's portrait. Hand it over and I'll be on my way. Like I said, you don't have to get hurt."

"No," she said, her voice as final as nails thudding into a coffin lid, "you can't have it. It's my landmark work. The defining moment of my career as a painter."

"Hand it over. From what I hear, you painted it twenty years ago. Have you gone downhill since then?"

Her lips tightened, but she said nothing.

4

"Don't screw with me!" he growled. His legs, however, felt like they were made of jelly. *Why in the world am I so scared? It makes no sense! I'm wearing a mask and gloves, for heaven's sake—she can't see my face. Even if I leave now, the cops could never . . . . And I've got a gun on her!*

He had no intention of shooting her anyway. If she proved troublesome, a single sharp tap on the forehead would put out her lights.

She smiled disdainfully. "To hell with you. Go make your own painting. I retired from the world to pursue my art and since you refuse the recluse her seclusion . . ."

She flung the paintbrush at him. It hit him dead center in the forehead, stunning him like a punch, then clattered to the floor.

While he fought to recover his wits (it felt like the paintbrush was stuck deep in his brain), she crossed to him, hips swaying like a catwalk model's. "Oh, yes, you're going to pay for this."

She reached him and plucked the gun from his seemingly nerveless fingers.

He finally cleared his head, tried to resist her, to knock her out and leave. The painting he'd come for was now completely irrelevant. *Estrada can keep his blasted money—I just want out of here!*

To his horror, he found he was now frozen in place. He felt wrapped upright in a steel coffin, unable to move his limbs even slightly.

She pulled off his ski mask. "Well, at least you're good-looking; that's a pleasant change." She smiled. "You can still talk. Say something."

"Uh . . . uh . . ."

She laughed—cold, hard mirth. "You thieves are all the same—cowards with firearm spines. I wonder how many helpless women you've killed. Maybe even *raped* first. Left them torn and bleeding, wishing they were dead because of the shame of their violation."

"None," he muttered honestly. "None." In his mind he wondered why he'd decided to go this alone, to leave his bedridden darling at home. *Oh, God, help me.*

"Please, I'm sorry," he pleaded. "I honestly wasn't going to shoot you."

She smiled back, her eyes a touch less cold, now also simmering with lust. "Of course you're sorry, darling. A man should *never* point a gun at a woman. It could go off accidentally, and then you'd have a murder on your hands."

"I wouldn't have shot . . ."

She kissed him softly on the lips. Hers were soft like marshmallows. Her tongue probed the gap between his teeth. She pulled back, smiling, then felt him between the legs.

"I'm sorry. Please let me go. Raven will . . ."

"I'll get you another pet bird, darling."

"Raven . . ."

"Relax, baby, this won't hurt at all."

"I'm sorry."

"Everyone's sorry when they're caught. Would you have felt the same if I hadn't walked in on you?" She smiled. "Don't be afraid."

"I'm sorry."

"Stop it. Don't be a party pooper. We've already been through all that."

"I won't ever do it again."

"I assure you that you won't." His eyes bulged with horror, with terror. The fear-sweat that now plastered his hair to his scalp ran down into his eyes as he regarded her. He willed his muscles to move, to leave this awful place. They refused to obey his mental directives. He still felt them as part of him, but that was all. He had a sudden horrible understanding of how a quadriplegic must feel.

And out of the corners of his eyes? Her paintings seemed to mock him. 'We told you so,' they seemed to scowl, all those warped monster faces that questioned their portrayer's sanity.

Slowly, with firm strong hands, she lowered him to the floor. It felt like he was floating downward on feathers to a conclusion of some kind. Then his head touched the ground, and she was above him, straddling him. Her sex gaped at him like an eye.

Sexual wetness glistened on her thighs.

He felt her undoing his belt.

"What . . . ?"

"Do I really need to spell it out for you? At your age?"

She pulled his limp penis out. He felt her lips on him, her tongue licking and teasing. Deep sucking. And he was hardening in spite of his terror. He wasn't sure how—unless the same spell that had frozen his body was now freezing his manhood. But that was a lie, her mouth felt fantastic.

Then her mouth slipped off him and was replaced by her vagina. Slick and sweet. Irresistible despite his dire straits.

He felt like a bear hibernating in a dark warm cave.

Damn. The thought surfaced like a shark on the ocean of his fear. *Raven will be super-pissed over this.*

Fingers tweaking her nipples, the woman slid up and down on his erection. "You're fortunate that I like you," she said, a languid smile on her beautiful lips. She stroked his cheek. "Still, you'll be here a long, long time paying for your crimes; better start getting used to the feel of my pussy." She let out a long sigh of pleasure, then grinned. "Oh, by the way, darling, I'm Isis Lynch—one time leader of Pussy Transmission."

Frozen on the art studio floor while she moaned deliciously and ground her hips on his, driving his penis deep into her soft welcoming flesh, Jake Neville could only hope that she was jesting with him. *I can't stay. I have to get back to Raven, she's not feeling too good.*

***

She was outside now, in the large gallery with the statues and equipment. He heard her fumbling around to his left. Once she muttered angrily, cursing like she'd stubbed her toe.

He no longer lay on the floor. He now sat on a disused bench facing the gallery door. He was still frozen stiff, his limbs useless for anything other than keeping him propped upright.

He felt another sort of tired too. They'd had sex thrice without any pauses in-between couplings. Normally impossible for him, but his erection had felt like stone. He'd come too, but the sensation—it had felt more like pain than pleasure. Now he felt drained, like he'd sleep for days if the adrenalin rush of his fear would permit him.

His pants were down around his ankles, his penis (thankfully) limp again.

His phone vibrated in his pocket. That had to be Raven. Try as he might (his brain sweating from the exertion of willpower), he couldn't move to reach it.

He began worrying. *How's she feeling now? She looked okay when I left the motel . . . said she felt better too, just not strong enough to exert herself . . . but her fever had definitely reduced. By now—what time is it?—I should have been long out of here, should have called to let her know I'm fine. She must be worrying herself silly. And she really didn't want me coming over alone. Damn the damn flu! Damn Estrada's insistence! Damn my greed!*

The phone vibrated on. He imagined it as Raven's heart throbbing with worry. It was almost a comforting feeling. *Someone cares about me.*

The phone stopped throbbing. A pause, then a final, longer, telltale vibration. A beep in unheard frequencies. *Okay, now she's annoyed. That's the 'where in the hell are you, beau?' text message just come in.*

Only problem was, his girlfriend wasn't well enough to rush over and help him even if he could communicate his current problems to her. *How do I—*

Isis walked back in then, dragging something white after her.

Jake blanched. It was the skeleton he'd seen lying behind the Moog synth.

She dropped the skeleton in front of Jake, then, after blowing him a kiss, walked out of view behind him, swaying her hips for his benefit as she went.

He studied the skeleton, those disturbingly-fresh-seeming reddened bones. It had a wide pelvis, so was a woman's. *But what does she want with it?*

He heard her at work in the room behind. It sounded like she was slicing something. Like she was cutting meat. *Meat?*

Isis walked back into view again. He saw what she held and almost peed himself.

It was a severed human *face.* Just the skin and muscles, dangling limp in her right-hand grip like a dishcloth. Female, with pink lipstick on it. Dark eyeshadow too on its shut eyelids. Large fake lashes. Cut like a venetian mask from hairline to chin, the edges of the flesh mask were ragged and bleeding, running blood through her fingers and down her arm.

Where did she find a corpse? he wondered. *There's nothing up here in these rooms except me and these bizarre paintings. But no—the face is bleeding; corpses don't bleed. Shit, she just murdered someone!*

She draped the bloody mess of skin over the skeleton's 'face.'

"What are you doing?"

She smoothed the face mask over the bones, patted it down, then looked at him, her lips curling into a sneer. Some blood was splattered on her breasts.

"I'm tired of jerks like you endlessly coming here and trying to steal my art," she snarled. "Everything in this house took years and immense amounts of work to make. It's the singular legacy of a bygone, non-reproducible era. And though I'm unsung now, someday my genius *will* be recognized. But not if all my greatest paintings are in the hands of private collectors everywhere. Then I'll simply be a female hypothesis—an unprovable party joke."

She pointed to the skeleton with its face of human skin. "This lady will definitely keep my collection safe."

A murderess and mad to boot, Jake thought glumly. *And she's got me captive. Except I can somehow break this spell of hers, it'll soon be my turn with the knife.* "C'mon, get real," he said. "How can bare bones—?"

She silenced him with a gesture. "Leave *how* to me. You'll see for yourself in a minute."

Standing to one side of the skeleton, she bent over it and began chanting whilst waving her bloody hands.

"Yeba, yeba, coocha, coocha . . ."

The atmosphere in the studio immediately grew darker. Not the lighting, but the ambience. Jake felt it—*evil* had entered the room. There was no doubt in his mind: like it was a physical being, evil *had* walked in. The paintings he could see looked like ghosts, and now also, like they were alive. The hairs on the nape of his neck stood stiff like roaches were crawling through them.

"Coocha, coocha, Betty Butcher . . ."

The evil condensed—the air directly over the skeleton suddenly swirled red, then became a mass of floating midair flesh. A quivering shapeless mince that next tightened up into recognizable muscles and tendons, with organs (Jake clearly made out both heart and liver) mingled into it. Loops of yellow intestine and a purple kidney dangled from the underside of the mass.

Isis straightened up and stepped back from the skeleton. The hanging mass of flesh dropped 'splat' on top of it. The meat began squirming over the reddened bones.

"Betty Butcher, xalamina, kayill KUS!"

Isis stopped chanting. Gray eyes intense, she frowned at Jake, her face terrible with concentration.

"Keep watching. This part is almost art."

Jake watched. The mass of body organs now flowed over the skeleton like a tangle of solid rivers. Thick muscle strands slithered around the bones like serpents; white nerve threads flashed in and out between its ribs like thread being woven on a loom. Intestines wobbled like drunks around the spinal cord. Blood appeared from somewhere in the mix, coloring everything red and spreading below the mass.

Isis watched the ballet of flesh and bone with a grim smile. "Almost as good as PT's *Meat Symphony*," she said. "But that was . . . still is . . . in a class of its own." She smiled at Jake. "Since you'll be staying awhile, I might play *Meat Symphony* for you some day; we filmed the concert."

Jake had no idea what she was talking about. More madwoman's ravings, he supposed. He tore his gaze from the horribly writhing mass of flesh, rolling his eyes sideways, desperately seeking something sane to focus his attention on.

Now, finally, he saw what had brought him to this accursed place—Mary Sherman's portrait. Life-sized, it stood on the floor, propped against a wall, hidden in the shadows of other tall canvases. Eyes straining because of the angle, he stared at the painting, wondering if something similar to his current experience hadn't befallen Mary. *She disappeared, right? I hope she isn't frozen somewhere in this madhouse.*

In the room's current evil atmosphere, the painting's dark eyes seemed to regard him back miserably. If she'd willing sat for her portrait, Mary Sherman had clearly not enjoyed doing so. The teen brunette's pose was one of utter defeat; her face completely lacked the traditional party freak's brazen drugged defiance.

If I can get free, I'll come back with the cops and search—

A movement in front of him broke his train of thought. He looked forward again. He gasped despite expecting to see something like what faced him.

The meat had now totally smothered the skeleton, lying in perfect muscle arrangements on it. White skin was currently covering the muscle over, zipping closed over it, sealing up to a seamless surface.

Yes, it was a *woman's* body. In the period he'd looked away, blonde hair had sprouted around the face-mask. Also mounds of fat had grown at pubis and breast levels. Slim but curvy (the image of a bouncy, bosomy teenaged cheerleader cartwheeled into his mind and refused to leave). In her own gory way the corpse was quite pretty.

The skin zipped up completely over the body on the floor, leaving her looking totally normal. Except for her face, which was still the dead woman's, with bleeding jagged edges of skin all around it, like someone had slashed her around the head with a knife.

Isis Lynch laughed at Jake's confusion. "Meet Betty Butcher," she said.

He remembered the name mentioned during her spellcasting. *Butcher?*

Isis snapped her fingers. *"Allirrinz!"*

Betty Butcher opened cold, cobalt blue eyes. She smiled and sat up. She stood up, regarded Jake and Isis. She was tall and wide-hipped. Her breasts were massive, hanging heavy on her chest. Her hair hung in curls that spread over her shoulders.

She looks like a stripper, Jake thought. And yet there was still that bounciness to her movements, like she was athletic despite her build. *Cheerleader,* his mind kept insisting to him. He had no idea why.

His thoughts were interrupted. Betty was suddenly gripping a large bloody axe. A thrill of fear coursed through him. *Hey, where did that come from?*

Betty Butcher smiled. It was an intensely creepy expression, seeing as she was wearing another woman's face. Besides, the warmth from her lips never reached her frigid eyes. She looked pointedly at Isis, then pointed at Jake.

"Kill?" Her voice was a happy teens', which only made the question more horrible.

"Kill?" she repeated expectantly. "Him?"

"Yes, but not him."

Jake sighed with relief.

Betty looked disappointed. "Must kill. Like to kill. Who'm I gonna kill? When? When?"

Isis laughed. "Anyone else who enters this house. Anyone."

"I don't wanna wait." Spoiled brat's plea. "Please let me kill the people now in the house."

"No, Betty. John and Olaf are off-limits."

"The servant and the old guy? *Please?*"

"No. And that's final."

"C'mon, mistress, give me a break here. Don't wanna wait. Don't wanna wait."

"Don't worry your massive tits over it. In any case, I doubt you'll be waiting long. My darling here has a girlfriend he's worried about. Raven, I think her name is."

Jake's eyes widened in horror. "No, not Raven . . ."

She waved him quiet. "The girl's likely as worried about him as he is about her."

"You evil bitch. If you dare harm Raven, I'll—"

She silenced him with a backhanded slap, then turned back to the naked woman with the bloody axe. "You kill Raven and anyone else who dares show their face in this house without my permission. There's always lots of the fools. Is that okay?"

Betty nodded happily, hopping from foot to foot. She swished her axe around in a chopping motion, grinned her dead smile at the stunned Jake. "Oh, yes. Thank you so very much, mistress."

"You can go now," Isis said. "The stairs are that way. Remember, John and Olaf are both off-limits. Mess with either of them and I'll send you back to—"

"Okay, don't rub it in my face."

Betty bounced off out of view. *Yes*, Jake thought through his headache, *definitely a cheerleader. From Psycho High.*

He focused his thoughts on getting free. *I must escape from here before Raven comes looking for me. I've got to keep her far away from this madwoman— this witch with her paralyzing spells and psycho bodyguard.*

Then he saw Isis was smiling at him. *Oh, no*, he thought, recognizing the lust in her eyes.

"I can't make it again so soon!" Blood dripped from his mouth with his weak protest.

"Aw, shut up! You know you're lying!"

"I'm not." But his penis was already springing erect again. He desperately tried to think down his erection, thought of war and blood, of car crashes and NFL football, but it was no use. Her witchcraft(?) was too strong. Even thoughts of how much he truly loved Raven (and how incensed at him she'd be if she ever found out about this) had no effect on his swelling manhood.

He soon felt himself once again stiff as a sword.

A sword Isis Lynch quickly sheathed in herself.

"Aaahh," she moaned, sliding down to his testicles on him. "You're so good in me."

"I don't love you."

"Nice that we agree; it uncomplicates our relationship. I don't love you either—I love my husband." She laughed. "This isn't meant as pleasure for you. It's punishment—one you'll suffer for a long time.

"I won't be here long."

She slid up and down on him, rubbing her breasts in his face. "Oh, but you will. You can bet my next orgasm on that."

She came, gripping his ears tight like they were handles, like she'd rip them off his head in her passion. Her body squirmed against his like a mass of worms. Her vagina squeezed him, wet and tight—irresistible to mere male flesh.

He came again, emptying himself deep inside her, detesting himself for doing so.

Isis collapsed limp on him. Licked his ear. Whispered: "How many pussies can you stick your dog into at once, anyway?"

She laughed at his lack of an answer.

Looking over her shoulder, Jake's eyes once again fell on the portrait of Mary Sherman that had gotten him into this mess. Once again he was struck by the painted girl's utterly inconsolable expression, her frown so deep that the edges of her mouth seemed to be trying to tear out of the sides of her face.

"I totally know how you felt back then, girl," he said miserably. "Believe me, I do."

Then Isis spoke a spell that rendered him mute.

PART ONE:
THE PORTRAIT WITCH

CHAPTER 1

Raven

Concealed up in the branches of a roadside silver maple, Raven Perry regarded Lynch Place with major misgivings.

It's even more creepy-looking than I remember, she decided. *And the name . . .*

Raven, a pretty young woman with black hair that looked like someone had poured ink over her head and shoulders, was finally well enough to get out of bed.

The flu had been bad this time. *So then, why'd Jake and I ever bother having flu shots in the first place? Well, they worked for him apparently; though from the look of things now, it might have been better if they hadn't—if we'd been stuck together in bed.* Five days of lying in bed, watching Sex in the City and Ally McBeal reruns, eating acetaminophen pills like they were peanuts, drinking tea and lemon, feeling like a kebab being roasted, sinuses feeling stuffed with tar, waiting for the fever to subside, for her joints to stop aching . . . endlessly dialing Jake's number . . .

But I'm okay now. Only . . . only now, I'm almost sick with worry. It's the worst thing in the world to know the person you love the most is in danger and that you're unable to do a thing about it. Jake never came back to the motel, and his phone's been dead since. It clearly ain't the cops; no one's come knocking on our door, so . . . And all because of one stupid painting? And there's something odd here that I'm missing. Something I'm staring at that I'm not seeing. But what?

From her vantage point up on the branch, concealed by her veil of leaves, Raven regarded the house again. Her gaze scaled its walls like a spider. This wasn't her first time out here—before taking ill she'd cased the house together with Jake.

(At Jose Estrada's request, Raven and Jake had driven over to Zanesville from Pittsburg, Pennsylvania a fortnight ago. The Latino millionaire, who ran a supermarket chain out of Columbus, had learnt of them from a close friend whom they'd helped 'acquire' the Marriage Scarab of Amenhotep III [a priceless ancient Egyptian relic] from its rightful residence in Boston's Museum of Fine Arts. Raven and Jake found great amusement in imagining the reverential expressions on the faces of museum visitors/tourists all nodding sagely at the artificially-aged plaster-and-fiberglass model they'd replaced the original scarab with.)

Lynch Place was a solitary suburban residence on Smithfield Avenue, a hundred-fifty meters west off Route 22/93 (which ran south out of Zanesville to Lancaster and Circleville). It was a big and ugly white edifice. Four floors studded with wide balconies, arched bow windows, and a vermillion slate roof. It sat alone, clearly visible to passersby in its isolation, a concrete ship sailing a sea of mown grass that extended a hundred yards either side of it to a high green metal picket fence.

The few trees in the grounds, sparse-leaved despite the lovely warm summer, looked perfect to hang people from. In the fast-falling twilight their branches seemed ghosts' fingers.

Yeah, this was one damn creepy joint alright.

A red Mercedes sedan was parked by the front door. For the three days Raven and Jake had cased Lynch Place, no one had visited or left the building except for a single manservant who'd twice departed to return with bags of groceries.

Meaning Isis Lynch was as reclusive as their client Jose Estrada claimed.

Who was she? According to Mr. Estrada, some kooky expired middle-aged painter who'd once almost been a genius before drug burnout. There was practically nothing about her online—Isis Lynch had apparently run out of creative juice before Wikipedia and compulsive blogging became the order of things.

Raven mentally reviewed she and Jake's plan. *Enter through a fourth floor wind—*

Suddenly realizing what she'd so far missed noticing (*but how could I? I've been staring straight at it all this while!*), she grew scared. Like a worm, fear wriggled down her back. She felt it rise like vomit out of her stomach, up her throat, on its way to her brain, seeking to drive her hysterical.

Lynch Place had no fourth floor windows anymore! Just blank walls faced her up there.

Raven calmed herself, forcing her fear way back down into her guts. Further down still, into her mental rectum, like it was the next turd she'd pass. Black-denim-sheathed legs swinging below the branch she sat on, she reached inside her black leather jacket and scratched an itch under her left breast while considering the problem.

How can all the windows just vanish? Magic? Clear your head, girl, this isn't a movie!

But the weather-streaked plaster where there'd previously been glassed-over arches made her look around to check if there really wasn't a director somewhere with a cameraman.

Raven now didn't feel anywhere nearly as prepared as before to enter Lynch Place. Sneakers kicking palmate maple leaves, she leaned back against the gnarly tree trunk, fingers tapping the gun stuck in her waistband, and rethought her strategy.

Her initial intent had been simple: enter the house after dark, snoop around, find Jake, shoot his captor(s) if necessary, flee . . . with or without the Mary Sherman portrait.

Now, however . . .

She got out her cellphone and dialed.

"Miss Perry? Estrada here. Has Mr. Neville returned yet?"

"No, no, I'm out at the house now looking for him. . . . No, he's not run away with your painting—our car's still parked down the road, its windshield spattered with bird poop, meaning he's *still* in the house. . . . Yes, Mr. Estrada, I'll still try to get the painting for you, or die trying. . . . Now, I need you to tell me everything you know about this Isis Lynch woman. Every darn thing. . . . Why? Oh, you won't believe this . . ."

She explained, he talked, she listened. Around her, dusk fell into night.

Jose Estrada hung up. Raven put her cellphone away, sat staring at the house. The ground floor lights were now on, the manservant's stooped silhouette visible at intervals behind windows.

Leaves rustled around Raven as birds made themselves comfortable for the night.

A totally weird story she'd just heard. Jose Estrada, clearly shocked by her tale of the vanishing windows, had gone into a lot more detail about Isis Lynch, gossip and speculation inclusive. *Wow, I'd no idea she was once famous—I was just out of diapers then. But that stuff Estrada mentioned? Dude, c'mon! You've got to be . . . Well, I'm going in no matter what—*

Her thoughts were cut off by a car driving past her tree. A yellow Corvette convertible with the top down and two giggling women in it.

She was surprised when the yellow car stopped just in front of her, by Lynch Place's front gate.

Oops, I thought they never had visitors.

Her face grim, Raven swatted away bugs and watched the new arrivals, itching with impatience for them to leave so she could break into the house.

CHAPTER 2

Lily & Nina

Lily McLean palmed the car horn again. Three long toots.

"He clearly doesn't intend letting us in," Nina Kissing said.

"It's impolite to pretend he can't hear us. We can clearly see him at the windows."

Nina yawned. "It's late; she probably told him not to. Let's go find a motel and come back tomorrow. Maybe that Super 8 we passed driving over."

"It's just seven-thirty." Lily honked again, then sat back, a grimace on her face.

Lily McLean was thirty-two years old. Good-looking, with short chestnut-brown hair, and dressed in a white pantsuit, she was a reporter for the underground publication Dirty Vagina.

Nina Kissing, Lily's current companion and girlfriend, also worked for Dirty Vagina, as a photographer. Nina was twenty-six, a tall thin blonde with watery blue eyes, a massive nose, an equally large mouth, and a predilection for drugs. Uppers, downers, weed, coke, speed, E— whatever was available, she'd do it. She had needle marks on her thighs from her six-month addiction to heroin a few years ago. 'Whatever doesn't kill me makes me stronger,' was her favorite quote. Nina had OD'd thrice, most recently three months ago and intentionally, when Kiki, her last girlfriend before Lily, split with her. At the moment there was a vial of coke in the pocket of her black leather jacket and a bottle of multi-colored pills in her purse.

The pair were here to interview Isis Lynch. Flying in from Denver, Colorado, they'd landed at Columbus's Rickenbacker Airport two hours ago, then, after resolving some confusion over Nina's misplaced luggage, had rented the car and driven over.

Lily said, "It's bad enough that she won't even answer the phone to give us an appointment. Even Marilyn Manson did; and he's a *real* star."

Nina shrugged. "She's a recluse; like Garbo or Phil Spector. Too much hype and drugs fries their brains and that's what you get." She pouted, ran cool fingers across Lily's cheek. "Darling, I told you it's a bad idea coming here. She's not given an interview in fifteen years. She's likely old and senile now."

"She's forty-eight."

"Senility comes early in some families." Nina got out her pill bottle. "Wanna red?"

Lily shook head. "Easy with those. I want to make love tonight." The warm dusk was filling her with romantic feeling.

"Me too—it isn't a downer." She popped a red pill, then pulled up her black skirt and tapped her yellow panties. "My pussy's dripping for yours, honey."

Lily's gray eyes widened with desire at the revealed expanse of creamy thighs above the laced-up white knee-length boots. She pouted a kiss at Nina, then her face turned serious again. She pointed through the gate. "Look. There he is again. Watching us—the Peeping Tom."

"Blackwash. He's inside; we're outside."

"We're not peeping at him, he's peeping at us."

"I already told you: let's check into a motel and screw the night away. Come back tomorrow."

"From what I've heard, it'll simply be more of the same." She frowned. "Like you said, Isis Lynch hasn't given an interview in fifteen years. If we get it, it's the scoop of a lifetime. It'll make our careers."

Nina yawned affectedly. "Yours, you mean. You just brought me along for cunnilingus."

Lily rolled her eyes. "Darling, you're taking the pictures. Duh? This is a *we* deal. I get famous, you get famous."

Nina wiped her lips with the back of her hand. "Nah, the magazine wins. Only Dirty Vagina's getting famous."

"We're too underground for that—our name alone scares off anyone who isn't fanatically avant-garde."

"I'm just joking. You know I love your drive—not just your sex drive, but how you're always striving to get the most out of life, to be the absolute best you can in this male-dominated world, no matter what." She sighed. "Maybe it's the drugs, but I've no motivation whatever to be someone popular." She gestured at Lynch Place. "Not like Isis and her combo, from what you say."

Lily smiled. "Pussy Transmission? PT, they did whatever it took. Rachmiel Donovan once said their motto was 'Stardom by any means necessary.' Isis and her husband John clearly agreed. I mean . . . you saw some of their multimedia escapades, right?"

"My favorite was *Meat Symphony*. Now that's extreme."

"And it worked big time for them. Early to mid-90s, PT were the darlings of the extreme underground. Isis's paintings, her brother Rachmiel's sculptures, John Lynch's videos, that Elektronik music . . ." She gave the peering silhouette at the window another angry blast of car horn. "Which makes it so bloody odd how they vanished. One moment they're about to break out of the underground and become a nationwide . . . possibly a *worldwide*, sensation, the next moment they disappear."

"Oh, I really like how Tricky Dick put it—'They vanished like three stones beneath a lake surface, leaving not even a ripple trace.'"

"That's just it. They're practically erased from art history. Even an internet search yields nothing. And it's apparently by their own doing. Isis and John never sold any of their art, and they spent a lot of money buying back all rights to their public work. So there's really nothing to see."

"Those tapes Dick showed us?"

"Were copied secretly by one of John Lynch's old assistants. PT have no knowledge of their existence." She gestured at Lynch Place. "All their performance sets, stage equipment, everything, is reputedly in this house."

"A treasure trove for art thieves."

"Only die-hard collectors. PT are too obscure now for anyone else to trouble themselves."

"Isis and John clearly don't think so. Notice how there aren't any windows on the fourth floor?"

"Yeah, I've been trying not to mention it. That's real odd."

"Has to be where all their gear is stored."

Nina yawned. Lily glared at her. "Hey, don't you dare fall asleep on me! I told you not to Quaalude your ass. I want some lovin'—just looking at you makes me horny."

"It's okay. I'm just bored waiting out here. I've already told you twice—let's go party and come back tomorrow." She yawned again.

"Besides, if she keeps playing hard-to-get, we can go interview her brother in New York."

"Rachmiel Donovan? Tricky Dick's still sniffing the Big Apple's ass looking for him. Unlisted number and the whole shebang. Rach's made a post-career career of remaining anonymous." She scowled, ran a hand through her hair. "Thing is, Isis and Rachmiel were rich kids from the get go." She sighed wistfully. "Being loaded makes it so easy to disappear."

"Look upstairs," Nina said.

"Huh?" Lily did so. A clearly female form stood framed in a lit third floor window. Naked. Willowy body, large breasts. Long blonde hair.

"It's Isis Lynch!" Lily whispered, bouncing excitedly in her seat and clapping her hands. "She's seen us!"

"Calm down!"

Instead, Lily gave the Corvette's horn several honks. The woman at the window pulled the blinds closed.

"She's gone."

"She's telling *him* to come open the gate and let us in."

They waited. "Where's her husband anyway?"

"Inside. Likely doped out on drugs like you."

"Hey, I resent that."

"It's been ten minutes since she left the window. Nobody's coming."

"You're right. Arrgh, this bitch is totally pissing me off now. Doesn't she know our careers are on the line here?"

"Look, Nina, screw Isis Lynch. For tonight anyhow. You're right—let's go find that motel and get stoned and make love till daylight like you've been suggesting. You still got that new Columbian blow, right?"

"Yeah, but . . ."

"Hey, where you going? Get back in the car."

"No. We're going in."

"You're stoned, honey. Get in the car and let's leave!"

"No. Get your stuff out and lock up. We'll climb the fence, go knock the front door."

"Two words—electric fence."

"Then we'll die together and make love in paradise instead. Who're you kidding? No way in hell is this fence electric—it's painted *green*. Hurry your ass up, let's go!"

"You *are* stoned."

Nonetheless, Lily followed her girlfriend's lead. She raised the Corvette's top, then got out and locked the car. Then both women climbed over the green pickets.

CHAPTER 3

Raven

From her perch in the silver maple tree, Raven watched the two women cross the fence. Once on the other side, they giggled, kissed, then started up the short driveway to the house.

Both carried handbags; the one wearing a suit also carried a laptop case.

The taller woman, in shiny black clothes and equally shiny white boots, walked with a swaying, unbalanced gait like she was drunk. Once she stopped, placed her hand to her mouth, and jerked her head back like she was taking medication. Her dark-haired companion, hair a compressed storm cloud in the dead twilight, walked briskly on ahead of her, her strides purposeful like there was something in the house she wanted and intended getting, no matter what.

Raven, who'd also noticed Isis Lynch's brief appearance at her window, doubted they'd be let in. Both women, however, presented an additional hindrance to her plans. She was already tired of waiting for the coast to be clear so she could enter the house.

CHAPTER 4

Lily & Nina

Lily was about ringing the front door buzzer when the door altered.

For a brief moment she and Nina stood staring not at a wooden entrance, but one made of meat. She jerked her hand back in fear and gaped at the wet throbbing expanse of muscle and gristle facing them, the red mass interlaced with thick veins that pulsed like a heart was pumping blood through them.

Nina goggled. There was no mistaking what she was seeing. The entrance archway they stood in was lit by a recessed lamp that enabled clear vision.

The door was undeniably meat, like someone had opened up a cow and made a door from it. The door handle was a bloody rib.

The shocking image held for two seconds, then abruptly—

The door was normal again. Dark hardwood in need of cleaning with a spyhole and a normal brass handle.

Lily, her heart racing double-time, looked at her girlfriend and just managed to gasp out, "You saw that too, right?"

Nina, her eyes worried, shook her head. "Don't involve me. I'm an unreliable witness—too many drugs in my past."

"Be serious."

"I am. I see weird shit regularly. What did *you* just see?"

"The door became meat."

"Yeah, that's what I saw too. Looked like USDA prime beef. Or mutton, if you could find a big-enough sheep to skin. Just don't count on me to back up your account anywhere. You know I'm registered with the government as a habitual liar."

"Darling, your drug busts are neither here nor there." She grabbed Nina's hand. "Let's get out of here."

"Yeah. Mrs. Lynch can go—"

They turned away. The door swung open behind them. Both women immediately spun back to face it.

The man framed in the doorway was tall and stooped. He had short black hair and a long, thin face ending in a prognathous jaw. His ears and nose were large, his lips thin. Pale wet eyes peered reprovingly at them from beneath bushy brows. He was dressed in an old grey suit and seemed about fifty-five years old. A smell of mothballs preceded him.

His voice, when he spoke, was hoarse, with an east-European accent.

"Good evening, ladies. My name is Olaf." He pointed a large hirsute hand back towards the gate. "You are trespassing on private property. I must ask you to leave."

"We're from Di Va magazine," Nina said, regaining some composure. "We're here to interview Mrs. Lynch." (Where avoidable, one never called the mag 'Dirty Vagina' in public. 'Di Va' was the code phrase—you let the unsuspecting think you were a fashion/showbiz reporter. Using this dodge to get interviews had one major drawback however: they were eternally having to fend off threatened lawsuits from UK lesbian mag DIVA, who called Dirty Vagina a 'male-fantasy-fuelled, rape establishment sexist dishrag,' and claimed that the magazine's very existence relegated women back into the stone ages. Indeed, Lily and her Sapphic office sisters had more than once found themselves publicly snubbed by their feminist peers.)

"The mistress doesn't grant interviews," Olaf retorted. He gestured again with his massive hand. "It's common knowledge. Now please, go, or I'll call the po—"

"Why the hell did the door just change to meat?" Nina interrupted him.

"What?" he stuttered.

Lily got out of the way. Nina got all up in Olaf's face, her voice loud and insistent. "You heard me. This door just became meat." She peered around Olaf into the house. "Are you guys running an illegal slaughterhouse in there? Is that why you don't want anyone snooping around?"

Lily rolled her eyes. *Stay off the drugs, honey. What was in that white pill you just popped again?*

Olaf, meanwhile looked confused. "Meat? I assure you this door is wood, lady. The finest teak." He looked pleadingly over Nina's shoulder at Lily. She shrugged back.

Nina poked Olaf in the chest. "Yeah? Yeah? We'll see about that!" Then before he could stopped her, she'd pushed past him into the house.

He turned and rushed after her. "No, come back here! The mistress will be livid!"

He'd left the door open. Still bothered by its odd transformation, but unwilling to pass up this opportunity, Lily followed them both inside.

***

Olaf and Lily dashed after Nina into a large oval living room, where Nina immediately plumped herself down in a teal armchair, crossed her legs, and began whistling *Smells Like Teen Spirit.*

Like Olaf himself, the living room smelt stale and unused. As though, like its owner, it too was retired from dispensing hospitality. There were several leather chairs and a television. A phone on a wall shelf. A thick brown carpet. Seemingly thicker drapes. Three severe-looking portraits. Little else. A room oppressive in its reserve.

"Listen," Olaf said, his long face severe, his gruff croak perfectly fitting these neo-gothic surroundings, "you both have to leave this instant. Mrs. Lynch . . . the mistress . . . is sick and mustn't be disturbed."

"You're lying," Lily said, shaking her head so her brown hair swirled round her face. (Now they were inside the house she felt more confident. She intended pressing their advantage, no matter how slight it might be.) "We saw her at her window twenty minutes ago. She gestured at us to come inside." She looked slyly at the manservant. "You're not keeping her prisoner up there, are you?"

"She looked terrified," Nina added. "In an absolute torment of dread and fear."

Olaf looked first flummoxed, then outraged. "I assure you nothing is further from the truth. Mrs. Lynch is perfectly fine. This is *her* house after all. Don't you dare suggest any foul play."

"I notice you keep saying *Mrs.* Lynch. Where's her husband John? We know he lives here too."

Olaf looked suddenly pained and ill at ease. "The master is . . . is . . ."

"Is dead?" Nina finished with a wink. "Murdered? Buried in the basement? Spread out as meat over the front door?

"Stop saying that! There was no meat on the door!" Olaf yelled, calm and gentility dispensed with for the moment. A mothball smell poured from his old suit. His thick eyebrows heaved like they'd leap off his face.

Lily too sat down now, on a wide blue sofa, dropping her handbag and laptop on a coffee table. "Yes *there was* meat on that door, Olaf. It looked human, had arms and legs." She smiled coldly. "And . . . you're clearly hiding something about Mr. Lynch's true whereabouts. Where is he?"

"He's . . . he's . . . Look, you two ladies are trespassers. You've no permission to be in here. I don't have to explain anything. I'm calling the police to remove you."

"You do that, and we'll explain about the meat on the door, and also how Mr. Lynch seems to be missing—"

"And also how Isis Lynch is clearly a prisoner in her own house."

"Yep, we both saw her screaming for help at a window before she was dragged away from the curtains and bludgeoned bloodily silent."

Olaf sat down, looking totally confused. "You ladies wouldn't do that."

"You clearly don't know us very well."

Lily winked at Nina. This *was* nasty and wholly unethical, but . . . She was suddenly certain of foul play somewhere in this house. *I mean, where the hell is John Lynch? And why is this haggard old guy so scared of a police investigation?*

"Talk, Olaf. What the hell going on here?"

"All we want is to interview Mrs. Lynch about Pussy Transmission for our mag. Then we'll be gone and you can resume stuffing corpses in the basement."

"You kick us out now, though, and we're off to the nearest cop shop."

Olaf sat with his head in his hands, staring miserably ahead. "You two don't understand. This is for your own good."

"We'll look after ourselves. Just get on the damn phone and—"

The phone rang.

Olaf leapt up like he was waking from a nightmare and rushed over to pick it up. Lily and Nina were surprised to see the man was shivering.

They looked at each other. "Maybe this isn't a such a hot idea after all," Lily whispered. "He's scared shitless over something."

"Sshhh!"

"Yes, madam," Olaf said into the mouthpiece, "they're absolutely refusing to leave unless . . . Okay." He looked over at both intruders. "Your names and your magazine again?"

They told him.

Olaf winced and relayed the information: "Lily McLean and Nina Kissing. For Dirty Vagina Magazine." He listened awhile, then nodded. "Okay, madam. As you wish."

He put down the phone, then looked at them both in surprise. "Mrs. Lynch agrees to see you."

Lily drew in a sharp intake of breath. The smell of the room filled her nostrils. "When? She's coming down now?"

"Unfortunately not. She's busy painting at the moment. She requests that you both stay overnight and she'll answer your questions in the morning." He gestured overhead. "You'll have comfortable lodging on the second floor."

"Fair enough," Nina said, uncrossing her long legs. She got up and strode towards the front entrance, patting Olaf on the cheek as she passed him. "See how easy it is to cooperate with us?"

She didn't feel as blasé when she withdrew her hand however. It was wet with Olaf's sweat. Yes, the man was clearly scared of something. But what?

"Come on, Olaf," Lily said. "Give us a hand getting our stuff out of our car."

He shambled after them out of the house.

CHAPTER 5

Betty

Betty Butcher paced restlessly back and forth along Lynch Place's third floor corridor.

Betty (born Elizabeth Morning Genevieve Buchwald) was very upset. 'Mistress' had just informed her that the two women she'd earlier noticed in the yellow car while peering from a window weren't to be killed either.

Betty found it immensely frustrating, having warm bodies full of blood nearby and not being let loose on them, not being permitted to separate their flesh from bone and bathe in their shredded remains.

Betty lived to kill. Once reanimated, it was her only pleasure (besides sex, which she found less satisfying). She wondered when someone, *anyone* (innocent or guilty, it didn't matter—everyone, particularly the innocent, were guilty of something anyway; their sins just weren't public knowledge yet), would turn up whom she could smash her axe into.

She raised the weapon, kissed the flat of its blade. (It was a good, reliable, friend, one that had given her much pleasure in different times and places.) Then she walked into the bedroom she'd previously looked out from, and peered down from the window again. Olaf was just locking the gate behind the women's yellow car as it rolled up the drive.

She sat in a chair and scratched in front of her left ear, pushing back her long blonde hair to reach the itching raw skin at the edge of her current face.

She smiled, vividly remembering her last kill . . .

***

A dim alley somewhere. It didn't matter where. The man's name didn't matter either. What did was the fear in his eyes. His abject terror . . .

He turned and fled, rushing to reach the alley's farther end.

Wan moonlight glowed overhead.

Naked, her hair billowing in the wind, her bare breasts bobbing furiously, her feet splashing in dirty puddles, Betty rushed after the fleeing man, thrilling in the dark chase.

She trampled a startled rat that hadn't scampered away quickly enough. The hapless rodent exploded beneath her foot, its guts spurting from mouth and anus. A tiny treat of death as she chased the real prey.

The man looked back and saw her gaining on him. His mistake. He tripped and fell forward on his face. She kept running, leapt at him. She stepped once on his back, then was over his body, standing by his head.

He tried to get back to his feet. She kicked him viciously in the head, then stood a moment regarding his stunned prone form.

But not for long.

"Please, lady . . ." were the only words he groggily managed before she struck.

Leaping atop him like a lion, squatting with both feet on his shoulders, she smashed her axe down into the crack of his buttocks. "Die!"

He screamed. Blood spurted out of his trousers, up to wet her face. The blood turned her grin red.

She hacked down again and again, chopping deep through his buttocks, breaking through his pelvic bones into his guts.

While he screamed tormented gibberish and pleaded and tried to understand why a naked giggling woman with a dead face was murdering him in a dark alley, she hacked him in two from between his legs up into his chest.

Then she dropped her axe, lay down in the mess she'd created from him, and rubbed it wet and red over herself.

***

Betty surfaced from her reverie. It was almost satisfactory. Nothing like the real thing though. But where, oh where, and how soon, would she have someone, an unprotected intruder to kill?

CHAPTER 6

Raven

Once Lily and Nina had reparked their Corvette beside Olaf's red Mercedes and the trio had entered Lynch Place, Raven pulled on a black ski mask. After a five-minute wait to ensure no one came back out again for something they'd forgotten, she dropped down from her tree perch, landing inside the house grounds.

She swiftly crossed the lawn, stopping beneath a dark second floor window on the far left of the house, one hidden from roadside view by a large buckeye. (She was avoiding the third floor for the moment. She'd twice noticed a nude blonde—who had to be Isis Lynch—peering from one of its windows.)

Using a grappling hook, Raven hauled herself up to the window.

She reeled up her rope, collapsed the grappler and snapped it back onto her belt, then sat on the projecting ledge a moment getting her breath back.

It wasn't a high climb, but since she'd been ill . . .

Okay, she thought. (For a moment she worried that her influenza had left a residue to hamper her rescue attempt. But flexing her muscles revealed no residual aches and her body temperature seemed normal enough.)

Light and loud giggles poured from the window on her left. The happy visitors. She listened a moment:

"She let us in, darling. Our careers are gonna skyrocket after this."

"Don't be too optimistic; she could still refuse to talk to us. If she does, there's nothing we can do."

"I thought you just took uppers, not downers. Just stick to taking snaps, Miss Pessimist, I'll get her to talk."

"Kiss my ass, darling."

"Are you speaking literally or figuratively?"

"It's an insult. And no pussy for you tonight."

A smack of hand on flesh and an excited yelp followed, then the sound of both women chasing themselves about the room. One finally loudly caught the other. Loud laughter and the yielding creak of bed springs as the women fell on it.

Outside, perched on the ledge, cold wind in her black hair, the sound of their happy love-play upset Raven. She imagined both women kissing passionately in an ornate bed with gold rails and perfumed pillows. *Dammit! Jake and I should be doing the same right now.*

Her threatened depression galvanized her into action. *Okay, I've been out here long enough.*

It took her two minutes to quietly cut through the glass by the window latch.

So far so good. She waited another two minutes to see if she'd triggered an alarm. Once certain she hadn't, she opened the window, dropped into the room, closed the window again. She crouched beneath it awhile, scanning the dim interior with a penlight.

She was in a storeroom. Stacks of boxes everywhere, racks of clothes. Odd carvings. Some paintings done in odd brown textures. Metal tripods supporting racks of colored stage lights. On her left were two female fashion mannequins, on her right a stuffed six-legged dog.

Between Raven and the door stood a large sculpture of a flower. A truly monster bloom it was—pink and webbed with thick blue veins. Its massive stamen rose like a red obelisk amidst its exploded petals.

She regarded the sculpture more closely, recoiling in horror when she realized what she was actually staring at. It wasn't a flower, but a skinned penis—a huge erection with its skin split in six at its glans, then peeled halfway down its length like it was a banana. And it was painted realistically bloody. Now the veins made sense. And yet it looked so much like a blossom . . .

Horror filled Raven. *Ugh! What sort of woman . . . of person . . . considers such a monstrous object art?*

She crossed quickly to the door, wanting to be away from the disgusting sculpture as fast as possible. *Two floors to climb. Jake must be on the third or fourth floor. She wouldn't room the visitors near him.*

Her eyes worried, she opened the door and peeped out. Light spilled in from the corridor. She looked left. Over the corridor's near end a glass semicircle showed the outside sky darkening. She looked right. The stairs began ten yards away. *Coast is clear.* She snapped off her penlight, clipped it to her belt.

Gun in hand, she stepped out of the room and headed for the stairs.

Loud laughter sounded from behind the next door. The visitors were definitely partying it up. She wondered what their business was here. Some kind of cult? Or were they simply relatives, unaware of the sinister happenings in this house?

She pushed the thoughts from her mind as she reached the staircase. *Questions are just distractions. I need to be focused now; there's danger in this house for sure.*

Raven ascended the stairs. Quietly, like a ghost, the sound of her footsteps muffled as if the carpeting was eating it up.

The stairway folded back on itself halfway up. Almost at the bend, Raven heard soft sounds overhead. She stopped dead, peered up over the upper staircase.

She stared in confusion at the naked blonde sitting on the topmost stair with a pair of scissors in her hand. *And, is that an axe by her butt?*

Then she saw what the woman was doing with the scissors, and her blood chilled in her veins. She covered her mouth, stifling the gasp that threatened to betray her presence on the steps. *She's cutting . . .*

Unaware she was being observed, Betty Butcher was trimming the excess skin from her face. The seam of joined skin around her head kept itching, a bother she could do without, particularly with no one in sight to kill. In previous incarnations, she'd discovered removing such 'spillover flesh' reduced her discomfort.

Her flame of urgency quenched, Raven watched Betty work. She quickly noted that Betty's face had a different skin tone from the rest of her body. She considered also the raw flesh edges at the join and the woman's unnatural facial expression. *How come she doesn't feel any pain while cutting herself? And who is she anyway? She seems more dead than alive!* Raven lowered her pistol. It suddenly seemed very inadequate. The axe by Betty's buttocks gleamed wickedly. *Wow, that thing looks like it can slice through metal!* She was suddenly perspiring inside her ski mask. Sweat dribbled down between her breasts.

Raven left Betty fixing her face and padded softly back down the way she'd come. *There should be another stairway to the third floor at the other end of the corridor.*

***

Betty finished trimming the excess skin off her face. To dispose of the jagged wet strips, she ate them.

CHAPTER 7

Lily & Nina

Lily spread Nina's legs wider, dug her tongue deeper into the wet crevice of her vagina. Nina moaned, ran appreciative fingers through Lily's hair.

Lily licked upward, dragging her tongue out of Nina's sex and over her purple pee-hole to her clitoris. She swirled around the engorged bud like a tornado, round and round like she sought to make her mouth dizzy.

Nina's moans deepened, quickened. Her hips lifted up off the bed, grinding her vagina into Lily's mouth. Her trembling thighs clamped tight against Lily's ears, then jerked apart again.

Her fingers flowed like water from Lily's head down her back. They moved sideways to grip her own thighs, then (as if controlled by a sexual puppeteer) leapt up to her breasts, raising each creamy orb to her lips so she could suck its swollen purple nipple. Then, as her orgasm rushed over her like a beast of prey, she gave up caressing herself and flung her arms sideways, digging her fingers deep into the mattress and weeping tearlessly.

Lily (loving being able to satisfy her so) ate Nina straight through one orgasm into another. Her slick fingers traveled back and forth inside the wet vagina. Her lips tightened on the clitoris, vacuuming the little bud hard. Then she reversed the arrangement, her tongue slurping down into the tangy welcoming wetness, her fingers massaging Nina's clitoris.

Nina arched up off the bed. She held the position like she'd never break it, forcing Lily to rise with her, propping herself up on fingertips as she licked and sucked the blonde crotch.

Nina collapsed again. She lay trembling, eyes open and staring at the ceiling.

Finally, she found words: "Oh my God, that was incredible!"

She pulled Lily up to her, kissed her long and deep, savoring her vagina in the other woman's mouth like it was life-giving nectar. Then, she rolled Lily over on to her back and bent to suck her nipples, one hand straying down to play beneath her pubic hair.

Lily gasped as hooked fingers penetrated her sex. One, two, three! She opened up like a wellbeing excavated. She bit her lower lip as the fingers began sliding in and out, stroking her vaginal walls. Panting, she reached across the bed, her hand unzipping her bag. The hand returned a moment later holding her black strap-on harness with its pink dildo. "Use this," she moaned. "I want to *really* feel you in me."

Nina grinned. "I thought you'd never ask." She strapped on the proffered sex toy, then pushed her girlfriend's knees up onto her breasts and penetrated her.

"Drill me hard," Lily moaned when the dildo was nested in her like a bird. "Fuck me like you want to teach my vagina to behave itself."

Nina did so, bracing herself up on her arms and pumping Lily as hard as she could. The bed shook from her violent thrusts. Sweat poured off her, falling like rain onto Lily. She drove the pink plastic phallus into Lily's vagina with force, piercing her deep with it, ramming it home like the dildo was a nail, and she, Nina, a hammer.

Moaning deliriously beneath her, Lily took everything Nina had to give and begged for more, finally spattering into orgasm like semen glazing a porn starlet's face.

CHAPTER 8

Raven

Raven padded back past Lily's and Nina's room, rolling her eyes at the sound of the women's loud impassioned moaning. *You guys clearly have no idea of the sort of crap going on out here.*

She hurried on.

Positioned like sentinels on either side of the middle of the corridor were life-sized sculptures of people. All the statues had distorted bodies. One, a nude woman, had four long tentacles in place of her nose and blue claws for fingers and toes. The male statue beside her had feet where his eyes should be and large eagle's heads grafted like shoulder pads on each shoulder. There were six or seven other sculptures, each more disturbing than the last in their lifelike surrealism.

"Damn," Raven muttered aloud, speeding up her pace so as to pass them by quickly. "Whoever did these was screwed in the head like no woman's business."

"You're gonna die," a squeaky voice said.

Startled, she stopped and looked around. *Who said that?* There seemed no one in the corridor except herself and the statues. *No, I'm not imagining things. I did hear a voice. These statues aren't speaking, are they?*

"You're gonna die," the little voice repeated.

She located the speaker—a black rat perched on a female statue's shoulder.

The rat was humping something flat, wet, and pink. Raven gasped on recognizing what it was having sex with—a severed human ear. She watched the rodent grunt and pump its hips, slamming its little penis into the earhole. Each time its erection reemerged, it had a fresh coating of brown earwax.

41

The rat looked at Raven between strokes, its beady black eyes like oil spills. "The witch—she don't take no prisoners."

Raven ripped her mind from the disgusting sight. She ignored the obvious insanity of a rat talking to her. "What do you mean?" she whispered back.

"Just that—you won't leave here alive. Except you leave now."

Fear, dread, horror now flooded Raven's thoughts. She forced them back out, clamped down on her urge to flee screaming back to the window through which she'd entered the house. "Do you know where my boyfriend Jake is?"

The rat didn't instantly reply. It stiffened atop the ear it was copulating with and gasped, its entire body shaking. Semen began spilling from beneath the severed ear. Finally, the rat collapsed on the ear, squeaking softly.

Raven considered slamming her gun on the rat's head and killing it. She cautioned herself: *The noise will likely alert Miss Deadface back there. And concerning her . . .why can't I shake this feeling about the woman, that I just looked at a reanimated corpse? Come to think of it, she did smell decayed. No, that's just my imagination.*

The rat peered at Raven, baring its yellow teeth. "Your boyfriend's in the house."

"Where?"

"I won't tell you. Isis will be mad at me if I do." It sat back on its hind legs, its penis now shrunken again. "Best thing for you to do is leave here."

"I'm not leaving."

"I am, though." And with that, the rat leapt down from the sculpture's shoulder to the floor and vanished into the shadows.

It was only after it had disappeared that Raven realized she was breathing hard and fast. She stared a long time at the severed ear the rat had just had sex with. The semen trails emerging from beneath it made the organ look like an insect with liquid legs. *I knew this wouldn't be a walk in the park before I broke in. I've just had irrefutable confirmation. Hell's going to be let loose at some point, if it isn't already.*

She frowned, her lips set in determined lines. *But I'm getting Jake out of this place, no matter what.*

***

Raven reached the farther landing without incident and headed up the stairs there.

She refused to dwell on the rat's warning. It was either that or give up her rescue quest.

The third floor corridor was dimly lit but deserted. She peered hard down the passage, but saw no sign at its other end of the naked blonde with the axe. *She must have headed downstairs. Hopefully she'll stay there.*

She returned her focus to the doors flanking her. *Now it's a process of elimination,* she figured. *Up one side of the corridor, down the other. Then up to the top floor and repeat the same. I either find Jake or I find Isis and convince her to tell me where Jake is.*

She tried the first door on her left. It opened quietly. She stepped quickly inside, leaving it ajar so she'd hear any approach from outside.

The room was empty and dark. It was a large bedroom, with windows affording a wide view of the front yard.

She slipped back out into the corridor and into the next room. Another dark bedroom, this one with a mussed-up bed.

The next room was (by Raven's calculations) the one she'd noticed Isis in while scouting the house from the maple tree. A seam of pale light delineated bottom of wood door from floor. She tried the door carefully, nodding grimly when it opened.

She's in here, Raven realized, slipping quietly into the room. Soft sensual moans reached her from the bed to her left. *What? She's wanking?*

Raven pulled off her ski mask and stuffed it in her left rear pants pocket. *The time for masquerades is over. We do this woman to woman—face to face.*

"Hey, Isis!" she called out, pointing her gun at the bed. "Get your punk ass up."

Then she noticed the masturbating woman's dirty feet and realized her mistake.

Betty Butcher lay in the bed with her thighs spread wide apart, her right hand fingers dipped deep into her sex. Her pale flesh was sweaty. Her blond hair lay in disorder across her face and large breasts; her expressionless blue eyes stared through her spread tresses at the ceiling.

Watching the busty blonde pleasure herself, Raven couldn't shake off a horrible returning thought: *Why do I keep thinking that this woman is dead?* Try hard as she might to be rid of it, the impression remained with her that she was looking at a zombie. *And yes, she does smell of decay a little bit. Not much, but . . .*

In the bed, Betty finally stiffened, moaned deliciously through a sequence of blissful orgasmic shudders, then went corpse-limp. Then, realizing she had company, she sat up and looked at Raven.

She smiled, her eyes cold above her spread lips. "Hello, honey, I'm Betty Butcher, and I'm about to kill you." She giggled. "Sex is nice. Killing's a lot better though. But sex and killing? That's best of all. Just had me one, time for the other."

Before Raven could retort, Betty had grabbed her axe off the bed covers and leapt at her.

Raven had good reflexes. Even so, the speed of the attack so surprised her that she couldn't shoot. She only just got out of the way before Betty smashed the axe into the bedroom door. She gaped—the force of the blow had driven the axe blade completely through the thick wood.

Betty yanked the axe out of the door and spun to face Raven, who was now trapped inside the room, Betty between her and the exit. Vaginal secretion dripped down Betty's thighs.

Raven smirked. "Stay back, girl. What I'm here for doesn't concern you in the least."

Smiling, Betty stepped towards Raven. "Doesn't matter. I'm going to kill you anyway—for fun. The mistress says I can. You aren't one of her visitors."

Mistress? Yeah, that must be Isis. Visitors will mean the lesbian couple.

She waved her gun warningly at Betty. "Now, look here. I've no quarrel with you, but if you come any closer—if you rush me again—I'll shoot you. Get it?" (She recalled how Betty hadn't seemed to feel pain earlier while cutting her face, but even that had to have limits, right?)

Betty laughed. "Oh, I'm not scared of guns. I've been shot many, many times." She stepped closer, axe raised overhead in a double-handed grip.

Raven shot her in the face. The bark of her semiautomatic sounded excessive in the room.

Betty staggered, but didn't fall. Raven shot her in the face again. Betty dropped the axe backwards, then went down to one knee.

Raven stepped up close to her. Betty's left eye was now a destroyed bloody pulp. Blood dribbled also from a little hole in her left temple.

The rear of her blonde mop was red with blood that streaked down her back.

Still, she reached up a hand toward Raven. "I'm gonna kill—"

"Frigging die, will you, zombina?" Raven hissed, firing two more bullets into her skull.

Betty flopped over on her back, blood spurting like wet horns from her temples. She, however, *still* wasn't dead. Raven pondered what to do about her. *All the books and movies say headshots are what kill zombies, but here I've got a live one who still isn't dying after four bullets to the brain.*

Then her eyes fell on Betty's axe.

Oh, okay. I'll just relieve you of your head. I'll see how you keep messing with me when that's downstairs and outside and your body's up here.

She bent to pick up the axe.

Before her fingers reached it, Betty grabbed her wrist, then sat up. "That's mine, bitch. And I'm killing you with it."

Raven looked sideways at her and winced. The undead blonde's head was completely repaired again, her previously exploded left eye normal once more. She was bloody all over, but that was all.

Betty let go of Raven's hand and grabbed the axe. Raven immediately leapt away from her. Betty leapt to her feet. She crouched like a tiger, breasts like pale bullets, reddened curls whipping around her bare shoulders.

She smiled without mirth, her eyes emotionless. "Bitch, I'm chopping you into a billion pieces."

A gust of cold wind separated the window drapes. Outside, the sickle moon looked as sharp as Betty's axe. Raven imagined Death's cold fingers gripping a monumental handle beneath the moon, lifting it overhead to slice down into the world.

Betty lunged at Raven.

Raven ducked the violent axe-swipe. A chair shattered in her stead in the space she vacated. She fired twice more.

Both bullets hit Betty in the chest. Other than for twin explosions of yellow fat from her right breast, there was no effect. Betty Butcher came on relentlessly, a pretty female engine of destruction.

Raven ducked another violent swipe and rolled aside. Her hand struck a chair, her gun flew from her grasp like a startled bird. Betty instantly leapt at her again, the axe moving like it was piston-powered. Raven leapt up quickly and backed away. The look on her attacker's face appalled her. Animated, grinning with glee, but dead, the eyes colder than those of a sheep with its throat slit.

Raven didn't panic over the loss of her gun. The way she viewed it, her biggest problem now was that Betty once again stood between her and the door to the corridor. And she just knew she'd never make it past the blonde alive.

Screw this. And I'm too high up to jump out of the window.

She discovered a temporary escape route. To her left was the open bathroom door. Flinging herself over a recliner to avoid being decapitated, Raven scrambled into the bathroom and locked the door behind her.

CHAPTER 9

Lily & Nina

Nina, exhausted by her energetic sexual thrusting, fell asleep immediately after Lily's second orgasm.

Lily covered her up with a duvet, then got out her laptop. Propped up against the headboard on a pillow, she powered it up. The sex had energized her; she felt like doing some work. With the occasional loving glance at the softly snoring blonde beside her, she began typing:

'The Rise And Rise Of Pussy Transmission: What Really Happened To The Groundbreaking Underground Trio?
A Dirty Vagina Exclusive Interview With Isis Lynch, by Lillian McLean.

Stepping into Lynch Place, one may be forgiven for believing one has walked through a time warp back to the age of Count Dracula. All the trappings are here: the stolid manservant in his musty attire who gives gothic credence to the solid oak and pinewood furniture, the dark mahogany cabinets, the maroon carpets that seem almost never walked on.

Or possibly only ever glided over by ghosts.

But most of all, it's the ambience that traps you. Almost like a scent of vanilla orchids, Lynch Place gives off an overwhelming feeling that time has made no impression here and may never do so. Indeed, since Nina and I arrived, we sense the reclusive mistress of the manor (who we're yet to meet, by the way) in the very air trapped inside this building . . .

Then there are the paintings and sculptures, each of them stranger than the last. And more warped. Opposite me as I write this is a life-sized sculpture of a naked three-breasted woman breastfeeding a baby, unmistakably the work of Rachmiel Donovan . . .'

Lily's cellphone rang. She got out of bed and picked it up. It was her editor Tricky Dick, back in Denver. She accepted the call quickly so as not to wake Nina, then shut herself in the en-suite bathroom.

While talking she had a nice long pee.

"Hey, Lily, what's up?"

"Dick, we're in, dude! Isis has agreed to do the story."

There was a shocked pause, then Dick's fat-guy growl of a voice squirted from the phone. Big, bold, not caring what anyone thought about him. "What!? Yaay, Lily! I just knew if anyone could get this scoop, it'd be you . . . What did she say?"

"We've not seen her yet. She's busy. She gave us rooms at the house and will see us tomorrow."

"Cool, just cool, yeah, frigging great. That means my bad news is irrelevant now."

"What bad news?"

"The kid brother Rachmiel. He's nowhere to be found, senorita."

"I thought you said he was in New York."

"I thought so too. He ain't. Remember PT were big down there back then. If he was in town, someone would be bound to recognize him."

"Not with cosmetic surgery, they won't."

"True, but even a recluse keeps in touch with some people . . . there's this rumor that he emigrated to Europe. Germany or Switzerland."

"Any proof?"

"I just said it's a rumor."

"Don't be a dick, Dick. You know what I mean."

"Girl, watch your mouth before it cuts your expense account in half."

"Like you cover anything at the moment; if we keep freeloading much longer we'll have to change our name to Dirty Panhandler magazine."

"Don't you dare besmirch an already filthy cunt further." Then he laughed. "Okay, Where's Nina?"

"Out cold in bed."

"Just sex? Or is she 'luded out of her numbskull again?"

"Lay off her, okay?"

"She messes up this photo-shoot 'cos of drugs, I'll lay her off."

"I'll keep her in line; the pix will come out fine."

"They'd better. I'm only keeping her here because of you . . ."

"And before me, because of Kiki? And before Kiki, Jennifer?"

"You're the one implying she's the office groupie, darling, not me . . ."

"Suck my dick, Dick."

"I would, but I suspect at the moment it smells of our druggy photographer's anus."

"I hate you."

"Love me—I pay you. In fact, kiss my ass like you do Nina's."

"You got anything to say that won't piss me off?"

"Yeah. You two girls watch your backs out there. I'm beginning to suspect Rachmiel hasn't emigrated."

"What do you mean?"

"Well, like I said. No one that popular simply vanishes without trace, do they? I think Rachmiel might have been murdered."

"C'mon, you can't be serious."

Tricky Dick laughed his fat-guy laugh. "Maybe not, but . . . watch your asses anyway. I was able to dig up details of old man Donovan's will."

"Who?"

"Spencer Donovan, Isis and Rachmiel's father."

"Oh. Okay, I'm listening."

"Neither of the siblings inherited anything outright. Donovan set up a trust fund that pays them both a . . . call it a salary . . . six figures a year, close to half a million clams each. But there's a catch. If either of them dies before the other—"

"The survivor gets the whole sum, double what they're now getting; am I right?"

"Yep, senorita. That's close to a million a year. Fantastic motivation for murder in my book."

"Dude, I'd hate to be your sister. But . . . it doesn't make sense. There's no reason for Isis to kill him. She apparently hasn't left this house for God-only-knows what number of years. What does a recluse want with a fortune?"

"She sets up a trust fund for her dog or budgie when she dies? C'mon, don't be naive: who else but Isis has a motive to kill Rachmiel?"

"I dunno; an ex-girlfriend?"

"No one would go to such extremes to hide a crime of passion. And, if a woman killed him, it'd likely be because of another woman, and there'd be a loud stink raised by the bereaved chick. No, if he's dead, it has to be his sister who did it."

"We're just *assuming* he's dead. He could have emigrated like the rumors suggest."

"Curiosity killed one cat; a lack of it killed the other. Don't thank me if you like, Lily, but I'm just watching out for both your behinds."

"You just want your damn story. Okay, thanks, Dick. Appreciate it. Haven't seen Isis anyway, or anything suspicious. Okay, *there was* the front door . . ."

"What happened to the front door?"

"It opened . . . get it? Ha ha ha!"

"Arrrggh!" Tricky Dick hung up.

Lily smiled at his displeasure. She wiped dry, then left the bathroom.

She didn't immediately return to bed, however. She stood by the bathroom door staring out the window at the risen moon, a blazing white sickle that looked about to cut someone up.

She looked down at the rented yellow Corvette, then out toward the front gates, her gaze sweeping over trees that now seemed alive, their moon-shadows loaded with ambient menace.

She shuddered. She'd almost told Tricky Dick about the door's strange transformation. But the editor would never have believed her.

She looked back into the room, over at her slumbering girlfriend, body spread out in bed as carelessly as that of a murder victim. Sexy Nina, still slumbering serenely. *Yeah, she is a pill-head, and very unreliable, but . . . hey, everyone has their good points. What's that old saying? Even a broke-down clock is right twice a day? Without her, we wouldn't be about getting this story now—so that's one benefit of drugs.*

Lily McLean had a well-developed sense of right and wrong. She had no idea how long herself and Nina Kissing would last as a couple, but for as long as they did she intended to protect Nina from people like Tricky Dick, who didn't care about her beyond her immediate usefulness, and the other multitudes of emotional leeches who were only out to milk her dry and discard her.

For Lily, that's what love was about—cherishing and protecting each other from the hostile/unwelcoming/disapproving world.

She frowned at her sleeping girlfriend. *But that's the easy part of loving you, darling, ain't it? How do I protect you from yourself? Ensure you don't self-destruct?*

Standing there, left hand resting on the sculpture of the three-breasted mother, Lily was suddenly taken by a thought. Maybe it was the light, but she was suddenly struck by how birdlike Nina's face seemed—the high and narrow forehead, the massive beak of nose that would have embarrassed even Cyrano De Bergerac, the large wide lips; the chin so weak that Nina's face seemed almost arrow-like, pointed forward like it was headed somewhere. By a coincidence, the duvet was yellow in color.

Lily grinned. *She looks like a canary . . .*

Then she was suddenly aware of something odd, of a wetness under the fingers of her left hand. She looked left at the sculpture of the three-breasted mother . . .

And gasped and jerked her hand away, reeling back in shock.

Like the front door had been earlier, the statue was now meat. Skinless raw flesh that wept blood down in red runnels to the green carpet from exposed arteries and veins. Bleeding mother and child throbbed in synch like a massive heart.

Lily's rising scream died in her throat as the meat mother and child turned to gaze at her with pleading eyes. *Help us!* their joint stares screamed in psychic silence. *Help us!*

In her shock, Lily dropped her phone. It crashed to the rug, spilling its battery.

She stood shivering, hand in mouth, staring at the bleeding pair who in turn stared back at her, the horror on their skinned dripping faces the torment of the forever damned.

She found her voice. "No . . . No!"

"Lily? What's the matter?"

With a start, Lily turned to face the bed.

Nina was sitting up in bed and staring at her oddly. She stifled a yawn. "What's the matter, honey?" she repeated. "You look like you've seen a ghost."

"I-I-I . . ." Lily gibbered, spinning back toward the sculpture, and pointing. "Wha . . . ?"

The three-breasted woman and her child were normal painted clay again. Frozen and innocent, their faces models of contentment.

Lily jabbed her finger at the statue, too bewildered to say anything.

Nina yawned again, then rolled her eyes. "Just don't tell me you accidentally took some mescaline from my bag instead of a sleeper—that stuff'll give you frightmares. C'mon, baby, when're you ever going to learn the difference? The sleepers are red with white stripes, the mesc . . ."

Nodding without listening, not trusting herself to explain what had just happened, Lily hurried over to the bed. Quickly, she shut her laptop and put it aside, then leapt into bed beside Nina and held her tight.

"What is wrong with you?"

"I hate this house," she squealed piteously. "I want to go home!"

Nina regarded her curiously. "What happened to the story we need so desperately?"

"Screw the damn story."

"Dick will be pissed."

"Dick can go suck himself."

Nina giggled. "Yeah, right. I'd so *love* to see that—him doing a Ron Jeremy act." She cuddled Lily close, then after a wicked wink at the three-breasted Madonna, fed her girlfriend her left nipple. "Have some tit, darling. It'll surely help you sleep better."

Lily locked her lips around the proffered nipple and sucked and sucked and sucked.

It worked. Her terror left her and they fell asleep like that.

CHAPTER 10

Raven

Locked in the bathroom, Raven looked around for a possible weapon.

The black rat's words replayed in her mind like a gangsta rap crew overdubbing background vocals. *You're gonna die. You're gonna die. Gonna die . . .*

She smirked. *Not yet, homies. But how do I get out? That woman outside simply can't be killed, and all that currently separates us both is—*

Thunk! With a dull thud, the door splintered in the middle of its top half. Raven winced at the gleaming axe head embedded in the wood, then watched it withdrawn. A blue eye peeped in through the hole. Blinked.

Fierce blows began raining on the door. *Wham! Wham!* Wood splinters flew everywhere. The axe blade penetrated deeper each time, a silver prevision of violent death to follow.

While the bathroom door disintegrated, Raven quickly examined the medicine chest above the sink: shaving cream, a pack of Gillette Mach 3's, dental floss, spare toothbrush . . . Night Light glow-in-the-dark condoms, a pack of Lixx Dental Dams . . . She gave up in disgust. *Nothing of any use in here. And how did I forget to bring my knife with me?*

She checked Betty's progress with the bathroom door. The barrier now sported a head-sized hole in its middle. *Shit.* Wood chips covered the floor. Some had sprayed into the bathtub, more splattered with each axe whack. The door would clearly soon be history. Indeed, it was so destroyed already that Raven felt Betty was still hacking into it just to prolong her intended victim's agony of anticipating a gory death.

Well it ain't working, bitch—I'm not pooping my thong in here.

But she was definitely close to doing so. She searched urgently for something, anything, to fight back with. Then she remembered the grappler on her belt. She unhooked it, sprung the release and smiled. Its three metal hooks would wreak havoc on human flesh and bone. All she needed was to time her attack right so she caught Betty as she rushed inside, smashing the grappler deep into her head. Then, before the blonde recovered, she'd dash across the bedroom and out into the corridor. *Okay, I mustn't forget to retrieve my gun on the way. I think it ended up by the foot of the bed.*

The axe blows to the door stopped. Betty giggled. "Killing you will make a great main course, honey, then I'll jerk off again for desert." Her left hand came in through the hole, feeling for the lock.

Raven smirked. *You're not too smart, are you?* She decided against savaging the probing limb. Doing so would alert Betty that she was armed.

Betty found the lock and began fumbling with the key. A loud click announced her success with the lock. The arm withdrew.

Raven, urine hot in her bladder, raised the spread grappler overhead, waiting for the door to open. She poised, tensed to leap, anticipating her first sighting of the blonde's head. *I'll dig these hooks so far into your airhead skull, bitch, they'll scoop all your brains out!*

The door burst open. Betty strode in smiling, her axe raised.

"I ain't gonna kill you quick, honey. I gottta enjoy—"

Raven rushed at her, bringing the grappler down hard.

Then, with no idea what had happened, Raven was suddenly somewhere else . . .

She checked her charge, just managing not to topple over. Breathing hard, wide-eyed with shock from her abrupt transition, she studied her new surroundings.

She was now in a green corridor, or rather, an elongated room—it had only one door, a red one directly ahead of her.

I'm alone in here, she realized with relief. *Where the hell is that maniac? Okay, I'm glad I'm out of that mess, but . . . what the hell just happened?*

And what to do now? She was clearly meant to walk through the red door facing her, so she did.

***

The red door opened into a white bedroom. A dark-haired, mustached man reclined in the bed watching television. He wore blue pajamas and was covered by a blanket from the waist down.

He smiled on seeing Raven. "Come in, come in. I brought you here."

Naturally distrustful of him after her recent experience, she checked quickly for signs of an ambush.

"Don't worry about Betty," he said. "She's still in the bathroom wondering where you disappeared to."

Nodding cautiously, she fully entered the bedroom. The blinds were drawn and the room smelt musty, like the man never went anywhere. Up close, she saw that his eyes were blue-green like seawater. He was handsome, seemed about forty-five.

He indicated a chair by the bed. She sat. He indicated that she watch the TV. She did so. The television—a 55-inch Samsung LED model—showed the bathroom she'd just been in. Inside it, Betty Butcher stood axe-in-hand, looking perplexed. Behind the bloody blonde, the hacked-out hole in the bathroom door gaped.

"That woman is an irredeemable psycho," the man said.

Raven regarded him suspiciously. "Who are you?"

"John Lynch."

"Isis Lynch's husband?"

"One and the criminally forgotten same." His voice was bitter. It made Raven additionally wary of him. "And who are you?" he asked.

"Raven Perry. I'm looking for my boyfriend Jake. He came here—"

"Two days ago. To steal the Mary Sherman painting, right?"

"You saw him?"

"Yes . . . at first anyway." He sighed. "He's not the first to attempt it. When the hell will Jose Estrada—that jackass—learn to leave a bad scene alone? So he loved the girl, but . . ."

Raven regarded John Lynch. *Mr. Estrada knew this might happen?* "Where is my boyfriend?" she asked coldly.

"Don't take that tone with me. Your boyfriend's in a mess of his own making. You'd be too, if I hadn't pulled your ass out of the fire just now." He pointed to the TV, where Betty was just leaving the bathroom. "You should be grateful I stopped *her* from hacking *you* to bits."

"Okay, thanks." Something about the way the man sat in bed made Raven think his legs didn't work, that he was a cripple. But there was no wheelchair in sight.

John Lynch stretched. "You're surely wondering why I brought you here."

"Yes, and *how*."

"Don't worry about *how*." His expression turned serious. "I need your help."

She looked at him in surprise. "Huh?"

"I'm a prisoner here."

She laughed. "Yeah, like this isn't your house."

His expression turned sullen. "I'm not joking. *I am* a prisoner."

Raven's eyes widened. "I don't get it."

John Lynch sighed deeply. Then with intense anger written on his face, he pulled the blanket off his lower body.

Raven's mouth formed an 'O' of surprise and remained like that. John Lynch was a merman. Instead of hips and legs, he had a fish's tail from the waist down. Large shiny green/blue scales that matched his eyes, dark brown fins that matched his hair. The transition from man to fish looked natural, like he'd been born that way.

"I wasn't born this way," he said miserably. A previously smothered faint fish pong wafted from him to Raven's nose.

She considered the merman, his pain and anguish. "How then?"

An exasperated gasp. "Isis. My *darling wife* did this to me."

"But why?"

"I kept telling her to leave magic alone. She didn't like the advice and shut me away down here." He winced. "I should just have kept my mouth shut. Now I can't even get out of bed."

"Look, man," Raven said with forced calm, "since being in this house, I've had a rat tell me I'm going to die, fought a woman who can't be killed, and now . . ." she pointed at his fish-tail, "I meet . . . you. Please explain what the hell's going on."

John began covering up his lower body again, then flung the blanket away in disgust. "I wonder who I'm hiding it from anyway!"

Raven thought he'd left himself exposed for her benefit—seeing his fish-parts was extremely convincing. "Calm down, man. You were saying?"

"The rats work for Isis; Betty Butcher works for Isis, and I—"

"Yeah, and that reminds me: that zombie chick, why can't she be killed?"

"Betty?" He laughed. "She isn't a zombie."

"She isn't alive either. I blew her psycho brains out the back of her head and it didn't faze her one bit."

"I saw you do it." He raised hands to forestall the question forming in her eyes. "Betty Butcher is a curiosity—something much worse than a zombie. She's not from our reality either, but from a parallel dimension. Betty somehow got unstuck from her home realm, and now there's bits of her scattered throughout the different layers of space-time. Also, she's tied to that axe of hers, like Thor and his hammer? And I think Isis also mentioned an odd knife with the power to summon her."

Raven considered. "It looked like . . . I mean . . . is she *really* wearing another woman's face?"

"Yeah. The ritual to awaken her involves . . ." He frowned. "Look, it'd take ages to properly explain."

"And time isn't money either of us have to squander, right? Okay, I'll concede that."

"Just stay out of Betty's way. Isis never told me how she can be defeated. I'm not sure she can be."

"Okay."

A loaded silence followed. John scratched his tail scales while looking moody.

Raven plugged up the hole in their conversation by studying John's room. The metal rack on which the TV rested housed four video players, two of them old VHS models. It also held a row of VHS tape cases with 'PT' written on their spines. Another compartment held marker-labelled DVDs.

Directly opposite her, thick crimson drapes covered something large and rectangular that bulged slightly off the white wall. *No, that's not a window,* she reasoned. *The window's behind me.* She carefully considered what the carmine curtains concealed: *Another door? No, it's raised too high off the floor for that. It's most likely a dumbwaiter so the servant can supply John with food and drink, unless he also gets zapped in and out of that green room like I did—like Star Trek. But John can't walk, so it's too far from the bed to be a dumb—*

"Okay, now down to business," John Lynch said finally, breaking her chain of thought.

She looked at him, glad the conversation was resuming. "I'm listening."

"We need to trust each other, so I'll level with you. Firstly, your boyfriend isn't on any of the lower three floors."

Raven nodded. "I suspected as much. All the windows on the fourth—" she stared pointedly at John. "Hey, if you can't leave this room, how'd you know that?"

"Same way I saw you." He picked up a remote control from a nightstand and trained it on the TV. "I'm connected to everywhere in the house except my wife's rooms."

The TV image switched from its previous bathroom display to show the bedroom beyond it. "Hold it!" Raven exclaimed as the camera (Who was handling it?) swept across the bedroom.

John froze the scene. The screen now displayed the bed. He zoomed the view in. Betty Butcher lay splayed-legged on the bed sheets. She was masturbating again, fingers stuck deep in her sex, licking her lips.

"That slut," Raven spat. "Is masturbate and murder all she ever does?"

"Mostly. Look, forget her." He clicked twice. The onscreen view 'leapt' outside the building to show the trees and parked yellow Corvette, then back inside, where it framed a corridor.

"Dude, I'm not even going to ask *how* you can do that."

"*All-view*, and I'm not explaining either." He zoomed the view along the corridor to a door, then through the door.

"Ah, the visitors," Raven said, seeing the sleeping women entwined in each other's arms. "I heard them making love earlier."

"I *watched* them make love. That blonde has huge pussy lips. And she moans like . . ." He shrugged at the reproving look in Raven's eyes. "Voyeurism isn't my first choice for recreation either—I mean I clearly couldn't even jerk off to those two—but it passes the time." He grinned slyly. "Would you like to see the recording I made?"

"You didn't!"

"Why not? They'll never know."

"We're getting off track. You were showing me all this for a purpose."

He adjusted his sitting position, his tail slithering snakelike across the sheets with a paper-like rustle, the motion spilling fish smell into the room. "Ah, yes, yes. Forgive me, I've been captive in here so long that while I desperately desire to leave . . . I mean, if you've been imprisoned for ten years, what's one more day, right?"

"I'm in a hurry."

"Which is a total waste of your time."

She looked angrily at him. He raised hands in a gesture of peace. "Okay, I was just trying to show you that *I can* see everywhere in the house from here. Isis left me my *all-view* so I don't get bored. Your boyfriend has to be on the fourth floor."

"I figured that out too."

"Getting up there, though, is a problem." The TV view flipped from the sleeping women up through the ceiling and out into the corridor, then along the corridor to what was clearly a stairway entrance, only it was blocked off at the second step, leaving an arched niche. "Same thing at the other end of the corridor. You want to see that one as well?"

"No need, I believe you. The outside windows are all missing too. Will explosives make any impact?"

"No. Watch along the edges of the concrete filling."

"What? Oh, you mean the crackling. What's that? Some kind of electric defense?"

"Worse. It's a magical one. Nothing can get through that barrier. Nothing. Same thing with the blocked windows."

He pressed a button on his remote and the TV screen suddenly displayed just whiteness. "Normally, I should be able to see both our PT museum and the corridors, just not Isis's studios or bedroom. Now, nothing." He looked at Raven. "As far as we both are concerned, my darling wife and your boyfriend might as well be living on another planet."

She gawked at him, horrified. "So how do I get up there?"

He smiled (which she thought totally out of place considering the situation's gravity). "You take the train to the fourth floor."

"*Train?* You're shitting me, right?"

"I wish I was. Trust me, I haven't popped a turd in ten years."

Raven rolled her eyes. "You know what I mean."

The merman's handsome middle-aged face turned dead serious. "*There is* a train to the fourth floor." He forestalled her question. "No, the station isn't in this house. It's . . . Look, Raven. You have to go on a trip."

Raven scowled. "This whole scene is a trip—a bad one. Stop messing with my brain. You lost me ages ago."

"I'm sorry, but there's no easy explanation. You have to go see DOG in Absurdia." Seeing Raven was still scowling at him, John switched off the TV and dropped the remote control. He pulled himself to the edge of the bed and sat with his tail fins on the floor.

He leaned forward. "To really explain, I need to tell you a story: And you need . . . despite the pressing urgency of your . . . our . . . quest, to be patient and listen to it." He looked at Raven inquisitively. "Can you do that?"

She nodded back. "Okay. Shoot me with the info."

CHAPTER 11

Nina

She was tied down in the middle of a barren plain, secured by cords around her wrists and ankles. All around her rose black mountains, immense ebon crags from the tops of which lava spilled. Deep red clefts in their slopes looked like the eyes and mouths of demonic faces.

(The sky was a dirty off-white expanse. A huge black sun floated behind transparent clouds.)

She fought against her bonds. Her exertions were useless—the cords restraining her were tied to stout metal pegs driven deep in the ground.

After numberless futile attempts to gain her freedom, she collapsed, exhausted.

Then she heard it—the pattering of a million little feet mingled with loud insistent squeaking.

An instinctive fear welled up in her. *Oh, no! I know that sound!*

Seeming to come from behind the black mountains, the storm-like noise of feet rumbled louder and louder, until it shook the ground she lay on.

Then she saw them. Like black puke, they spilled from the mountains' red 'mouths' and 'eyes.' A million rats, no, a billion of them—an endless multitude flowing like toxic sludge across the distance between the mountains and herself.

She resumed desperately fighting her bonds. "Somebody help me!" she screamed, but no help came. "Help me, goddammit!"

The rats reached her. Like she was drowning in hairy black water, they covered her . . .

And began eating her.

She screamed as their sharp little teeth dug into her soft skin and flesh, ripping her to pieces; spilling her blood in little jets that quickly became sprays and then a shower of red rain. A group of rats chewed their way up her vagina into her womb, and fed on her from the inside.

Others ate her head, their incisors gnawing holes through her hair, scalp, and skull into the soft brain. They bit holes through her cheeks, ate her nose and tongue, ate her eyelids.

Her eyes . . .

Before the black rats ate her eyes, she managed one last look at the mountains. The red demon faces (from which rodents still ceaselessly poured) were laughing at her.

***

Nina Kissing jerked awake, sitting stiffly upright in bed. Her heart pounded hard and fast like a drum roll and she was literally drenched in sweat. She breathed in short dry gasps that felt asthmatic.

Rats were eating me . . .

She calmed herself. *A nightmare, that's all it was. I'm safe and warm in bed, and*—she looked sideways at Lily— *my darling's here with me.*

All of a sudden, she felt foolish. *And I'm going to murder Z-Lo for giving me the wrong pills again. What was that nonsense?*

But . . . *was it* the pills? Nina wasn't certain. *This house has a complex vibe to it. It's ordinary, and yet extraordinary. I can't really finger the oddity, but it's there. It's much more than just that creepy Neanderthal Olaf . . .*

She smiled down at Lily, feeling a warmth in her crotch. *At least one of us is having a good night's . . . no, she looks like she's having nightmares of her own.* She ran appreciative eyes over her partner's nakedness. *Damn, my baby's hot—check out that sweet ass!* Her thoughts turned serious again. *Hey—wait a minute! Earlier, when Lily came out of the bathroom, she looked like something had spooked her. I wonder what—*

Her thoughts froze. A black rat sat on the dresser to her right, watching her while eating something pink that dripped blood.

Nina sat motionless, just staring at it. One part of her mind wanted to wake Lily up; the other cautioned her against doing so, insisting that Lily wouldn't see anything odd and would accuse her of being a pill-head. *Which I am,* she agreed, *Oh, Z-Lo, I am so going to—*

The rat flung what it had been eating at her. Nina gawked down at the object that landed in her lap, cushioned in her blonde pubic bush. It was a well-gnawed, freshly severed (she deduced this from the blood coating it) human finger.

Scared to touch the gory object, she looked back up at the rat. Her scream of terror was locked in her throat; she'd somehow lost the key to her vocal cords.

The rat blinked thrice at her, then it leapt down off the dresser and exited through the wall.

No—it didn't just do that! Nina thought, her mouth agape. *That wall is solid . . .*

As if to convince her that it had in fact done what she doubted seeing, the rat's tail momentarily reappeared through the peach-toned wall paint. The scaly black whip wagged twice then vanished again.

Nina stared long and hard at the patch of wall the rat had vanished through. Then, with a jerk of horror, she suddenly remembered the gnawed finger in her crotch.

She looked down. The finger was gone. What lay on her pubic hair was one of Lily's red lipsticks.

Nina picked up the lipstick tube and examined it for trickery. Then, holding it carefully (like she expected it to once again become a finger), she got out of bed and placed it back on the dresser.

Her dread slowly submitted to common sense; her jagged breathing returned to normal.

She looked at the wall clock to the right of the dresser. *2 a.m. What a horrible time to wake up.*

She entered the bathroom to pee, sat on the toilet watching Lily snore delicately, her girlfriend's breasts rising and falling deliciously with each breath.

Lily turned over; her vagina opened gloriously. Nina felt her lust return. *Oh, mama, I just want to taste that pussycat.*

Her thoughts turned serious. *Okay, so there was no rat and no finger. I just carried my nightmare over into waking. It's the damn drugs. Oh, Z-Lo, you're history. I'll*— Then she grinned. *Just forget it already, wilya? Everyone has a bad trip occasionally.*

But . . . the question nagged her like a shrewish wife, *if I imagined it all, how'd the lipstick end up in my lap?*

She wiped, flushed, returned to the bedroom. There, after a look around to confirm there weren't any rodents in the room (*Frigging stop it! There never was any blasted rat!*), she got out two yellows from her pill bottle. *Otherwise, I'll be wide awake till morning.*

This time Nina Kissing saw nothing when she slept. She instantly dropped like a stone into nothingness, splashing into a lake of endless peace like death itself.

CHAPTER 12

Raven & John

Despite the compelling urgency that pressed on her like a weight, Raven found John Lynch's tale of Pussy Transmission an absorbing one.

"We originally just intended to have a few laughs," the mustached middle-aged merman said. "We had utterly no idea we'd get so big. You know—three rich kids with nothing better to do than party?"

"But you did," Raven commented drily. She shook her head, causing her black hair to flow like water. "So why'd you break up?"

John placed both hands flat on his tail, slid each sideways to grip a brown fin. "Personal problems: I got addicted to booze and cocaine. Isis got addicted to magic. Rachmiel had an addiction to fourteen-year-old girls . . ."

Raven sniffed. "I can imagine that last one would be a problem."

John scowled. "Don't get judgmental. He was only eighteen himself, so it wasn't as bad as it sounds." He saw Raven's replying scowl. "A teen's a teen, right?" He frowned. "We didn't like it either—it was a clear invitation to trouble to come visit. Rach? He never forced any of them, but they were always all over him. Come each summertime, it was like God had built a factory that made pubescent girls and was raining these teen chicks down on Rachmiel. They literally seemed to pouring out of the walls in each town we reached." His eyes shone with memory, "You should have seen the kid back then: Handsome mo-fo, dark and broody like James Dean—"

"Still, someone might have gotten the wrong idea."

A cold laugh and a shrug. "People *did*. Two newspapers were going to run stories; we bought their silence. Frigging journalists. One of them put cameras in Rach's dressing room and got X-rated shots of him doing some teen girl in the ass. Can you believe that? Got the creampie too—the little slut's anus looked like a volcano spewing white lava. Shit! Cost us a hundred grand for the prints and negatives."

"What'd your wife say?"

"Isis? She was utterly furious; their parents even more so. Mr. and Mrs. Donovan had never approved of our larking about to begin with. And when we began getting famous for stuff like our movie *All Cats Are Gray*—"

"What's that about?"

"Three hours of intercut footage of cats and vaginas set to an electronic dance soundtrack. Ha ha. There was also *Ass-Collage*—four hours of exposed male and female anuses—"

Raven winced.

"—but Isis's most outrageous media feature was—"

"I get the point. You were talking about Rachmiel?"

The merman traced a finger between the aquamarine scales of his tail. Each semicircular plate glittered with rainbow colors as it caught the light. Raven was struck by the fish-tail's beauty (it was like a compression/convergence of a thousand prisms), but also by how incongruous it was attached to a human.

John Lynch cleared his throat. "Us rich are a curious breed: we're fine with bad behavior—it's indiscretion we can't stand. Remember, this was well before reality TV became a way of life. So Isis's parents got on her back, and mine got on mine, both families threatening to cut off our allowances if Rach didn't stop his newsworthy behavior. So we both piled pressure on Rachmiel to quit with the sweet-fourteens. 'Oh, but there's just something about their breasts, John,' he replied me. 'So firm, so . . .' 'Stop fucking the little bitches already, kid brother,' was Isis's response. 'Mum and dad are threatening to write us out of their will.'"

"And did he keep off the high-school cuties thereafter?"

John smiled, stroked his mustache. "Oh, he most definitely did. That was the end of that. Rachmiel wasn't ready to be left without any money. He felt passionately that, despite its widely touted character-building value, working for a living was grossly overrated. I concur."

Raven detected a thread of sadness in his voice. "W-Why don't you sound pleased about his decision?"

"Because . . . we'd have been a lot better off if we'd left him to keep banging his Lolitas." His voice turned melancholy. "Try to imagine this: Three spoiled brats who no one expects to ever do anything of value—hell, we never expected to accomplish anything either— suddenly are on the verge of becoming famous . . ." He fell silent, like what he had to say was too heavy for his lips and tongue to form.

"And . . . ?" Raven prompted.

"And everything falls to pieces because of Rachmiel's first girlfriend of legal age."

Raven gaped at him. "*How?*"

John sighed. "The girl in question was Mary Sherman."

Raven was now totally intrigued. "The girl in the painting Jake came here for? What in the world happened to her?"

He sighed again, louder. "Yes, the same Mary. What happened? Okay, so I had a drug and booze problem, and Rachmiel had his girls. Then Isis got into magic . . . You know she was a painter . . ."

Raven wondered what he was finding so difficult to say.

He shrugged, threw up his hands. "What happened? Mary *became* the painting."

Raven looked at him blank-faced.

John laughed coldly. "You don't get it, do you? That portrait of Mary Sherman . . . isn't a *painting* of her . . . *it is* her."

Raven had no words. She stared at him while running nervous fingers through her hair. What he was saying was clearly impossible. But, John Lynch himself—half-man, half-fish and seated beside her— was an impossibility.

John went on: "Mary had been modelling for both Rachmiel and Isis—they shared a studio, he sculpted while she painted. I'm uncertain if Isis did it intentionally or not that first time—you know, just to see if it worked? Afterwards I know it became intentional, but I digress. Okay, try to picture this scene: Here I come climbing the stairs to the studio, only to see Rach emerging from it, his face pale. I hurry him back inside and Mary is stuck in a life-sized frame, flattened just like Isis had painted her. Only thing was, the painting was breathing."

"I find this very hard to believe," Raven said. This was untrue, merely the first sentence that came to mouth.

The merman John Lynch laughed bitterly. "You doubt that's possible, right? Oh, I'll convince you alright." He pointed to the strangely covered portion of wall opposite Raven. "Pull those drapes back."

Raven got up and did so.

She gasped. Sliding the heavy crimson curtains aside revealed an oil painting—a life-sized frontal depiction of a nude male lower body (without underwear—the genitals projected out of the picture) that ended just below the navel. And just by looking, she could tell the painting was thicker than it should be.

She looked nervously back at John.

"Yes, yes," he said impatiently. "Those are my legs—penis and testicles inclusive. Feel them—my legs I mean—run your fingers over them."

Apprehensive as to the result of such tactile exploration, Raven nonetheless touched the 'painted' legs. Her hazel eyes widened as she felt the hair growing out of both frozen limbs. They widened even more when, resting her fingers over a foot artery, she felt the weak beat of a pulse.

"Believe me now?" John asked.

She nodded mutely.

"Good. Explaining everything else will much easier now."

Raven nodded again. She stopped stroking the legs in the painting when it began to get an erection, the penis stiffening out into the air as if it was still connected to its owner.

CHAPTER 13

Isis

Isis Lynch considered the picture on her easel with a cold, expert eye.

It depicted a barren red surface riven with deep cracks, over which tawny eyes floated in a yellow sky containing neither clouds nor sun. A naked woman floated over the largest foreground crack, at the bottom of which a large silver fish stood upright on its tail with its mouth open. The woman was bleeding from her vagina. The blood streamed down her legs, dripping off her toes into the fish's mouth.

Vaginal Odor, the painting was called.

No, Isis decided finally. *It's not right yet—too Dali.* Displeased that she'd once again failed to transcend herself, she dropped her palette and brushes, got off her stool, and paced around naked.

Isis always painted naked now.

Whatever her other failings (real or perceived), there could be no denying the fact that Isis Lynch was a committed artist. She lived for *ART*—ate, breathed, and slept it. Even copulated with it occasionally.

Even now, twenty years into her retirement (the fact that Mary Sherman's 'accident' had forced her out of the public eye still rankled greatly—but John had insisted), Isis painted with as much dedication and fervor—'furiously' a casual observer might say—as someone sitting before a blank canvas for the first time.

Fuming, she stalked between rows of canvases, barely resisting the urge to kick holes through them. (*No! Even if they're failures, I can't destroy them—they took too long to create! Months, years! More's the pity!*) Her motions were those of a caged beast, a tigress ready to rend apart the slightest intruder into her solace.

Truth be told, Isis Lynch wasn't a bad painter. She was in fact very good—exceptional even, many art critics agreed. But she set unrealistically high standards for herself—every brushstroke had to be perfect, the colors appearing at once both brilliant and subdued; each angle had to be sharper than a razor blade, each curve smoother than her breasts. And so on. Isis was the sort of person who painted a teacup like she was painting the Mona Lisa, and she regularly suffered the resultant frustrated lows demanded by her overambitious aspirations.

Another problem was her subject matter. Isis Lynch had looked into some very strange places. Extremely strange—like the landscape with the flying eyes depicted in the painting presently annoying her. To the average person, her depictions (she paused momentarily before a painting: a crew of warrior rats sailing a boat over a river of liquefied flesh) were those of a madwoman. Isis, however, knew a lot better. These places (and others even weirder) existed in the realm called Absurdia.

She stopped pacing before a framed painting on the wall. More Absurdia—*War at the North Pole*. A woman staring through an open window at a beach and sea where a monstrous transparent dragon fought an equally huge dinosaur. Far off behind the giant combatants, a massive purple penis rose skyward like a nuclear mushroom.

Isis returned to her stool and sat. She stared hard at *Vaginal Odor*, wondering what was wrong with it. *Is it the lighting? Or does the woman need nipples? They seemed superfluous—they still do! Maybe another eye . . . in her navel?*

She yawned and stood again, too tired to attempt another brush stroke on canvas.

It's two in the morning now. Whatever the problem is, It'll wait till after my interview with those reporters.

***

En-route to her bedroom, Isis walked through her studio annex.

She winced on sighting a pile of rat droppings by the door. *Another one? I have to do something about these vermin. And exactly where am I magicking them in from?*

As she always did, she paused in the studio annex and regarded her framed captives—her rogue's gallery of people she'd caught attempting to steal her work.

Her captive's 'portraits' were arranged around the room. Some hung on the walls, some were suspended from the ceiling. Six stood upright in stands, two sat on stout tripods. There were thirty-two framed people—twelve women, twenty men—all life-sized, flattened to an inch thick, and held motionless on canvas in a rune-decorated wooden frame.

The runes were simply for insertion purposes, there was no undo.

Except for one of them, all the trapped women and men in the pictures were still alive, all could hear and see her. All their eyes seemed to track her across the room. It was a private joke to her: *My personal Mona Lisas?*

Did she feel guilt over what she'd done to these people? Yes . . . No . . .

It's a horrible punishment, for sure, Isis thought, *and I'm a truly horrible person to dish it out to them, aren't I? Oh, no—I'm not! These philistines all deserve what they got. Steal the art that I labored to create? You jerks are lucky I don't decide to burn you in your frames!*

Seeing as Isis Lynch wouldn't directly stoop to murder (her summoning Betty Butcher was a panicked last resort), 'framing' was the next best thing. Oddly, she'd never considered simply spiriting art thieves out of her house with magic and letting each go their way. (She actually couldn't either, having never really bothered to learn too many additional spells that didn't directly facilitate her creation of art.) She considered punishment for their crimes essential—just payment they'd labored hard to earn. And if others might consider the punishment overkill? They'd never know to complain anyway.

The human 'paintings' were all kept in this room adjoining the bedroom (rather than out in the PT museum) so Isis saw them constantly. Sometimes, when starved for inspiration, she painted in here; something about having an audience . . . (She sighed, it looked like she'd need to take that approach with Vaginal Odor.)

Occasionally, when bored, Isis re-posed the frozen figures in their landscape backgrounds; she switched their clothes, changed the tone of the skies, the color of the suns, etc.

She also painted over her captives, altering their faces and bodies as she pleased. The man to her right currently had three eyes and two noses, the woman on her left had penises for nipples. Another man was now a ram-horned cyclops with four ears and vampire teeth. It was fun, was all. Maybe not for the captives, but definite comic relief for herself.

(Of course, John had never approved of any of this; Which was why [*You know I totally love you, honey, don't you? I just can't have you messing with my stuff!*] her husband was currently resident downstairs with a fishtail, playing voyeur. But even John utterly detested the art-thieves: one of the female captives—the fat blonde with penis-nipples—had carelessly trampled one of his most prized film collages, irretrievably ruining it. He'd been irate—Isis was sure he'd have strangled the woman if she'd not already 'framed' her.

The oil-painted penises now adorning the woman's breasts were actually exact replicas of John's, not that he'd ever appreciated the gesture.)

Isis Lynch didn't consider framing people art. Painting was ART; music and literature were ART. John's multimedia (*Oh, I wonder how my darling's doing?*) was ART; cool sculpture too like Rachmiel used to make . . .

The thought of her brother made her wince. She gazed across her gallery of captive people to the oldest of them all—the portrait of Mary Sherman. The one that had started her down this dark path.

The frozen brunette (returned inside here from Isis's studio after the latest attempt to steal her) regarded Isis back, her face a mask of despair.

Isis sighed. *Oh, poor Mary!* She still remembered the horror on Rachmiel's face—the utter disbelief in his eyes—when he'd seen what she'd done to his girlfriend. "Get her out of it! Fucking get her out of it!" he'd screamed at her non-stop for fifteen minutes straight.

She sighed. "Rach," she muttered to the portrait like a prayer of penance, "I know you still won't believe me—but it honestly *was* an accident. The runes were simply to catch a 'ghost image' of Mary that I could use as a body template."

Tears filled her eyes. She stopped speaking. She stood, a chill in the room stiffening her nipples, trying to dispel the strong emotions the memory built in her breast. Long ago as it was, everything was still crystal clear, fresh in her mind as the pain from a wound suffered just yesterday.

One moment Mary Sherman had been smiling at Rachmiel (who sat across the room from her, clay-sculpting a dwarf woman with Mary's face and two side-by-side pregnancies, one of which had a bushy tail), the next . . . Isis winced . . . Mary touched the magically prepared canvas . . .

Isis suddenly felt cold all over. The chill in her nipples had spread like an invading army over her body, coating her skin with gooseflesh. Mary's becoming stuck in the canvas had been the end of Pussy Transmission. The one thing no-one had foreseen was Rachmiel Donovan, previously celebrated playboy fan of pubescent high school vaginas, falling head-over-heels in love with his first legal-aged girlfriend . . . and his having a nervous breakdown when she had her 'accident.'

Isis's and John's parents had both paid out fortunes to keep the story out of the news. It had helped that Mary Sherman had been an orphan with no one really asking questions about her. Except for one person . . .

That single person was Jose Estrada, Mary's last boyfriend before Rachmiel. Jose had sensed foul play, but there was too much money involved for him to do anything about it. (He'd been just a geeky, twenty-three-year-old broke-ass postgrad student back then, with no pull whatsoever.)

Also, he had no idea of what had really happened. He still didn't, in fact. In Jose's mind, Mary had gotten caught up in some weird *Portrait of Dorian Gray* scene.

And he wanted the portrait in question.

Isis was bemused by the level of Jose's commitment/besottedness. She stared coldly at Mary Sherman. *Twenty years on and he still keeps sending people to find out what I did with you? To steal you back?*

By her count, fifteen of her thirty-two captives had been dispatched by Jose Estrada. *The damned thieves!*

Suddenly enraged, Isis walked briskly over to Mary. This close, she could sense the trapped woman's hatred mingled (like ratsbane in coffee) with her despair.

At this moment, however, the hatred was mutual. "This is really all your fault, you dumb bitch!" Isis raged at the painting. "You're the reason PT broke up! Do you get that, you fool? Do you?"

She flipped Mary's carmine skirt aside (odd though it was, she *could* do that) and stroked the flattened white thighs. "I know what Jose wants, girl," she said, slipping a finger up between Mary's legs. "It's your tight, eternally-teenaged kitty. Too bad he'll never have it to fuck again."

On a sudden evil impulse, she dug her fingers into Mary's flattened sex. She sensed Mary's hurt and pain at the penetration.

It was scary—her fingers entered deep into Mary's sex, further than the depth of the portrait, like she was only flattened on the surface.

Then the painting began weeping, cold tears spurting from Mary's eyes, raining outward onto Isis's nakedness, down on her penetrating hand.

Isis froze as the wetness splattered her. Shamefaced, she removed her fingers from Mary's vagina, smoothed her skirt back down.

"I'm sorry," she said sincerely. "I really wish I could free you, but . . . it's too late now."

The painted woman kept weeping, tears flowing down to pool on the floor. Isis leaned forward and kissed her gently on the cheek, then turned away before Mary saw her own responding tears.

Seeking distraction, her eyes fell on her latest captive: Jake Neville, the young man she'd caught two nights ago, who'd tried to shoot her. He was handsome, most definitely her type, and with John currently unavailable . . .

She'd 'framed' him naked, posed as a Playgirl model, complete with a black bow-tie. *Hmmm, he has nice muscles.*

She walked over to Jake's portrait and began rubbing his genitals, smiling when, despite the resistance she sensed from him, the penis became stiff.

She stroked his flattened cheek while cupping the hairy dangling testicles. "Stop pretending, kid, I know you want me too—you've nothing to do all day long but stare at my ass."

Lust radiated from the picture, along with intense hopelessness.

Laughing, Isis knelt and sucked the stiff phallus—it looked like one of those dildos with suckers that one attached to a wall—for a while, taking amusement in how it throbbed helplessly in her mouth, like a worm being tormented.

She pulled her lips off Jake's penis and straightened up. "You know," she told him, "I could just leave you here like this, unable to come. Blue balls are scant payback for your pointing a gun at me. But I'm a generous woman, so . . ."

Turning her back to the portrait, she positioned herself carefully, then slid down on its erection.

She began moving slowly. "Now don't you dare come before me," she whispered. "In this case, art serves its mistress, not the other way around."

She groaned softly as her sensations rose. *Oh, no—I'm not cuckolding John—I'm just literally loving art!*

Isis Lynch reached orgasm. It felt like a flock of birds had been unleashed in her womb and were flying through her, seeking exit through the pores of her skin. She rose and rose and rose . . .

Afterwards, she smiled at Jake while gripping his still-turgid penis. With her other hand she fondled his balls. He'd not come yet—his testicular eggs felt harder than his penis. "You know what?" she told the framed man. "I've changed my mind. No orgasm for you tonight, honey. Maybe tomorrow, if I'm in a good mood after my interview." She squeezed the erection hard and laughed. "Don't count on it, though—I never really liked reporters. But you might be lucky—I could even give you anal if I'm happy enough."

After a last look at Mary Sherman (*Thank goodness she's stopped crying!*), Isis left the gallery annex for her bedroom and sleep.

She sensed Jake Neville's frustrated anger radiating from his portrait as she walked away from it, shaking her behind for the trapped man's benefit.

What I don't understand, Isis thought as she dropped off to sleep, *is why Rach's never forgiven me for what happened. It clearly wasn't intentional. All these years later and he still isn't speaking to me? Not even one phone call in twenty years?*

PART TWO:
2nd FLOOR STATION

CHAPTER 14

Rachmiel

It's a strange day, thought Rachmiel Donovan. Seated with legs crossed in his first class compartment on the Berlin–Warszawa Express, he awaited his traveling companion with a mix of excitement and trepidation.

Rachmiel had booked all six compartment seats, essentially rendering it private. Blue curtains drawn over the corridor-access door, he watched the milling crowds outside the train.

(These days, Rachmiel—to the German government, on social media, and to everyone else except his wife, his aged mother in New York, and his closest friends—was known as Peter Donovan. ['Peter' was his middle name—a clue which Tricky Dick of Dirty Vagina magazine had overlooked during his searching.] Nowadays, too, Rachmiel listed his occupation as 'Food Critic,' not 'Sculptor' or 'Artist.' This, in addition to his now residing in Berlin [where his face was easily imagined as Nordic once the suggestion had been made] was responsible for his general anonymity.)

It's a strange day.

Rachmiel Donovan—one time sculptural anarchist—had aged well. Now a trim good-looking thirty-eight years old, his brown hair was still thick, his brown eyes still bright. He was still wealthy.

He could be happier, however, if only Maxine would allow it.

Maxine Donovan. His wife, his soul mate—the source of his perpetual torment. Even now 'Rach' saw her intense glower of displeasure as she accused him of not loving her enough. That was Rachmiel's eternal crime in Maxine's eyes, that he didn't reciprocate her affection to the same degree she showed him hers.

And she did show it to him. *She loves me like a flame loves a moth, like fire loves wood, like water loves salt; like lions, tigers, and wolves love raw meat . . . she wants to consume me, to make me part of herself, to use me all up if she can till I've nothing left.*

He grimaced, eyes rising toward the networked arc of metal girders outside the train. *And now? Will she be satisfied to know she's driven me into the arms of another woman?*

Rachmiel pulled his outside gaze down. The Hauptbahnhof's Platform 12 extended before his eyes like the rest of his life, the soon-to-be passengers it brought to the train his fading days. *And I, why am I so melancholy? I should be pleased. It's a strange day. The day I gain freedom from Maxine, from the chain of my love.*

But . . . will she come?

Olga Franck. They'd met online (who didn't nowadays?), a Facebook friend request from a woman who felt his face looked interesting. He'd almost ignored it, but . . . she looked interesting too.

Her interesting face? That's a laugh, Admit it, you dog! You just want to bed her, to fuck someone who doesn't dig her nails into you like she's trying to rip you apart at the seams!

He forced a laugh. It was that and much more complicated.

Shadow fell over the platform—passing clouds. Shadow fell over Rach's mood. This was too easy . . . too simple. In his experience, his karma was a convoluted one—it detested resolutions. Every complication was a flight of stairs to his next entanglement. *I'll likely discover that Miss Franck is even more intense in her love—*

His cellphone beeped. Heart in mouth, he studied the screen. *She's here, she came after all! And me? Why is my heart beating like I'm fifteen again and on my first date?*

Their arrangement was simple: Olga had a seat in the last first class compartment. She'd join him in here once the train had passed the Berlin Ostbahnhof station and was speeding toward Frankfurt (Oder). Money wasn't an object, discretion and privacy were.

He calmed his nerves, then pulled aside the corridor curtains to see the platform on that side. A slim blonde in a zebra-striped coat was crossing the concrete toward the train. Her clothes seemed a disguise—wide blue hat, gloves, huge dark glasses, dark blue knee-length high-heeled boots. She carried a massive fur-trimmed purse. She was totally overdressed for a warm summer Saturday.

He laughed. *That has to be Olga—she looks like something from a seventies spy thriller.*

The blonde walked past Rachmiel to the front door to board, then passed him again headed to the rear of the carriage. It was her! Otherwise there was no need for such an embarking rigmarole.

He closed the curtains again, realizing he had an erection.

His phone beeped. A text message. "I'll be with you soon, darling."

Rachmiel relaxed back in his seat. Suddenly he felt happy. He had no idea how things would play out between himself and Olga Franck, but the simple excitement, feeling his blood rushing for the first time in years, was something to treasure.

And Maxine? She thinks I'm meeting an old artist friend in Konin, to return tonight, maybe tomorrow Sunday if we drink too much while reminiscing. Damn— it was the devil to get her to let me out of her sight! He smiled. *Well, I'm not exactly lying, am I? I am travelling to Konin for the day, only I'm taking the friend along with me.*

Rachmiel pushed thoughts of his wife and her reaction (that didn't bear considering) if she ever found out what he was doing now, out of his mind.

He relaxed and mentally prepared for sex with Olga Franck. He'd packed a lot of condoms in his briefcase. It looked to be a busy time of getting properly acquainted for them both.

***

The fields approaching the Germany–Poland border were in full bloom. Cultivated in geometrically perfect rows (Rachmiel just loved German efficiency!), trees, flowers, and the occasional distant house all streamed past at 70 miles per hour.

The corridor curtains parted.

"Peter? Peter Donovan?" The voice was soft and timid; seductive as an airbrushed Playboy bunny fanny.

He looked up. There she stood, wrapped in her zebra coat, a massive red scarf additionally enclosing her neck and chin. Total overkill even for an illicit affair.

He leapt up. "Olga!"

He embraced her, tried to kiss her. She turned her lips away from his. "Not yet, darling."

He pointed to the seat opposite his. She sat.

Rachmiel studied the little of Olga Franck that was visible. She was twenty-six and just divorced. She was thin, her build almost childish—

the same as Maxine's. He fiercely pushed away thoughts of his wife. *Seeing as the little bitch'll never let me go, nor I her (for reasons best know to Satan)—I might as well enjoy this brief intermission in the drama of our tortured existences.*

"It's safe," he told Olga. "You can get rid of the ridiculous goggles and hat."

She giggled throatily. "Are they that terrible?"

"Darling, you look like you're about to explore the Arctic."

She giggled again. "You're right. I do look absurd. It felt safe though. I was just so nervous that someone might recognize me with you, a married man. Okay, darling, I'll take them off."

She unwrapped her scarf.

Rachmiel was later unsure exactly when he first sensed he was in deep trouble. Was it when Olga peeled off the scarf? Or when she removed her gloves? Or when she took off her massive glam-rock goggles? Or when her voice altered?

Whichever of those actions first alerted him of a looming crisis in his life, he knew for certain when Olga Franck removed her blonde wig (*It's a wig?*), revealing herself to be his wife Maxine.

Rachmiel had one moment of clarity to reflect on how completely she'd fooled him and suckered him into her trap. He had no time to regret his actions.

The next moment, like the hellcat she was, Maxine Donovan launched herself through the air at him, raking at his face with her nails.

"You bastard!" she screamed in a violent whisper, ripping a bloody series of gullies down his left cheek. "You lying, cheating bastard!"

Rachmiel, stunned by what had just transpired, managed to grab her hands before she gouged his eyes out. Outside their window, Germany flowed like a river into Poland.

"Just calm down!" he pleaded as she fought to savage him further. "I can explain."

To his disbelief, his plea worked. Like she'd had her violence switch flipped to 'off,' she went limp against him for a moment. Then she stepped back and again sat in the seat opposite his.

Maxine got out a cigarette from her handbag and lit up. She dragged deep on the pale tube, then smiled coldly. Her green eyes were fierce, but for the moment she seemed pacified by the blood she'd drawn in their conflict.

"Go on, darling," she said smoothly through a gray cloud of cigarette smoke. "I'm dying to hear what you've got to say." She sucked in another deep drag, then rummaged through her handbag and threw him a handkerchief. "Wipe the blood off your face, you look like an unsuccessful rapist."

Still stunned by the current turn of event, Rachmiel dabbed at his wounds, trying to work out which excuse he could give that would sound the least stupid.

CHAPTER 15

Raven & John

Raven stared into the mirror, watching the ivory comb (which belonged to Isis) as she drew it through her hair. *White on black, like a shark slicing through a sea,* she thought. *And I'm wasting time here. Everything's conspiring against my attempts to reach Jake.*

Her face was pale, almost goth-white, the result of both her recent illness and her worry. *Gosh, I look like I've aged overnight.*

"The door into Absurdia opens at fixed times," John had explained. "Next one is at six in the morning. Get some sleep—I'll wake you."

She had no reason to doubt him now, but . . .

"I'm worried that your wife has made a picture out of Jake. If she has . . ."

"There's no way to reverse it," John had assured her solemnly. "Your only chance of saving your boyfriend is reaching him before it's too late."

He'd woken her up as promised. The time was currently 5:53 a.m.

She looked now at the merman, who, fingers tapping nervously on his glittering tail, regarded her back, his eyes far from calm.

She smiled. "Don't worry, I'll make it to the station alive."

"It may be more difficult than you imagine. Maybe I should come along."

"You know that won't work. If Isis senses that you're gone—"

"It's not just that."

"I won't forget about your legs."

"I'm not saying you will—"

"Don't worry. I won't. I'll mention it to DOG when I see him."

"I'm counting on you, Raven. You've no idea how crappy its been down here for me these last years, seeing only Olaf—"

"It's six o'clock."

"Yeah, time to go. And Raven?"

"Yeah?"

"Just remember—you're *not* going insane out there. No matter how weird it looks, everything you see and encounter is as real as it seems. Take Absurdia completely at face value. Forget that for even a second, and you could be dead."

"Meaning you won't get your legs back, right? Sorry, I didn't mean that. I'm just nervous. Best I get my backside to the other side already."

They both smiled weakly at each other, then Raven opened the red door and stepped out through it.

She took one look at where she was, then, her eyes fixed on the landscape, tried to retreat back through the door. The door, however, had disappeared. Instead of its handle, she now gripped a tree branch that had gray feathers in place of leaves, and huge dangling orange fruit.

Oh, I really am stuck here now, and Absurdia is a very appropriate name for this realm.

The sky was yellow, the sun green. The landscape was orange, just like in all those Martian sci-fi movies she'd watched with Jake.

Other weird stuff (She smirked: *Like a feathered tree ain't odd enough, right?*): On the ground below the tree she stood by were several small—two foot long—skeletons. Of winged humanoids—their pinion bones spread behind them like fingers.

Having no idea what had killed the little winged people (or if it was still nearby), Raven walked quickly away from the tree, off towards the green sun.

She was armed again. In addition to a red switchblade ("You never know when you'll need to cut something or *someone.*"), John had also given her a .38 Smith & Weston Airweight revolver and a box of bullets. The bullets were in a fanny pack, the weapon stuck in her belt. She'd left her grappler behind.

He'd also packed her a bag of food and drink. As she walked, she unwrapped a ham-and-rye sandwich and bit into it, sipped water from a bottle.

She trudged on, seeking a break in the seemingly interminable sandscape. *DOG, DOG, DOG. Where the hell is DOG? Don't worry, he said. Just look for a road, any road. DOG's like ancient Rome—all roads lead to it. Okay, that may be so. But where are the roads then?*

CHAPTER 16

Rachmiel & Maxine

Adversaries in love, they stared each other down across the first class compartment, each waiting for the other's defenses to crumble so they could enter and ravage and wreak emotional ruin on the tender exposed psyche.

Rachmiel's face stung and he was embarrassed. Opposite him, Maxine kept smoking, her eyes seemingly calm behind a nicotine-scented haze. It was a ruse, of course. She had a hair trigger—all she needed was the right combination of words to come at him again.

Finally Rachmiel said, "I'm glad it turned out to be you."

She stared at him a long time, her lips pursed around the cigarette, sucking, flaring its tip in an endless mini-inferno that reflected her desire to burn him up in her flames.

Yes, Rachmiel thought distractedly, *smoking in women is fellatio practice.* She spilled smoke through her nostrils. *Yes, I married a dragon.*

She blew a smoke ring. *Behold the nicotine vagina!*

While she consumed her cigarette, he studied her.

She was small. Not a child—she was twenty-three, eighteen when he'd married her. She'd been fifteen when they'd met in Hamburg. A runaway.

Eager to not to repeat the behavior of his youth, he'd initially not slept with her even though the German age of consent was fourteen. It had been hard—she was so beautiful, and, pubescent hormones aboil (in addition to her craving physical affection after fleeing from an unpleasant family situation), had desperately wanted him to fuck her, feeling he was rejecting her because of some physical flaw. He'd finally given in to Maxine's urgings after she broke up with him for the third time over the issue, but up till then, he was glad he'd controlled himself. It had felt good to be in control of something.

Not like with poor Mary, where he'd had no say . . . Despite his current emotional straits with the angry woman opposite him, just the thought of Mary Sherman . . .

He forced Mary from his mind, commanded it to process the data his eyes fed it about Maxine.

Maxine looked elfin. Her face had a triangular aspect to it—from being wide at temples and cheeks, it tapered to an almost-point at her chin. Her green eyes were large, her mouth very small—when she fellated him it looked like he was plugging her face with his penis. Her nose was also small, her ears completely hidden by the neck-length red hair . . .

Her torso was bony. Her breasts were little, almost all nipple. She had broad hips. Her pubic hair was thick—a lush, curly red expanse that foretold of deep pleasures to come.

Her slim legs, sheathed in black leotards that dipped into the long boots . . .

Don't eye-fuck her, he thought, *you've sufficient complications already without adding a boner to the mix.*

She caught his appraising eyes on her and stubbed out her cigarette, loving him as intensely as she hated him. "Well, do I have to scratch your other cheek before you say anything?"

"I just said: I'm glad it turned out to be you, darling."

The reply momentarily confused her. Emotions warped her face as she reorganized her anger.

The train thundered on through the placid green ocean. Outside was birds, clouds hung in layers . . . the sky a pale blue canvas. Forests, fields, roads running parallel to the rail line, buildings . . . Normalcy— new country, same world, same people. A cool summer mid-morning.

Inside, anger boiled.

"I want a divorce," she said.

He nodded. "I suppose you do." He smiled. "How 'bout we enjoy the day in *Konin* first, get divorced once were back in Berlin?"

"I don't believe this. You're planning to fuck me anyway?"

"I would have anyway if it *wasn't* you."

She nodded coldly. "Be more creative, or I'll go for your eyes this time."

"Don't. Seeing as you're leaving me, I just think it a good idea to feed your vagina enough penis as possible first so it doesn't starve to death before you remarry. If you ever do."

"You bastard. I'll—"

The curtains parted. "Damen und Herren, Ihre Fahrkarte, bitte."

Rachmiel and Maxine both gave the inspector—a smallish woman with tightly pursed lips and dyed-blond hair pulled back in a tight ponytail—their tickets.

She looked them over, handed them back. "Danke, Herr und Frau Donovan." She departed.

Rachmiel regarded his furious wife again. "You were saying, dear?"

She didn't reply. Instead, she launched herself at him like a tiger.

This time Rachmiel was ready for her, catching both her hands inches from his face. She fought him silently, with all her energy. It was useless. Once she'd lost the element of surprise in their conflict, she was helpless, her childlike frame no match for his masculine force.

He quickly turned her round, forcing her to kneel on the seat by the window. Restraining her arms with one hand, he peeled down her cream pants with the other, then pulled aside her thong. He fondled her exposed buttocks roughly, slipped a hand between them into her vagina. He laughed coldly; her sex was dry and unwelcoming. All good then.

He unzipped his pants, freed his penis, and lubricated it with spit.

"No!" Maxine gasped. "Someone might come."

"That person just left. The next person coming is myself. Now shut up and take your punishment."

She shut up, her body tense against his. Dreading what was coming.

Her anus was a creased crater between her buttocks. Slowly, savoring the feeling, Rachmiel forced his penis into it.

Maxine shuddered and fought to get away. She whisper-screamed as the stiff organ penetrated her.

He held her down, her face pressed against the window glass. He worked the penis deep into her rectum, doing his best to hurt her. He knew she hated him using her anus—she felt it was the ultimate in subjugation, like he preferred her excrement to herself, implying she was less than feces—which was why he did it.

He stabbed her anus viciously, savaged the unwelcoming hole mercilessly. There was blood, but he ignored it—it was merely lubrication. While he sodomized her, she wept, tears streamed down her face.

He enjoyed it, but not much. She was incredibly tight there, like she intended never to defecate again. Using her this way felt like opening up a virgin forest. He knew she didn't enjoy it at all. It was a ritual of power between then—him relaying to her in this most brutal of ways who was in charge in their relationship. While sodomizing Maxine, it felt to him like he was destroying her, reducing her to less than she was meant to be. And clearly she felt it too: each time he sodomized her, she was docile for the next few days, no more rebellion in either eyes or voice as she walked gingerly around their house pampering her backside.

The last time he'd done it, she'd been stuck in bed for two days afterward, unable to poop at all, all talk of her leaving him gone. Of course, by the end of the week, she was her brash, confident self again. The bitch he loved.

Damn, he thought, slamming into her over and over, while she gripped the seat back and bit her lip to keep from screaming out with pain, *maybe I should let her go. It's like she's only with me to prevent me raping her.*

His climax built up in him. His body trembled from the pleasure of hers. He pumped the semen into her. He grimaced, imagining blood, excrement, and male seed mingling in her rectum.

He pulled out of her. She made to straighten up; he held her in place. "Don't move. I want to watch it drip out of you."

"I hate you," she moaned as the blood and come bubbled out of her hole. A tint of fecal brown . . . red, white, brown, her anus's national colors—the proud flag of the kingdom of sodomy.

Outside, Poland raced by them.

"I hate you." Her voice was a tortured, trembling gasp.

He grinned at the sound. *Oops. She must have come too.* "A one-sided opinion. I love you."

"I hate you." Her voice was wet with her tears.

He watched the mingled blood and semen dribble down her thighs. "So leave. Go away like you intend to. Slut."

Her response was a hurt moan, as if the slur on her sexual character pained her more than her torn backside.

He smirked. "You're mine forever, Maxine. I'm stronger than you, don't you ever forget that. And if you dare me again, you'll get more of the same."

Stronger? It was a lie, he knew. He was weaker than she was. And one of these days she'd kill him for sure, maybe while they had violent sex, maybe when she was high on drugs—coke or speed—or maybe in a fit of rage. Maybe even just as a gag. But she'd definitely murder him. Their love story would have no happy ending.

But till then . . . she was his jones . . . like heroin in his blood . . . he'd never be free of her. He loved her more than life itself. When she spilled his blood, it would have been worth it.

He let go of her hips. Her buttocks plopped back together. She straightened up, cleaned herself off, turned to face him.

She was still crying, her makeup ruined. He smiled at her. She stared dully back at him. No, there would be no more stupid talk of divorce— the rebellion was far gone from her eyes.

He saw her gaze was fixed on his exposed penis.

She grimaced through her tears. "Put it away, will you, before that fat inspector comes back down the corridor—she looked a nosy sort."

He moved to do so. She passed him some tissue. "Wipe it clean first, for goodness sake," she snarled, purple lips curled downward in a sneer. "Never forget commonsense hygiene."

CHAPTER 17

Lily / Nina / Isis

At 10 a.m., after a hearty breakfast of wheat toast, scrambled eggs, potatoes, turkey sausage, and coffee, Olaf escorted Lily and Nina up to the third floor. Lily wore a white sundress; Nina, a black T-shirt over faded denim pants.

The gothic manservant seemed well recovered from his previous day's experience of meeting them.

"I imagined I heard gunshots last night," Lily commented. "But I must have been dreaming."

"Me too," Nina added, hiding her surprise at her girlfriend's statement. "They sounded like they were coming from up here."

Olaf shrugged off both their comments. "Occasionally, the mistress finds sleep hard to come by. She passes the night hours watching TV cop dramas." He grinned a mouthful of broad teeth. "This house has freaky acoustics. Things can get distressingly loud."

"I hope she isn't woozy and cranky as a result this morning."

"Not to worry, coffee works early morning miracles."

"Why aren't there windows on the fourth floor?"

"Yeah?"

"The gallery. It's—"

He fell silent as the door ahead of them opened and Betty Butcher stepped into the corridor. She looked the approaching trio over with an angry expression, then audibly sighing, retreated back into the room.

"A model," Olaf quickly addressed his companion's quizzical expressions, both women visibly shaken by the blonde's appearance. "The mistress is currently painting a barbarian—"

"You're lying again, aren't you? She's naked and bloodstained."

"Not to mention carrying a massive axe."

"Were you raping her?"

"Or was *she* raping someone? She looks tough enough to."

Olaf gulped but recovered quickly. "Mistress Isis demands superlative realism in her models—make-up, paint . . . I'm sure you noticed how dead her face looked."

Lily nodded. "Yeah like a corpse—"

"Okay, here we are," the manservant interrupted her, pushing open the next door with a deferential attitude and gesturing that they enter. Remember, Mistress Isis is an exceptional woman; treat her with the proper respect."

Nina patted Olaf on the cheek. "Don't worry your moldy pants 'bout that; you'll be able to resume worshipping her once we leave."

To the sound of Olaf huffing in indignation, they stepped into the room.

The door shut behind them. Isis Lynch sat before them on a green couch.

"Come, come, girls," she said, pointing to the seats opposite hers.

***

It was all Lily could do not to wet herself from excitement on actually meeting Isis Lynch in person. She clamped down hard on her bladder to prevent the embarrassment.

Staring at the satin-wrapped middle-aged blonde on the couch, her jaded gray eyes seemingly custodian to impossible secrets, Lillian McLean couldn't but see her own future swinging open like a door through which eternal sunshine blared into what had previously been a dimly-lit career room. While not exactly bottom-of-the-barrel, reporting for Dirty Vagina didn't exactly promise great advancement prospects.

She smiled at Isis while setting up her laptop on the coffee table between them. *Well, I've got the great woman here now. This is that chance of a lifetime that I don't screw up, no matter what.*

She looked left at Nina, who, if anything, looked even more enraptured that herself—*She's probably wondering what her pussy tastes like*—and grimaced.

Against all Lily's remonstrations/pleadings/threats/good advice/better judgment, Nina (claiming she'd taken downers to get back to sleep after a nightmare and needed a fast pick-me-up, and no—

92

coffee just wouldn't do the trick!) had insisted on doing some pills and coke before breakfast.

Lily just hoped Nina would be able to hold it together now, she already had that manic look in her eyes. *Girlfriend, if you dare mess this up for us, Tricky Dick won't need to fire you—there won't be enough pieces of you left to fire . . .*

"So, girls," Isis Lynch said with a wry smile, finally giving birth to the conversation which the almost-full-term pregnant pause had presaged, "you wanted to interview me. Here I am."

"Just getting set up," Lily said, arranging a Samson USB condenser microphone facing Isis, plugging in a mouse, then clicking record in Audacity on the laptop and checking her input levels.

"Just one caveat . . ."

"What's that?"

"My husband John utterly refuses to speak to you. He's busy with some complex multimedia entanglement."

"That isn't a problem," Lily said, hiding her disappointment behind a smile. "We're delighted at *you* lending us your time."

Nina was already knelt in front of her chair, zoom-lensed Nikon pressed to her eye. "Thanks so much for agreeing to see us," she chatted between clicks. "I hope we're not imposing too much if we ask for some shots of the house's interior as well."

"Di Va's entire October issue will be devoted to PT," Lily added, pulling up the Open Office document containing her carefully prepared questions. "Everything about you three and your subsequent lives and lifestyles. So we need lots of pictures."

Isis waved dismissively. "Oh, that's no bother at all. Take as many pictures as you like, it's the least I can do."

"And can we also get a few shots of you in more formal attire, possibly working on a canvas at your easel?"

Their hostess laughed. "You're requesting two mutually excusive things."

Nina lowered her Nikon, perplexed. "How so?"

"I always paint in the buff." She adjusted her position on the couch, her blue robe splitting to give an impression of pale pubic hair.

"Naked? Why?" Lily realized the interview had gotten off to an odd start.

Isis laughed again. "Inspiration is in the air. It seeps into me through the pores of my skin. Obviously, clothes hinder that osmosis."

"So you don't feel inspired now?"

"Not as much as I could," she replied simply. "Don't worry, you'll have both sets of photographs." She frowned. "You'll have to wait till tomorrow for the dressed-up ones, though. I'm currently busy finishing something off and don't want to put on makeup only to have to take it off again immediately afterwards. And if you want me in different outfits . . ."

"Oh, that's perfectly fine," Lily quickly replied.

Nina nodded assent, then got to her feet and moved to a position behind Lily and focused the camera lens again.

Lily consulted her laptop notes. *Okay, first coup's been won; we're in her good books—she's invited us to stay one more day.*

She grinned at Isis. "So, if we can begin at the end: The question all your fans—all our readers—will be wondering is: Why? Why break your silence now?"

Isis smiled tightly. "Primarily so you'll both go away."

"C'mon, you're playing with us. There has to be more to it than that."

Isis sighed. "There is. I do think it's time I said something. Despite being a recluse, I've kept up with the latest trends in avant-garde over the years, and really, I'm not impressed in the least. And my disgust always stems from the same root: Can one lay claim to living on the cutting edge—to being the cutting edge—if all one does is repackage and recycle what was done when they were still in diapers?"

"You're of course making reference to Diane Fader's Temple of Cosmic Color Composition?"

"Not directly, but if the cap fits . . ." She scowled. "Pussy Transmission did what hadn't been done before. We were the Star Trek of our rebellious generation, fearless pioneers blithely unconcerned about the commerciality that ran rife in modern art circles back then."

"You were all rich," Nina injected. "You didn't need to be commercial successes."

Lily spun to glare at her angrily.

Isis waved the comment off. "No, no, she's quite right. *We were* rich kids. Brats. Totally arrogant in our self-belief. And that in itself fostered a purity in our art—we were able to seek out things not usually considered 'art' and show the public that whatever *entertains* is art. And what is entertainment? Whatever distracts us from mundanity—and here's the catch—whether we want or like the distraction or not."

Lily was almost defecating with glee now. *Yes, she's even better than I expected!* "But don't you consider this an extreme point of view?"

"Which part of it?"

"Well, for one thing, your suggestion that entertainment is entertainment, whether we want it to be or not. That's essentially saying that art exists independent of the spectator."

Isis smiled. "Almost every definition of anything is simply a question of interpretation. War, famine, murder, rape—these are all downright horrible things and yet . . . CNN for instance, exists simply because people find war and misery entertaining. The thrill of fear you get on hearing the Dow Jones stock market reports, realizing that your life's savings—all your careful painstaking investments—may be worth less than the cost of a bottle of Coke by tomorrow morning, that's entertainment too."

"Entertainment?"

". . . Properly defined, is simply whatever distracts you from boredom. Almost having a heart attack definitely qualifies." She nodded, agreeing with herself. "But like you say, it is an extreme point of view. What I'm getting at here, though, is that even art you hate is art just the same. So, on to the question of if art can exist independent of our recognition of its existence. The answer has to be *yes*—art is art is art is art, or else Pussy Transmission would never have been so successful." She laughed aloud. "Art must exist—no, it DOES exist, parallel to the spectator, or how would you describe, as in . . . okay, explain away all the books, movies, paintings you've never seen, both those made before and during your lifetime, and additionally, those you'll never even know exist—they do exist independent of you. Claiming otherwise is as myopic as saying the only people alive on the planet are those you've met personally. It's as daft as insisting that a tree falling in a forest only makes noise when there's someone around to hear it."

While opining, Isis's voice had gotten progressively louder. Placing a hand over her breasts, she took a deep breath like she was calming herself. "Oh, but now you've started me ranting. I hope we can edit that bit out. No, leave it in—it'll piss a few stuffed shirts off, but who cares? But I've gotten sidetracked. What I meant to say is that we— PT—actually brought new concepts of art to the public mind. Even the most jaded critic was confused when Rachmiel unveiled his Mona Kisser for instance—"

Damn straight, Lisa thought. She'd seen the Mona Kisser, a totally grotesque statue of a woman suckling a baby, only the mother had no face, just a massive set of lips on the front of her head. For a distressing moment, she remembered the three-breasted Madonna in her room, and that statue's odd transformation last night. *But did that really happen?*

"—So my beef with the so-called 'New School' is that they lay claim to inventing lots of things *we* came up with. The fact that we don't charge out blowing our own horns—masturbating in public—isn't license to plagiarize us."

"You're upset that they're not giving you well-deserved credit?" Nina asked.

Lily rolled her eyes. *Shut up, wilya!?*

Isis, however, nodded fiercely. "Yes. Every generation of artists, particularly uncreative ones, needs to show respect to those who've gone before them. Even standing on the shoulders of pigmies, you see a lot further ahead. So now, I think it's about time I break my silence—"

Watching Isis Lynch talk, her face fierce—eyes wide, nostrils flared with emotional heat—Lily was thrilled. *This is gonna be the best Dirty Vagina interview ever.* And after this, her career . . . she stole a loving glance at Nina who now stood by the door, attempting to catch Isis in profile—*Just get those snaps, babe—both our careers are blowing through the roof when this hits the newsstands.*

And yes, I do find Isis Lynch totally sexy for a middle-aged woman. Too bad she doesn't flow our way.

She checked her levels, then adjusted her microphone's position on the coffee table. "Now, Mrs. Lynch, let's go back in time to the beginning and talk a bit about how you formed PT. Whatever were you, your husband, and your brother thinking?"

"We were anarchists," Isis began. "All we wanted to do was blow up art—the entire bloated contemporary establishment—and rebuild the motherfucker from the ground up . . ."

Lily McLean grinned broadly. *Oh, this is going to be a great day.*

CHAPTER 18

Raven

Raven finally found a highway. A dusty cracked road that seemed rarely used. She followed it east (assuming her direction by the green sun's position). Soon, the orange-red landscape altered and she was walking between cliffs—sheer red rock walls that rose so high above her it hurt her neck to stare at their summits.

Ahead of her, the ravine seemed endless, the highway an asphalt river.

The transition had occurred in fast-forward. One moment, nothing. The next—like she'd descended a flight of unseen stairs—red rock flanked her left and right.

She smothered her apprehension, patted her pistol. The weapon's bulky feel beneath her black jacket reassured her somewhat.

She peered back. A good distance off, just visible between the walls of rock, the orange desert began/ended.

She turned around again, concentrated her attention on heading forward, between the skyscraper cliffs that seemed to extend forever.

Gosh, this place is just like the Grand Canyon. All roads lead to DOG, John said? Well, he'd better be right.

The highway soon curved sharply; her point of entry was lost from view. Above her the green sun burned hot in the yellow sky.

She blinked: *Was that a red woman I just saw flying through the air?*

Recalling the little winged corpses she'd earlier noticed beneath the feathered tree on her arrival, Raven remembered merman John Lynch's admonition. *No, I'm not hallucinating. This is real. To forget that is to die out here in Absurdia.*

She felt discomfort in her crotch—her thong had somehow gotten stuck between her labia. She adjusted it, then did same to her bra. She stood in the middle of the road staring down the highway.

Another winged red figure flapped across the distant sky ahead. Raven waited till it had disappeared from view, then resumed walking.

Looking at the sky had created an odd feeling of vertigo in Raven— it seemed like she was overhead, upside down, the yellow sky the ground she'd drop into. Walking was little better—she imagined the immense rock walls on both sides falling to crush her.

Depressing in the extreme. Nonetheless, she pressed on.

***

After a while, Raven began encountering turnoffs from the main highway, equally unused roads (and indistinguishable from the one she walked on) that vanished into the distance between similarly daunting walls of rock.

By one of these turnoffs, she found a parked motorbike. A red Harley Davidson. Dusty, but in good condition.

Appropriating it for her quest was a no-brainer—she'd long tired of walking.

After checking that it had sufficient fuel (an assumption—*how long is my journey anyway?*), she stowed her bag of food and drink in one of the Harley's side compartments, climbed on, and rolled off down the side road.

She quickly discovered her change of road and direction made no difference whatever—the immense red canyon walls continued with no end in sight.

CHAPTER 19

Lily / Nina / Isis

"You must understand," Isis Lynch opined fiercely, her gray eyes aglow with feeling, "That with PT—in my, John, and Rach's minds—art was supreme. You killed to make art. You died to make art. Your dying itself could be art, if it attracted sufficient attention to be a societal distraction. *You*, however, the artist, were *unimportant* . . . I mean, your sanity or lack of it, your wealth or penury—just ask Van Gogh or Mozart—and your relationships . . . get divorced every week if you liked . . . those didn't matter. What was important was that you created. That you damn well entertained every one. As John once put it: 'Bleed if you must, the damn show must go on.'"

She frowned at Lily, her eyes querying, 'do you understand?'

Lily nodded eagerly back. The interview was going great. Isis seemed much like a long-blocked pipe—once the obstruction was cleared, the backlogged buildup of pressure rushed to get out. Just give her the slightest prompting and she talked and talked. *At this rate we'll have enough for two issues of Di Va.*

She stole a glance at her girlfriend. Nina was done taking pictures for the moment and sat chin-in-palms, staring enthralled at their hostess. Lily sighed. *Oh, she's definitely thinking of screwing her.*

She returned her attention to Isis. "So," she began cautiously, "why the breakup then? I know this must surely be hard for you to discuss . . ."

Smiling like a sated cat, Isis waved the suggestion off. "Hard? Not at all. Why would you ever think that?"

"Well, there were rumors of a tragedy of some kind, of magic and such like."

"Tragedy? Magic? Ha ha ha! Nothing could be further from the truth."

"But you broke up right on the eve of your success . . ."

"Overwork. We were too new to the game, had no idea how to pace ourselves. Remember we had no idea we'd become famous."

"And the wild parties and drugs?" Nina asked.

Isis chuckled. "Whatever stories you heard about those are likely true. We were living a rock band lifestyle. Don't ask me, I was generally too out of it to remember anything, and darling John was even worse."

"But surely you must remember some things that happened. You can't have been *that* wasted."

"Oh, but darling—I was *that* wasted. Ha ha!" Her middle-aged face suddenly turned mischievous as a six-year-old's. "Hmmm, I do remember one. Have you heard of the shit-moustache incident?"

Lily and Nina shook their heads.

"Okay, there was this time at a party when John got so stoned that Diane Lisa Fielding—"

Lily's mind made a quick connection. "*Baroness* Fielding? The UNICEF Ambassador?"

"Yeah, the same. She was just fifteen then. Anyway, she had the totally mad hots for my brother Rachmiel, but John wouldn't let her near him 'cos of the potential scandal. So on the night in question, John's totally wasted on drugs—passed out cold, and Diane, who's herself higher than a kite—and remember she's still in high school—decides to have some revenge. So she gets out a Gillette Venus from her purse and shaves off John's eyebrows, mustache, and beard while he's out . . . then she does a little girly poop on a palette—it looked like chocolate ice cream—finds a paintbrush and proceeds to paint a mustache on John with the shit."

Lily gaped. "She did?"

Isis nodded seriously. "But that's not really the funny part. Now, I'm not there when she starts doing her poop mustache on my husband. I just walk into the room and see her using this brown paint on his face . . . and you'd not believe how serious she is at what she's doing—like she thinks she's Rembrandt. Anyhow, it finally hits me what's stinking up the room and what she's up to. I'm quite drunk myself; I'm just about to clobber the brat for abusing my husband when she wipes off all the shit on his face with a tissue, then turns to me, and asks sweetly: 'Could you paint him for me, Isis?—I'm crap at mixing poop colors.' Ha ha ha! Diane actually said that."

"And what did you do? Strangle her?"

"Ha ha ha! No! I was bombed myself, see, so much so that her request actually made sense to me. What's a painter do but paint, right? So I took the brush and palette from her, and actually did paint a shit mustache, eyebrows, and beard on my darling Johnny." She burst out laughing, then added. "What was worse? I recall at one point asking one of the girls—Rita Dennis it think it was—"

"Not *the* Rita Dennis?"

"Yeah, her, the snotty veggie movie star. It was either her or her sister Trina. I told her I needed a lighter shade of poop to give the mustache some definition, whereupon she instantly pulls down her jeans, squats over the palette and squeezes out this turd that looks like a filter cigarette. So I finish the painting."

"That's an incredible story," Nina said. "Rita frigging Dennis?"

Lily was laughing so hard there were tears in her eyes. "Wow! But we'll never be able to publish it—their lawyers would shut down the magazine."

"Not so," Isis said with a conspiratorial wink.

Lily leaned forward. "How, not so?"

"Well, because Rachmiel filmed everything. Remember, Diane was following him everywhere back then, so he was there. Once she stated her intent, Rach set up one of John's 16 mm cameras . . ." she sat back, fingers steepled over her breasts like she was praying, "and the rest, as they say, is celluloid herstory."

Lily gasped. "You're saying you have the movie of them doing it— pooping on palettes?"

Isis nodded. "Definitely. We even played it at several of our shows. It was good for a laugh back then."

"Your husband *allowed* that?"

"Sure. After he got over how ridiculous he looked, he was thrilled. He did a soundtrack for it of people farting. And that's how poop-art was born."

"What's poop-art?"

Portraits done with excrement. Oh, don't look so shocked. You must have noticed that every bowel movement you do has a different color. So I painted with them." She burst into laughter. "I did portraits of presidents Reagan, Bush, Gorbachev, Botha, Castro, Maggie Thatcher, and the Queen of England, all using excrement."

"*Your* excrement?"

"Occasionally. Most times no—there was literally no end of volunteers . . ." she made an expansive gesture, "people who felt crapped on by the establishment, and who wanted to donate their crap so I could paint the establishment with it. We just had to let everyone—the nouveau art crowd I mean—know when I'd be painting, and tell people what to eat to defecate the right colors. The vegetarians in particular made some remarkably pure tones."

"Do you have any poop paintings that we can photograph?"

"Mainly on film. John always filmed me doing them, then we took pictures. Most of the paintings themselves we destroyed—they smelled like shit. Ha ha ha!" She gripped her sides like she'd split apart with laughter. "You should have seen me: There's one film of me painting a poop copy of the Mona Lisa. I'm wearing a white gas mask—look like a Star Wars storm trooper—cos the stink's so bad!"

"Wow," Nina said, "you guys had a complete blast back then. Imagine trying that today!"

Isis laughed some more. "There was loads of other stuff I really was too wasted to remember doing. Which is a shame 'cos . . . hey wait—I do remember one more tale! There was this queer art dealer who used to follow John around. I mean Drew wanted to fuck John so bad you'd actually see him licking his lips whenever John was in the room. And he made no bones about it either. But of course, John wasn't having it. Nor was I . . . okay that's not entirely true—like lots of hetero women I'd often wondered what it'd be like watching two men get it on. Now, Drew's boyfriend Murphy got jealous of all the attention he wasn't getting, and so one night when we're all at Club 66Sex in the East Village, Murphy tells . . . Shit!"

Her expression had suddenly turned bothered. Very worried.

Oh, no, Lily thought, *now she's going to refuse us permission to print that great anecdote.*

"I'm sorry, ladies," Isis said, getting to her feet in a rush, "but you'll have to excuse me for a few minutes. I'll be right back."

Satin robe swishing about her, she left the room.

"She has a great ass," Nina said as the door shut behind her. She winked at Lily. "Nothing like yours, but you know . . ." she got her pill bottle from her handbag, looked pointedly at Lily. "You need any stimulation, honey?"

"Not the chemical kind. You can do me by hand later."

"O.K." Nina popped two white/yellow pills. "Why'd you think she just rushed off?"

Lily shrugged, leaned forward to click 'Pause' on her recording. "Maybe she remembered she left a tap running, or she needs to make wat—"

Her laptop mouse felt suddenly hairy beneath her palm. Then it twitched and moved. Lily shrieked and jerked her hand off it.

"What . . . ?"

The plastic mouse had become a live rat, the rodent's scaly tail disappearing into the laptop's USB port.

Lily and Nina both gaped at it in horror. The rodent—black, its body trembling like it had a fever—regarded both women with cold beady eyes. It sat there on its haunches, reeking like a gutter. Its bristling fur stuck out all spiky and disheveled.

Its mouth moved, whiskers twitching.

"You're both gonna die," it squeaked.

CHAPTER 20

Raven

Suddenly, there was a giant black rat blocking the road ahead of Raven. At least twenty feet high, the rat stank like a sewer. Smell rolled off it in visible grey clouds like it was a carpet someone was beating. Swarms of flies buzzed amidst the stink clouds. The rat stood with one clawed foot on either side of the highway's center line, its scaly tail extending behind it like an extension of the separation.

Its hairy bulk blocked off the entire space between the canyon walls.

Raven rolled her motorbike to a halt twenty meters from the massive rodent. *Where the hell did you just appear from?* Gun held at the ready, she sat there, bike engine throbbing like a penis beneath her, watching it uneasily. *Damn! There's no way around the frigging thing!*

The rat glared down at her.

"You're gonna die!" it said in a thunderous (though somehow also comical) squeak. "I'm gonna kill and eat your ass!"

She smirked back at it. "So you aren't friendly. You can talk anyway—that's a plus."

She did some quick calculations. *The last side exit from the canyon was half a mile back. They've been occurring say like every half-mile, which means the next one should be just behind this giant rat.* She considered the size of her gun: *To kill this creature, I need to shoot it in the eyes. A small target, but manageable, though I'll have to get up real close to it so as not to miss.*

"How do I reach DOG?" she asked the rat.

It twisted its head to one side, nose twitching like it could smell food. It scratched the canyon walls with a claw, triggering a rain of red dust. "DOG?" Its eyes blinked as they regarded Raven. "The hell if I know." It pointed a forepaw at her. "Gal, I'm just here for some breakfast, and that's you!"

CHAPTER 21

Lily & Nina

"You're gonna die." The rat repeated in a confident squeak.

"You already said that last night," Nina said in a strained voice, conscious of Lily's questioning gaze after the statement. "Can you be more specific? I mean, like, who's gonna kill us? Is it Isis? Her husband John? Olaf the goon? The blonde with the axe?"

The rat laughed. "Who or how doesn't matter. It's simply the nature of the thing. You're both going to die here."

Lily's initial fear of the rat had dispersed once she realized it wasn't itself dangerous. She leaned back in her chair. "And you expect us to lie down and take it like we're being raped?"

"There's nothing you can do," the rat insisted. "This house will kill you—it's your fate to die here."

"I disagree," Lily said tightly. "I don't believe in fate; I make my own choices and my own destiny." She was now worried again. This little beast's quiet conviction was getting to her. "I pilot the ship of my soul down life's river to my own destination, and I'm not going out . . ."

She ran out of words, looked to Nina for help. Nina wasn't even looking at her. She grimaced. *Trust my darling pill-head to take this moment to fiddle with her shoes.*

"Paddle your canoe however you like," the rat said, "Upstream, downstream . . . far out to sea even. You're still going to die. And then us rats will—"

"Shut the hell up!" Nina snarled, slamming the heel of her shoe down hard on the talking rodent.

The three-inch heel punctured through the black rat, exploding it like a bag of transfusion blood, red drops spraying everywhere. Then, all of a sudden, there was no longer any hairy rodent on the coffee table, just the scattered remains of Lily's busted-up mouse.

Both women looked at themselves.

"At least I got rid of the horrid thing," Nina said defensively. "You need a new mouse though."

"Yeah, the tiny fucker did talk too much," Lily said. Her expression turned serious. "But . . . we're gonna die?"

"Ignore it; it was just talking rat poop."

CHAPTER 22

Raven

Raven was about zooming the Harley Davidson forward to attack the monster rat, when, from out of nowhere, something struck it from behind.

That looks like the heel of a shoe! she thought of the massive spike which exited the rat's bristling fuzzy chest like a spear. *Yes, that definitely is a shoe heel. But no, it can't be!*

The impaled monster rat, bleeding out in thick red splashes, slumped to the ground in front of Raven, the piercing heel vanishing as it fell.

"Believe me, you're gonna die," it whispered.

"You first though, Hairy Scary," she whispered back. She was relieved that she didn't have to battle it anymore. *But . . . how the heck do I ride round it? It's blocking off the entire canyon!*

Then the rat exploded. Raven ducked behind the Harley, shielding her eyes as the air filled with flying lumps of flesh.

She peered out of concealment at the sound of crashing/clunking. *That doesn't sound like falling meat.*

It wasn't *meat*—large chunks of sizzling plastic were dropping all around her. Plummeting like bombs, streaking past like missiles, slamming into the red rock walls, ricocheting like bullets across the gap. She ducked one such ricochet aimed at her head, then stared confused at its 'Made in Taiwan' imprint after it bounced off the Harley's handlebars and came to rest by her feet.

The hard raining stopped. Raven got up and looked around.

There was metal mixed in with the shattered, scattered, plastic. Something about the arrangements, the curvature of particular pieces, looked familiar to Raven . . . *that massive red bowl spinning like a top . . .* She however couldn't assemble a recognizable whole in her mind.

The explosion had cleared the way ahead. She mounted her bike again and zoomed off between the chunks of fallen smoking plastic.

The erstwhile rat's tail had now become a thick gray cable lying precisely in the middle of the road. The cable bent out of sight around the next right turnoff. Raven decided to follow the cable to where it led. The rat had to have come from somewhere.

Body low to the floor, she swerved the Harley around the bend in the red rock. She leveled the bike out again and raced like the wind. Ahead of her, canyon walls and gray cable both extended seemingly forever after, the world contracting to a pin-point red aisle.

Then, as she biked along beside the cable, the landscape suddenly altered again, the forbidding red cliffs either side of her leveling down to orange desert.

She heaved a relieved sigh on once more seeing the sky everywhere ahead of her.

The gray cable continued along a dusty freeway through sand dunes. Between groves of feathered trees, Raven kept rolling: ten . . . fifty . . . eighty miles.

At one point, a bullet train—white, dark glass windows, blue longitudinal stripe—roared parallel to her for a hundred or so meters. Then, just as she was about heading towards it, it vanished again like it had been erased.

She blinked and rode on.

The cable ended at a cottage-sized model of a HP laptop. She stopped the bike and studied it. Large black steps with 'QWERTY' keyboard lettering led up to a massive screen that showed a continuation of the orange desert outside.

'Welcome to DOG Zone.' was printed on the screen. Beneath this followed a caution: 'All Vehicles are Parked Inside at Owner's Risk.'

Then a blue double door appeared on the screen and swung open inwards. Words appeared above the entrance: 'Enter here, all ye who dare.'

Well I'm here, wherever this is, Raven thought. She looked around. Everywhere was the same desert expanse. She looked back at the laptop.

And I do dare.

A ramp marked 'Enter' rose through the PC's right side from ground to screen. Hair flowing in slipstream, Raven zoomed the motorbike up this and through the door in the laptop screen. Somehow it seemed the right thing to do.

She felt herself pass through the screen, and then she was out on the other side. In the desert within.

CHAPTER 23

Lila & Nina

"Drat it, not now!" Lily said.

Nina looked up in concern from strapping her shoe back on. "What, baby?"

Lily pointed to the laptop screen. "I think I've picked up a virus."

Nina stared at the pretty black-haired girl riding a Harley Davidson across a desert landscape on Lily's monitor. "You're certain she's not some new screensaver?"

"No. I can't get rid of her whatever I do." She tapped the touchpad, right-clicked, selected 'Delete,' right-clicked some more. "See? She-it! Trust my luck to turn bad on today of all days. Has to be that damned rat!" She glared at the strewn bits of wrecked mouse like she wanted to kill it all over again.

"Calm down. Let's hope it clears up soon. Are you sure you didn't leave some file from YouTube running? What's that movie you keep streaming again?"

Onscreen, the 'camera' angle altered so the girl was now biking towards them, her hazel eyes squinting against the wind, her lips pursed, her hair a black splotching of ink. In her black clothes, she seemed related to Death.

"She's cute," Nina opined, "though I doubt I've ever seen anyone so grim-looking in my life."

Lily regarded the onscreen girl whose sable hair whipped around her head like a confused tornado. She *was* really good-looking, her features well-sculpted—a cute nose, full kiss-requesting lips, and a solid bosom that heaved rhythmically between the gleaming handlebars with her breathing.

She sighed; this was neither the time nor the place to dawdle. "Nina, baby, pull your horny nose out of her backside. Isis will be back any minute now. I need to record the interview."

"Here, darling, have a pill, a nice green Quaalude to calm you down. You'll feel better already."

"Thanks, baby. What'll I ever do without you? Yeah, I do feel better, but still—the interview?"

"Record it with your phone."

"Oh? Yeah . . . no, lend me your iPad, better audio quality."

"Okay, just don't accidentally delete my photos like last time."

"What? I apologized, didn't I? Just hand the frigging device over, darling."

"No need to. Look! She's gone!"

"Huh? Damn, now you've got me *too* relaxed; this feels almost like your tongue up my ass. I hope Isis doesn't notice."

"Darling, your onscreen biker chick just vanished. Well she didn't really vanish—a door opened up in midair and she rode through it . . . try and get your normal screen back now . . . there, see? Your virus troubles are over."

"Help me align the mic again. Careful—don't shift it too much! No . . . back left a bit. Okay, say something into it."

"Hi, everyone! This is Nina Kissing—feature photographer for Di Va magazine! Now, listen up, ya'll readers, while I explain how to eat pussy correctly. I'm totally appalled how, with all the great sexual literature out there now, even some lesbians don't know the right way to treat Queen Clitoris and get their girlfriends off. Yes, girls, being a lesbian doesn't automatically make you good in bed—we need to work at it just like the men do . . ."

"Stop it, stop it, Nina! You're cracking me up."

"I assure you our urethras are pissed-off by this neglect. Pussy isn't smiling at all . . ."

"Ha ha ha! Please stop it!"

"So that's been the Di Va Report by Nina Kissing. Tune in next week for Tongue-in-Cheeks: what gay girls *really* think about anilingus."

"Ha ha! Oh, you're totally incorrigible! Hey, what's keeping Isis, anyway?"

CHAPTER 24

Isis

A train! Isis Lynch thought in dismay as she opened the door to the sitting room where her guests waited. *A train? Damn those rats!*

The rats have become a huge problem, she lamented to herself. *I must get rid of them. Problem is—I can't remember which art spell summoned them here, and now they just keep getting into everything, with their endless prophecies of doom. And how exactly do I explain talking rodents to a pest-control company anyway? Thank goodness I sensed that they'd messed up the capture canvas and got up there in time; it'd have sucked in . . .*

Still preoccupied, she shut the door behind her. *But . . . rat pee? Yes, it has to be! After preparing the canvas, I left it by the wall . . . it was completely blank . . . it was the rats—one of them was butchered by the contact. Still, that doesn't explain how or why it's now showing a bullet train zooming across a countryside . . . and then, the other thing: Betty said there was a girl downstairs who disappeared inside the bathroom. And I checked—she's not with my darling merman. Heck! The blasted rats are getting more powerful!*

She sat facing Lily and Nina and forced a smile. "I'm sorry I left you girls so abruptly. I just remembered—" Her gaze dropped to the debris by Lily's laptop. "What in the world happened?"

The brunette reporter, who now looked doped, sighed. "I don't know if you'll believe us—"

"It was a rat," the blonde photographer interrupted her. "Her mouse became a rat."

"And no, we haven't been doing any drugs," Lily added seriously.

Isis sighed. *Yeah, darlin', that much is obvious from your dilated pupils.* But the pair were clearly otherwise telling the truth, they had a spooked air about them. *Ah, yes, the rats again, I leave here for just a minute and already they're . . .* For a moment, while she dredged up a good excuse for the women, she was taken by Nina's looks. *Her nose is really large—like an eagle's beak; massive lips too, and an incredibly weak chin, and yet she's somehow still pretty. Has to be those eyes—big as lakes, deep moody blues like Justin Hayward used to sing . . .*

She was clearly on drugs too—Isis had seen those spaced-out eyes too many times before. She wasn't one to judge, but . . . *I hope she doesn't louse up the photos. I suspect she won't though; people tend to have a talent for these things. I mean, John used to make great films even when he was too soused to walk straight.*

"I'm sorry about the rats," she said. "I asked my husband not to, but he insisted on demonstrating his skill as an illusionist for you."

Lily and Nina both raised eyebrows. "Huh?" the pair asked together.

Isis sighed loud and insincerely. "I warned him you'd both be scared out of your shoes."

"Illusion?" It was obvious neither woman really believed her, particularly Nina.

She laughed loudly. "Oh dear, please don't tell me you thought it was real? John's such a practical joker. Though he refuses to see you, he said he'd give you a special demonstration."

Lily nodded slowly. "The rat said—"

"That you're both going to die?" Isis finished easily, then laughed some more. "Just John's joke. Silly I know, but you know how men just have to act like jerks sometimes."

She gave an expansive wave. *Here's a good chance to clear up that mess Olaf reported happening yesterday when they arrived.*

"John does illusion experiments on lots of different things," she said, maintaining her bantering 'please don't tell me that scared you' tone.

Lily took the bait. "What . . . what kind of things?"

Isis laughed. "He has this Halloween trick where he can make doors look like they're made of meat. Great for a scare!" She'd anticipated the startled look that passed between both women—*Good! That fixes any awkward questions about last night.* "And another favorite trick of his is making our statues appear to come to life."

This time it was just the brunette's eyes that widened slightly—she'd clearly seen something.

"Wow. It would be just fantastic if we could interview your husband too, Mrs. Lynch."

"Not now at any rate, John's amazingly stubborn. But possibly, after your interview's published, he'll soften. Most johns do once they've been in vaginas, no matter how dirty." She laughed; Lily and Nina joined in once they got the joke. "But, girls . . . I was telling you a story, wasn't I, before I left?"

Lily looked thoughtful, trying to remember.

"The one about the art dealer with the hots for your husband," Nina said.

Isis clapped her hands with delight at the memory—it was a funny story, a good distraction to take the reporters' minds off the rat.

"Okay, where was I? Yes, I remember telling you what happened at club 66Sex. Did I mention that Murphy was a makeup artist? . . . No? Okay, he was. He also did a drag act at Lucky Cheng's on First Avenue, could look totally female when he wanted, just fabulous. So he made a deal with me. See, at that time, I wanted Murphy to introduce me to his buddy Mark Ryden, who kept snubbing PT but had clout both with David Zwirner and the Guggenheim Museum . . . and I *really* wanted to watch two men screw. Oh, I'll admit that bit—so our deal was . . ."

She burst into loud laughter. Lily and Nina waited patiently till she calmed.

"It's hard to tell this in proper sequence, you know—I have to rewind a bit. Okay, that night at Club 66Sex, Murphy bet Drew that he could get John in bed first. And that if he did, Drew had to leave John alone forever afterwards."

"Let me get this clear," Lily asked. "Two gay men—partners— made a bet that one of them could screw a straight guy first?"

Isis nodded. "John and I were both there. We laughed it off like it'd never happen; but when Murphy later approached me for my help, I agreed.

"So, fast forward to a week later. John's in Club 66Sex when this beautiful woman—who's also a dead ringer for me—walks in. John, who's dead drunk, assumes it is me and takes 'me' home. Once there, Murphy wastes no time getting him in bed.

"Now picture this: John's busy doing 'me' hard up the ass, when, as agreed, I walk in with Drew. John turns, sees me, and without batting an eyelid, slurs out, 'Darling, this version of you is so much better at sucking cock.' Then he turns away from us and finishes screwing Murphy. I mean, he's ramming so hard into him Drew and I can hear his testicles slap against Murphy's ass. Next, he pulls out leaving a massive creampie—it looked like someone had spilled whisked egg-white between Murphy's butt-cheeks—then falls stone asleep."

She resumed laughing. "I won't lie—that 'better blowjob' comment burnt me no end, still I kept to the deal: Murphy stripped off my clothes, I put them on and got into bed beside John like *I'd* just slept with him. The boys left, with Drew whispering angrily how Murphy had cheated by pretending to be a woman . . . and what did John's dick taste like anyway?"

"And John?" Nina asked. "What happened when he found out?"

"He never did. He really thought he'd fucked *me* that night—that's a testament to how sloshed he routinely got. He did wonder why I kept refusing to give him head for the next two months, however . . ."

Lily and Nina laughed loudly.

"You sure we can print this?" Lily asked, her expression dubious.

"Yeah, sure, go ahead. It's been twenty years—John'll just deny it anyway."

***

"So now on to your brother, Mrs. Lynch, can you tell us a bit about what he brought to Pussy Transmission? I mean I've seen some of his sculptures and . . ."

Isis had expected this, but nonetheless still felt a return of her old sadness at the questions. "Rachmiel? Oh I haven't seen him in . . ."

While answering Lily and Nina's questions about her brother, Isis once again tried to figure out why Rachmiel hadn't spoken to her even once since leaving his Gracie Square padded cell after his psychotic interlude.

As with all her previous attempts to figure out the coldness between them, she arrived at the same conclusion: *Rach's clearly pissed-off over something else other than my accidentally freezing Mary. But what? What the hell did I do to him that was so terrible? So unforgiveable?*

CHAPTER 25

Maxine

"You should forgive your sister," Maxine Donovan said.

Rachmiel kept staring out at the passing landscape. "You know, I sometimes wonder what use borders are. We're in Poland now, but everywhere looks just the same. And we'll end up conversing with most people we meet in English. We might still be at home."

"What did she do to you, anyway?" Maxine insisted. "Twenty years is a long time to remain angry at anyone."

"Let it go, will you?"

"No. If you expect me to forgive you for cheating on me, I expect you to forgive her too."

He groaned. "You're still angry over that?"

"My soul is currently bleeding worse than my anus. Trust me, your only chance at redemption is to tell me what Isis did."

"Let it go, Maxie."

"Not this time." Ordinarily, Maxine Donovan *would* have let it go. But now, she was intrigued, and still pissed-off at him.

"Please."

"No. Tell me."

Rachmiel sighed. "Okay, then. Mary was . . . still is . . . pregnant."

Maxine's mouth formed an 'O.'

Rachmiel watched her face change expressions as she processed the info. He shrugged. "Well you asked me; now you know."

"I'm so, so sorry. I had no idea."

He frowned. "So my unborn daughter or son is now stuck in a painting in Zanesville, Ohio, and will likely still be there when I'm dust and ashes."

Maxine was silent a long time, the only sound between them the train's rumbling. She'd grudgingly accepted that Rachmiel's sister was an actual, in-the-flesh witch. In the beginning of their relationship, acceptance had been simpler than arguing that such things were fiction. Now, however, she wasn't at all sure anymore. Right or wrong, her husband's convictions had slowly seeped through her defenses and become her own.

"I still think it's been long enough," she said softly.

He sighed again, sounding like he'd been punctured. "I've tried to forgive her. I just can't."

"But it hurts you too, darling, and that hurts me. You need to let this go."

There was torment in his eyes now. "If Mary and the baby weren't . . . if there was something I could do . . ."

"But killing them would be murder, right?"

He nodded, grateful she understood. "And I loved Mary too much to let that happen to her."

"Maybe you're *still* in love with her." This was spoke petulantly, with pique, anger.

"She's past tense," he said quickly to mollify her. "I'm just loyal to her."

"And yet you didn't insist on keeping the painting of her."

He laughed harshly, an ugly sound totally devoid of mirth. "Now you're being unreasonable. You know I can't even bear *thinking* of Mary, how do you think I'd be if I had to *see* her everyday? It would have ruined my life for good."

"I don't see much difference. *It is* ruining your life."

He stared cold-eyed at Maxine. "I also want Isis to suffer like I do, seeing Mary like that—"

"But she doesn't know about the baby?"

"No."

"Why didn't you tell her?"

Rachmiel fell into moody silence. It was a good question. *Why didn't I tell bitch sister?*

"No point stopping at Konin now," he said after a while, regarding Maxine evenly. "Quaint place, but . . . let's just go to Warsaw, get a suite at the Oki Doki, maybe even spend a week. Have fun. It may be possible to purchase a ticket extension onboard, or we could just pay the fine, or—"

"You haven't answered my question of why you never told Isis about Mary's pregnancy."

"Maybe I don't have an answer. Maybe I'm scared of the witch, in a fit of remorse, trying to birth the baby by magical means and foisting a monster on the world—some *The Omen* kind of shit." His expression turned sad. "Just drop it, *please*."

She nodded "Okay," then lit a cigarette. She smiled coolly, pulled on her cigarette, expelled two smoke rings at Rachmiel. "Let's go to Warsaw like you suggested. I want to do some shopping on Mokotowska Street. The fall fashions are in now, and I want something edgy from Acne Studios."

While smoking, Maxine studied her husband's face. Handsome, sad, his eyes pleading for her understanding, for her to drape an emotional blanket over him. For her to mother him, though he was her father's age.

She puffed out another smoke ring, wishing it was heart shaped. Her heart melted with love for him . . . *Oh, darling, I just love you so . . .*

Her stinging anus blew the pink romantic haze from her mind. *Rach was actually about cheating on me! And now he wants me to pamper him! The lousy son-of-a-bitch!*

She utterly detested sodomy, believed it the most unnatural thing ever. She always feared it would hurt, which made her tighten her sphincter, which made it hurt her more than it should, and yet seemingly made the sex more enjoyable for him (*the raping bastard*), so he'd spear her deeper and harder, right into her intestine even sometimes, so she'd almost scream from the pain, and he'd pump her still harder yet.

And when he ejaculated—mingling his semen with her excrement and agony? She felt totally humiliated, which she supposed was the point of it.

She hated him intensely while he sodomized her, yet loved him fiercely afterwards, much more than before. It made little sense, but made complete sense. Maxine reasoned simply in this matter: I *own* him, all of him; he owns me, all of me—he can use me as he pleases, it's his right to my body, I'll not complain.

Looking at his dark, uneasy face as she smoked, she wondered now in part-amusement what he'd say if she produced a femme cock—a strap-on—one day and demanded his anus as her wifely due. She giggled. *What could the bastard say? He'll have no choice but spread his buttocks for me and accept the pain—like I've just done, like I ALWAYS do.*

Maybe she would someday, but for the moment, their roles satisfied her, she sought and found her exaltation in this pseudo-degradation. *I ask for it, he gives it to me; I'm satisfied.*

But do I really ask for it? Or does he just assume I do? Ah, the eternal paradox of a woman: Am I doing this because I want to, or because I'm expected to want to? Or because I've been conditioned to want to?

She returned her thoughts to her primary anger. *He was about to cheat on me, the son-of-a-bitch. I should kill . . . Maybe I will still kill him; let's get to Warsaw.*

Her cigarette burnt down almost to her fingers without her dragging on it again. The long tail of ash behind the red glow hung on as long as it could before falling into her lap. Her lips locked in a fake smile, Maxine sat locked in her thoughts.

Their tragedy was guaranteed, she knew. *We're great for each other and yet totally wrong—horribly bad—for each other. I'll either kill him one of these days for sure, or he'll kill me, and it will be totally the right thing to do at the time—either in the heat of an argument, or he'll cheat on me and I'll catch him, or a vocal barb of mine will pierce him too deep . . . or . . . but one of us will justifiably murder the other in the heat of passion and afterwards be unable to explain satisfactorily our reason for doing so to anyone else, though whichever of us dies will totally understand and approve of being killed . . .*

Rooted deep in her anger, she noticed his mouth moving, but the words blew past her like birds. *Oh, get lost, darling!*

His mouth moved again. Then she saw him reaching for her handbag.

What? In alarm, she jerked out of her fugue, but was too slow to prevent him from taking the bag and fumbling inside it.

"Hey, give that back!" she yelped in horror, grabbing after it.

He held it away from her. "I just want a cigarette too. I've asked you twice, but you were comfortably resident in your little 'I hate him' world."

"Give me back my purse!"

His ears caught the desperation in her voice. His expression turned suspicious. "Why? What have you got in it that you don't want me seeing?"

"Please," Maxine pleaded.

Eyes on hers, Rachmiel felt through the bag. Then, his fingers touching cold metal, he froze for a moment while his mind assured him his senses were right.

He pulled out the pistol, a little silver revolver with a brown grip. He held it up in front of Maxine, dangling it between finger and thumb like it was poisonous.

"I'm not going to ask how you sneaked it through the metal detectors, but . . . Maxie, you were planning to kill me?"

Her silence was a LOUD answer in the affirmative.

"Maxie, what's the gun for?"

"Protection." But her voice wavered nervously and she couldn't look him in the eyes.

He gaped at her in horror. "You *were* planning to kill me? Why?"

No reply.

"Answer me, dammit!"

She looked at him then, her eyes hostile and tired. "I dunno. Same reason you wanted to screw Olga Franck? Boredom . . . something to do?"

"You bitch."

"You prick."

"Murderess."

"Philanderer."

"I haven't cheated on you yet."

A sweet replying smile. "I haven't killed you yet, have I?"

He put the gun away in his pocket. They sat together in silence in the rumbling carriage, neither daring talk for fear of what they'd say.

CHAPTER 26

Rachmiel

As the train sped on, Rachmiel attempted to make conversation with Maxine. A marital discussion that soon developed into an out-and-out argument:

"And your obsession with sodomy, hurting me—"

"I'm not obsessed with—"

"So you say. I've never consented to you using my anus, but you do so anyway."

"Only when you're behaving like an anus yourself. Like now."

"That's your excuse? You rape me because—"

"Maxine, please, I've *never* raped you!"

"It wasn't consensual."

"Maybe not at the start, but Maxine you came just now! You always come when I . . ."

She scowled, her face made intensely ugly by the additional lines. "I was frowning, grimacing . . . almost screaming." She smiled coldly. "You know, darling, psychologists say rapists generally imagine that the agonized expressions on their victims' faces—the painful grimaces as they rip their public lives apart through invading their private parts—are really those of ecstasy, and that their terrified screams of pain are actually expressions of pleasure. Sick, but true. The description fits you to a 'D,' darling—argue that off."

"Maxie, you always frown and grimace when you come anyway, so I can't tell the difference. And while we're on this topic—*Do you* fantasize that I'm molesting you to get off?"

She scowled again. "You bastard."

"Who totally loves you."

"Don't give me that 'love' crap! You were about having an affair!"

"Yes—with you!"

"You didn't know it was with me."

"But it was. So it works out perfectly for both of us. Sex with one's wife is generally better than with some unknown woman, even if she's a prostitute. Hookers may have great bedroom technique, but they're oh so lonely to screw."

She turned away to stare out the window. The pleasant scenery was too depressing, so she looked back inside at him. "I hate you."

"Last night in bed you loved me. You were moaning like my organ was the greatest thing in the world."

"Newsflash, darling. I was faking."

"How come our sex life is only crap when you're angry with me?"

"Whatever. Believe it or not, I *was* faking."

"You deserve the Oscar for Best Actress."

She looked then like she'd leap at him and rake his eyes with her nails again. He sat back, defeated. He couldn't help that he'd hurt her. He didn't like that he'd hurt her. He loved her after all, but . . . they kept fighting. Their endless fights had led to this, what was supposed to be a simple affair with Olga Franck (but was an affair ever *simple?*), which had brought him back to Maxine again. Full circle.

"I run away from you back into your arms," he said.

Her gaze was suspicious. "What do you mean by that?"

"Whatever it sounds like to you."

"I hate you."

"I love you . . . okay, maybe not very deeply at the moment."

Her gaze was hostile as an enemy soldier's. "You've an answer for everything, haven't you?"

"I wish I had one for our relationship. A fix for *us.*" He tapped her gun, safely hidden away in his pocket. "You were going to kill me, what kind of relationship breeds that?"

"I love you with all of my broken heart. No other woman can ever have you—I'd rather kill you than let that happen. Get it? It's that simple."

"And if I turned gay tomorrow?"

"See what I mean? How you trivialize my concerns?"

"I don't get it—can't we just be *happy?*" His gaze bored into hers. "Can't we just make each other happy? Is that really too much to ask of one another?"

"Now you've a *question* for everything. Screw questions and answers, okay?"

"You're asking a question too."

"Don't sidetrack me. What I mean is, you were going to cheat on me, and I caught you." She smiled, the curve of her moist lips saccharine sweet. "You're guilty, darling. I'm not. Just admit it and let's move on, go have some Polish fun."

That stumped him. Staring down at his feet, he considered his odd situation. It was odd to be both guilty and not guilty, or guilty, but not as charged. Emotional murder downgraded to manslaughter. And currently *it was* all his fault. But it also wasn't, it was *her* fault, though she clearly wasn't about accepting any responsibility. But then—he reasoned with her—*Why should she? Why should she expect anything less than total fidelity from me? We're married; I'm not supposed to be lusting for any vagina other than hers.*

And the gun? *But is that reason enough to murder me? And yet, I can't blame her, and I should be able to.*

So he had hurt her, but . . . in her own way, she was clearly more culpable than he. A wife wasn't supposed to go on Facebook and tempt her husband with Photoshopped pictures.

And how did he know even that she'd only been there looking for him (like she was certain to claim if he pressed the issue)? For all he knew, Maxine could herself have been playing the field. *Yes,* he decided on further reflection, *it could have been so. She's young and pretty—so why not?* It had been Olga Franck's Facebook profile—liking Rammstein, Kraftwerk, and Senor Coconut's music, Oriental sculpture, and Luis Bunuel and Jan Švankmajer films—that had attracted him to her. Thinking deep now, Rachmiel realized that these were the same list of attributes (in addition to her rather fleshy arms and large backside), that had attracted him to Maxine back then. The slim blonde Olga had also seemed slightly artificial (like a manga girl). Ladies with such looks were always a massive turn-on for Rachmiel—they looked like something he'd created in his studio.

I'm just dumb, he concluded. *I should have realized it was Maxine—smelt her poop a mile off. I've definitely tongued her anus enough to recognize its distinctive stink by now.*

"Rach, Rach!"

Her voice, suddenly not hostile anymore, roused him from his thoughts. He first looked back up at her, then sideways, his eyes tracking her pointing finger.

A large black rat lay on its back on the seat beside his. He blinked; the rat—a female—was dildoing itself with . . . It pulled the object fully out of its vagina, Maxine gave a yelp of horror . . .

A human finger, Rachmiel realized. *It's using a severed human finger as a sex toy!*

Squeaking with lust, the rat slid the finger back inside its sex, then looked at Rachmiel and Maxine.

"You're going to die!" it gasped, grinding itself hard on the penetrating digit. "Oh, you're going to die!"

Rach! Look outside!

Rachmiel ripped his gaze from the masturbating rat to stare outside their carriage. He blinked (*Hell no!*) then looked back inside at Maxine (who'd begun shivering with fear), then looked outside again at the impossible landscape now rushing past them.

They were clearly no longer anywhere in Poland, or Europe for that matter. The landscape outside the train now was a range of black mountains with monstrous faces cut in their slopes. Boiling red eyes, nostrils that seemed crimson tunnels to hell, mouths like blood-filled pits, black teeth the size of houses. Like burning hair, yellow-orange lava streamed down from the mountaintops.

"Where the hell are we?" Maxine asked, her teeth chattering.

"*Hell* may be right," Rachmiel replied her softly, his eyes as confused as hers. He retrieved her gun from his pocket.

"We might be able to call for help," Maxine suggested with little conviction.

Rachmiel got out his phone and checked it. "There's no network coverage," he said in disgust.

"You're gonna die!" the masturbating rat gasped like it was having an orgasm.

Rachmiel had forgotten the rodent. "You first," he told it, pointing the gun at it and firing.

The gunshot reverberated like an explosion in the compartment. Maxine grabbed her ears at the noise. The rat exploded into a mess of fur and blood. The finger it had been using as a dildo lay undamaged on the seat, the sight of it alone somehow all the more horrifying.

"The ticket inspector," Maxine mumbled. "She'll have heard the gunshot."

"She's the least of our concerns at the moment," Rachmiel replied, pointing out at the black mountains with their horrible red faces.

Above their bubbling peaks the sky was bone white, the sun black. The nylon-transparent clouds seemed painted on canvas.

Worse yet, from inside the train, from beyond the curtains shuttering off their compartment, came horrible noises—loud slobbering sounds mixed in with people screaming.

"It sounds like all hell's just broken loose!" Maxine screamed. She leapt from her seat into his lap and held him tight. "Rach, I'm scared!"

He gripped her close, pulling her into himself. He felt strengthened by her needing him. Suddenly, their recent hostility meant nothing. He'd die rather than let any harm come to his beautiful wife, his one true love. "Don't let the rat scare you, honey," he said softly. "We'll be fine. Together, nothing in the world can hurt us."

Only thing is, he thought to himself as the screaming continued around them on the hurtling train, *I don't think we're in our own world any longer.*

Outside, the mountain range's demon faces grinned in at them.

CHAPTER 27

Raven

The desert landscape altered into a ruined town.

Raven decided to rest awhile. She wheeled her Harley over to a doorless cottage flanked by large elms and demounted.

She'd been riding for four hours now. Her bike's tank still registered half-full. *So I ride another four hours. If I haven't found DOG by then . . .*

She rolled the bike inside the cottage through shattered French doors. In the front room, piled white/gray birdshit decorated the windowsills. The furniture was all coated with dust. A plasma TV stood in a corner, displaying mute static despite the decay of the place and its seeming lack of electricity.

She attempted dusting off an armchair, then gave up and sat in it anyway.

The TV static altered to video—a handsome middle-aged man violently sodomizing a young woman who was both crying and bleeding from her ass. He had her bent over a cabin chair, both her hands pinned to the wall over her lush red hair, while tears ran freely from her green eyes.

Alarmed, Raven cast a quick glance around the room, then at her motorbike. "Hey! Is anyone here?"

Only silence replied her. She returned her attentions to the TV. Back to the rape.

But no—she realized with shock—it wasn't rape. The young woman was panting hard and licking her lips through her tears.

From the rapidly shifting images visible through the oblong window beyond the lovers, Raven deduced that they were aboard a train.

Watching the violently coupling pair, she felt a rising heat in her loins and her sex growing wet. The man's penis seemed a white sausage he was feeding his lady friend's buttocks, her rear cleft a soft white mouth devouring him. He smacked her ass hard. Red marks appeared on the pale skin. She yelped in silent pain, shrieked back over her shoulder. "I hate you," Raven lip-read. "I love you," was the equally muted response.

Raven suddenly felt like she'd burst from pressure—sexual, her rescue attempt, everything. She needed release and quick. After placing the Smith & Weston Airweight within easy reach, she unzipped her pants and slipped eager fingers down into her sex.

She masturbated fast and soft, tapping her now dripping sex of the pleasure it offered. Her other hand roved over her breasts, softly squeezing them in milking motions.

At first she caressed her clitoris in rhythm with the marauding penis tormenting the bleeding onscreen anus. Then she forgot the lovers and dissolved into her own world of enjoyment, fingering herself faster and faster till she exploded with sensation.

She rubbed her orgasm out lusciously, melting into herself like chocolate in warm cream.

***

Raven suddenly jerked awake. *Damn! I fell asleep! How long have I—?*

She gaped at the TV. Onscreen now, a rat lay on its back, hind legs spread wide, sexing itself with a severed human finger and gasping, "Oh, you're gonna die! Oh, you're gonna—!"

Raven picked up her revolver and shot the TV. "Shut the hell up, bitch!"

She grinned in satisfaction when the television exploded, then became totally confused—the TV blew apart into a mess of meat and hair with twitching legs stuck in it.

She leapt out of her chair and peered in shock at the bloody mess. Amidst the meat and strewn wet guts, spilled body fluids and black fur, lay the rat's severed head, now large as a dog's.

The head gaped at Raven, its beady black eyes shining wet. Its jaws moved, blood draining from between them. She was certain it was trying to repeat its doomsday litany.

The rat's jaws locked open in death.

She turned away, stepping over puddles of blood and mounds of meat, suddenly very conscious of time's passage. *Damn, I can't believe I let myself get sidetracked from finding DOG. And I was jerking-off? What the hell came over me? Girl, this is neither the time nor the place for self-love.*

"What are you looking for here?" a voice said behind her.

Raven spun around, gun poised to shoot.

She stopped and gaped at the person who'd addressed her.

It was a man, only his body was covered with human fingers. Completely nude, he was also completely hairless, every inch of his skin other than his face, hands, and feet studded with fingers (many with long painted nails) and thumbs. Many of the fingers had rings (including engagement and wedding rings) on them. The multitude of digits (of many shades and sizes) constantly clenched as though seeking to form fists on his skin.

He was handsome, if thin-lipped, with a long nose and light brown eyes.

"Who . . . who are you?" she blurted out. *Holy cow! I seriously don't believe this.*

He smiled. "Fingers . . . Deacon Fingers."

She nodded back. *Dude, I've never met anyone more aptly named. You've even got fingers on your penis and testicles? Just don't ever bend over near me—I don't want to see your exit-works!*

"What are you doing here?" he asked, then gestured at the humps of hairy rat meat. "The gunshot alerted me to your presence." He grimaced. "Persistent buggers they are; it's great to see one dead."

"My name's Raven. I'm looking for DOG. I need to talk to it."

The finger-covered man nodded, the digits covering his head waving like they also agreed. "I can take you to DOG. What do you want to see it about?"

"Dude, it's a long story; best I tell you on our way there." She turned towards the entrance, pointed at her motorbike. "You can ride pillion, but"—she couldn't resist the quip—"no tickling, okay?"

He frowned. "No."

"Is that a no to 'no tickling' or a no to riding behind me?"

"No to both."

She rolled her eyes. "C'mon, dude, lighten up! I was only joking. Hey, you must be used to 'tickle' jokes by now, right?"

Fingers smiled. "Oh, I never tire of hearing them, particularly not from a beautiful woman." Like a normal person would stick his hands in his pockets, he locked his hand-fingers between two sets growing out of his hips.

Raven found the sight extremely disconcerting. And she'd also noted his 'beautiful woman' compliment. *I hope he isn't about getting an erection—No way do I want to see a boner with fingers poking from it.* "So—lets go?"

He nodded towards the front entrance, the empty French doors. "You misunderstand me. We're not going that way."

He turned and walked off towards an inner door, gesturing back to her over his shoulder. "Follow me—all roads lead to DOG anyway. It doesn't matter which way you go."

Raven hurried through the door after him. "I keep hearing that. If all roads lead to DOG like you claim, why not ride there on my bike?"

Smiling, Fingers waited by another, shut, door for her to join him. "All roads lead to DOG, true, but some are much longer than others. This one is very short."

He pressed a dusty button on the door. It slid aside to reveal a gleaming elevator cage. He stepped inside, gestured at his stunned companion to join him.

She finally did, getting over her heart's frantic beating. *How much longer?* she wondered, *does this unexpected weird stuff go on for? And I can't forget that rat—that's thrice now by the way—warning me that I'm going to die. And what did finger-man here just say? There's more of the things around?*

Fingers, sensing her confusion, smiled reassuringly at her. She was about smiling back when she noticed he had no ears, just a mass of little baby fingers waving on the side of his head. *Oh, no,* she thought, *I really can't endure this much longer!*

Fingers shut the elevator door. "We go up."

The cage rose. Raven considered the impossibility of their motion. "Up where? The building's a cottage."

Fingers' answer was cut off by the elevator's chiming their arrival two floors higher up. "We're here," he said instead.

The door slid open. Raven peered out and gasped.

Fingers laughed. "Like I said, some roads are shorter than others. Welcome to DOG Zone."

Raven nodded silently, her gaze rapt on the scene facing them.

***

They had to be about a mile away from DOG, yet it magnetized her eyes. DOG was unmistakable, a huge—'mountainous' instantly came to Raven's mind—metal dog.

The monstrous metal canine dominated the desert landscape ahead like it owned the world, its body gleaming dully beneath the yellow sky. Jumbo bolt-heads and rivets traced its joints. Its eyes, massive nine-faceted rounded rectangles, stared towards Raven and Fingers.

The pair stepped out of the elevator and walked toward it.

"Tell me about DOG," Raven whispered to Fingers.

The finger-studded man laughed. "Like what?"

"Like . . ." she searched for a question, "who built it?"

"No one did."

"Bullshit; it's clearly artificial."

"Yes it is."

"So?"

"It built itself."

"That's ridiculous. Nothing ever builds itself—"

"Except bodybuilders?"

"I don't understand."

"DOG . . . D . . . O . . . G, is a 'reverse-God anagram.' They're scattered all over the universe—auto-generated creatures with a claim on divinity, but who never truly achieve it."

Raven squeezed up her face at the metal-animal mountain they approached. "It's *divine*? John never said anything about that."

"John Lynch the PT guy?"

"Yeah, from Pussy Transmission. You've met?"

"Not really. DOG, however, is a great fan of his multimedia work." He smiled at her blank stare. "You'll understand in a short while." He frowned. "Now back to my explanation: GOD is simply an abbreviation for Generator, Operator, Destroyer."

Raven mused over the statement. "The beginning, the middle, the end? You know, I never viewed the Almighty—if he really exists—like that, but it makes sense." She gestured ahead of them. "And DOG?"

Fingers sighed; his light brown eyes filled with meaning. "Reverse the order of the words."

"Destroyer, Operator, Generator? What's the significance of that? It doesn't even sound logical as the name of a demolition company."

Fingers pulled on Raven's arm, indicating they pause. They sat side by side on a large tree stump.

"DOG isn't omniscient," he whispered, "but remember, canines have great hearing."

Raven nodded. "So what's the catch?" she whispered back.

"Remember I just explained how auto-generated creatures aspire to deity-hood?"

"Yeah, but they never actually get there?" Across from them, the air formed vague shapes, like a bedroom with two ghosts in it. The bedroom's farther wall was a mural of mountains with red eyes and mouths beneath a black sun in a white sky. A silver snake (*A train? Looks like the same one I saw a while back.*) slithered below the depicted black crags like it was scared. The mural mountains seemed to be laughing at it.

She returned her attention to Fingers. "I'm sorry, I missed what you were saying."

He waved it off, an odd gesture, since the fingers coating his arm all waved as well like a breeze was fluttering them. "Not really important. Just remember this—DOG is *almost* divine. Think of it as a metal genie."

"Oh, you're saying it grants wishes."

"Yeah. It can do most things, just be *very* specific in what you ask for."

They stood up and resumed walking toward DOG.

Fingers turned back when he realized Raven wasn't beside him anymore. "What the matter?"

She pointed ahead. The spectral bedroom she'd earlier noticed opposite them now lay directly in their path. Now too, it was more solid and . . .

Fingers understood, and laughed. "It's just an illusion. They're all over the place here. I'm uncertain if DOG's responsible or not. Come on. We'll just walk through it."

Raven joined him. Together they stepped into the 'room.'

Raven fought back her blushes. Two women were in the bedroom. A brunette was bent over a dresser, her hands gripping its edges. Her dress was pulled up high over her waist, her buttocks bare and spread like white moons over the face of the other woman, a skinny blonde who knelt on the floor between the brunette's legs, licking her anus.

"I know those two," Raven said when the brunette lifted her head and gasped.

Fingers smiled back tightly. "They're just illusions. Don't worry"

He seemed extremely discomfited, his face a mask of incredible strain. Raven wondered what the problem was, then she looked down at his crotch. He had an erection. And yes, fingers *were* sticking out of it like little penises themselves. A thumb with a long blue fingernail was tapping Fingers' glans like it was impatient for him to ejaculate.

"Dude, you know how bad this is for you," she said with genuine concern, grabbing Fingers' hand and pulling him across the semi-solid bedroom.

CHAPTER 28

Lily & Nina

Bent over the dresser, eyes shut tight, Lily was in heaven. The rug around the dresser was strewn with bottles of hair gel, perfume, and lipstick tubes knocked over in celebration of her intense pleasure.

"Yes, darling, rim me!" she gasped when Nina spread her buttocks even wider. The tongue in her anus felt incredible.

Nina had been tonguing Lily for five minutes now. Licking up and down her buttock crack, twirling her tongue in the tight fundamental orifice.

Lily felt embarrassed each time the wet lingua penetrated her anus. *Ooh, she's licking my poop! That's so dirty!* She'd almost push Nina away. Then Nina would spread her buttocks further apart and stick the tongue in deeper and Lily would melt again, her legs trembling. *Oh, darling—but it's so enjoyable!*

"Let's go over to the bed," she moaned. "Please—I can hardly stand up now. And you're not letting me touch myself." She stared at their reflections in the dresser mirror. Her eyes gaped wide like she was stoned, her facial expression desperate as a drowning woman's. Her brow and neck dripped with the passion-sweat that had already soaked her dress. Her mocha hair was mussed around her face like a used mop. "Please darling," she gushed in a voice that streamed from her soul like water, "I need you to fuck me. Dammit—my pussy's on fire!"

Nina laughed, pulling her tongue from her girlfriend's anus and spitting on the slobbered-up hole. Her massive nose was itself wet, a drop of saliva hanging snot-like on its tip. She wiped mouth and nose dry with her hand, then shook her head. "Not yet, girl. I love your ass. It's almost tastier than your pussy even. I could lick you forev—" She stiffened. "What's that?"

Lily, anticipating another sweet bout of tongue assault, looked back with dreamy eyes. "What's what, baby?"

Nina relaxed again. "Nothing, darling. Just your new laptop virus acting up again."

My new virus? As Nina resumed licking and sucking her anus, Lily looked weakly over at her laptop. *Oh, you're back, are you?* Hot with lust, she grinned at the image of the night-haired girl (now on foot) and her companion (a man covered with fingers) that the monitor displayed. *Yep, definitely a virus; maybe a video game ad even. . .*

Nina smacked her buttocks hard with a wet hand. "Oh, you've got the most pretty hole I've ever seen." Then her tongue returned to work—wet, thick, warm, tasting the outer anal ring then probing in deep, filling Lily with so much pleasure as it entered her that it took all her concentration to focus on her laptop.

Oh, screw it, I'll have it seen to once we're back at the office!

She wasn't really bothered. She'd already confirmed after the previous 'virus attack' upstairs that all her interview files were safe. And the interview had been just fab and afterwards they'd gotten to see Isis work, in the buff like she'd claimed she did (*Wow, that woman is a total genius once before a canvas—she paints easier than applying lipstick!*)—which was largely what had gotten them both so aroused now. (*Good golly, Ms. Holly—Isis Lynch has an incredible figure for her age!*)

She relaxed completely. *Like Nina says, it has to be the screensaver that's messed up. But, wow! Even for an animated screensaver, these are incredibly HD graphics.* She giggled on noticing the finger-coated man's erection, with a blue-nailed thumb desperately stroking it. *Ha ha ha! That must be so uncomfortable! And the way he's staring. . . one would almost think they can see us!*

Feeling great pity for the finger-covered man (*You should be glad you're not real, or how in the world would you ever have sex?*), she looked away from the laptop, letting her anus go slack so Nina's tongue could penetrate it again.

At least seeing those two onscreen was better than another stupid rat.

CHAPTER 29

Rachmiel & Maxine

Maybe we have slipped down into Hell, Rachmiel thought, peering out through the compartment curtains. *That explanation clearly fits the facts.*

Beside him, Maxine gaped speechless, her large green eyes now almost as wide as an anime girl's.

In the first-class carriage, all was pandemonium now, the noise increasing per the second. Blood was flowing like runoff water down the corridor.

And the source of the red gush? Creatures from insanity—monsters!

Either side of Rachmiel and Maxine, the outer corridor wall was warped, large portions of its plastic and steel stripped off from its framework and twisted into huge worms with grotesque demon faces—oblong red eyes, massive noses, lips blacker than coal, teeth the size of kitchen knives.

The corridor windows had all been destroyed by the monsters' forming, leaving just a single long hole through which the black hellscape rushed past, the demonic mountainside faces grinning in approval on the ensuing carnage.

The worm-creatures—their rear parts still attached to the train, their mouths dripping with the blood of those already slain—were attacking and eating the passengers.

Maxine yelped in horror when one monster jerked itself out of a compartment on their left, half of a woman's body dangling from its black lips. Blood spilled from its mouth down over the corpse's head. Two gulps, and the woman's head and shoulders vanished into the creature, converting into a lump behind its head that flowed down into its body. The monster licked its lips with a black tongue then darted its head back through the compartment door, emerging with a screaming, fiercely kicking man clamped between its jaws.

A sequence of loud noises made Maxine and Rachmiel look right. There, four of the demon-worm-creatures were pulling on the ticket inspector's arms and legs while she shrieked desperately. Each monster had one of her limbs in its mouth and was yanking on it fiercely. Suddenly, seemingly without warning, the hapless woman separated into pieces, exploding in a bloody mess as her limbs were ripped from their sockets. Her torso thudded to the gore-smeared floor, where it lay spurting blood while she vented her terror with wide-open eyes and mouth. Her screams were ear-splitting and pathetic. A fifth worm-creature, its eyes red lanterns, instantly slithered below the quartet gorging on her arms and legs and bit her body off the floor, muffling her cries as her head vanished down the carmine tunnel of its throat. The monster's jaws split wider . . . its horrid shiny teeth came together deep in her chest, cutting through her breasts like a spoon entering wobbling Jell-O . . .

Rachmiel had seen enough. He yanked the trembling Maxine back into their compartment, locked the door and shut the drapes.

She clung to him, shivering. "We're gonna die, darling!"

He peeled her off him, held her at arm's length. "Don't say that, darling!"

She forced her horror down (she considered it a miracle that she'd not peed or shat herself yet) and stared at him. "Those things, whatever they are, are going to—"

"You're going to die," a small squeaky voice interrupted her.

They turned to see a black rat seated on the windowsill.

Rachmiel (conscious of conserving bullets) pointed Maxine's gun at it. "You talking to us?"

The rat raised its forepaws in a gesture of peace. "Wrong compartment; I should be next door." It leapt down off the sill and ran out of the room into the blood and noise. (Rachmiel noted, but didn't point out to Maxine, that the rat had run *through* the shut door to get outside.)

Maxine stared at her husband. "What do we do now? As far as I can tell, they're working their way down the corridor from both ends. It's just sheer luck that we're right in the middle."

As confirmation, the sound of breaking glass erupted from the next compartment, followed by boisterous screaming."

"We get off the train," Rachmiel said.

She pointed out the window. "It's moving, darling!"

"It has to stop somewhere, then we'll scramble out through the holes left by the monsters' creation."

"We'll be dead before then."

He split open the revolver. "Don't believe the rats—they're full of rat shit. Okay, we've five bullets left. Have to make each shot count." He gave her a quizzical smile. "Or did you perchance bring the whole box of shells along, dear? Just to ensure you killed me properly?"

She scowled at him, about to make an acid retort, but the noise from the next compartment cut her off. That sound was now a wet slobbering. She felt an instant return of her dread and held him tight again.

A fierce banging began on their compartment door. Trails of blood seeped beneath it, flowing towards them.

Rachmiel flipped the revolver's cylinder back in. He pulled Maxine aside, pushed her behind him. "Time to find out if these things are bulletproof."

Holding him tight from behind, her little breasts soft against his hardness, Maxine moaned, "I'm sure they will be."

The door exploded inward. Expecting this, Rachmiel had shielded his eyes. The glass showered over him, ripping up his hands, filling his hair. Wincing with pain, he opened his eyes to behold the horror that was.

One of the monsters faced him—a huge, horned demon head on a thick, segmented neck. Its pink skin was like discarded-doll plastic; both its head and neck were dotted with tufts of black grassy hair. Its face was as terrible as those covering the mountains outside the train.

The monster spread its black lips wide. Rachmiel felt he looked into the abyss. Its mouth was a chasm, rings of triangular ebon teeth extending back ad-infinitum into an infernal blackness from which an equally black tongue poked.

The creature lunged at Rachmiel.

"Shoot it, darling!" Maxine yelped behind him.

Glad that she'd not fainted from fright, Rachmiel did so, aiming at its left eye and pulling the trigger.

The creature's head jerked back from the force of the bullet. It froze in space for a moment, then crashed to the floor. The impact with the floor seemed to break something inside it—pink goop gushed from its punctured eye like water from a hydrant. It tilted over and lay motionless, one of its horns stuck like a hook in the metal floor.

Maxine peeped out from behind Rachmiel. "It's dead?"

"Looks like it."

"But so easy? Just one shot?"

"It most likely has a very small brain." He pointed out into the corridor, where two more worm-creatures stared in at them with hungry expressions while licking their bloody lips. "We're in luck," he said in response to Maxine's shudder. "This dead monster has blocked the door. Not having hands, the others can't move its body out of the way and get in themselves."

"And they're clearly not smart enough—I think you're right about them having tiny brains—to pull it out of the way with their teeth."

"Don't put ideas in their empty heads."

"So what now?"

"We wait in here till we reach a station. Hopefully soon. Then we push this one out of the way and—"

His attention was diverted from the watching worms by Maxine's jabbing finger.

"*They* don't look too pleased," she said.

He looked out of the window at the live mountain range. The demon faces had lost their glee. Now their expressions were of intense disappointment, like those of a child who's just discovered he isn't getting the desired Playstation for his birthday.

"I'm thinking," Maxine said.

"Yes, darling?" He watched the door while speaking, checking that the worms hadn't smartened up to drag their dead counterpart out of the way.

She gestured at the angry mountains. "Well, the only reason they could look so pissed-off is if they realize we've escaped them. The monsters must have eaten everyone else on the train by now."

He looked at her thoughtfully. "You're suggesting that—?"

His words and the mountains were suddenly extinguished in an all-compassing grayness that resolved itself into the stone walls of a tunnel.

"And the train is slowing down," Maxine pointed out.

The tunnel expanded into concrete station platforms flanked with faded movie posters.

"Well, we've survived this ride," Maxine said.

Rachmiel looked over at the compartment door. The worm things still hovered there. "Time to get off, I believe, darling." He handed her the pistol. "I have to move this one out of the way." He bent and hooked his arms under the dead worm-creature's head, rolling it sideways so its trapped horn slid out of the hole in the floor. "Damn, it's heavy."

Rachmiel shifted the worm-creature by degrees, keeping his body behind its bulk. The most dangerous time would be when he got it out into the corridor, where he'd be exposed to the other monsters. He needed Maxine to keep her nerve then. There was only one way he could think of to ensure that she did—*I have to rile her up so her anger overrides her fear.*

He sighed. *Okay here goes.* Crouched beside the creature, he looked sternly back at his wife. "Now don't go on a shooting spree, darling. Remember, these are bullets, not my money you're spending. You've only four of them; aim for the eyes—one per monster."

She nodded back, pissed-off by his patronizing tone. "It's *my* gun, Rach. I know how to fire it."

The train rolled to a halt.

Rachmiel humped the monster up so it rested on his head and shoulders, then smiled coldly at Maxine. "That's wonderful, honey. Now I'm certain you won't *accidentally* hit me. *Intentionally?*—Now that's another matter."

Her green eyes flashed anger at him. Disturbingly, he'd never seen her look more lovely than she did now. "Just shift the damn thing and let's go," she spat. "We've no idea how long the train will remain in here."

"I'm warning you, Maxie: don't shoot me, or I'll fuck your ass as punishment. I'll do you so hard you won't shit for a week."

From the way her pretty little mouth squeezed tight with rage, Rachmiel knew the deed was done. *Mission accomplished.*

It's odd, he thought, grunting beneath the dead bulk while fighting not to slip on its spilt eye jelly, *women scare easily, but it's almost impossible to scare an angry woman. Stick a gun up a girl's ass even, and if she'd pissed-off enough, she'll still tell you to go screw yourself with it.*

"Okay, now here's the plan," he growled. "First, come over here beside me."

She did so, glowering at the demon-faced worms staring hungrily in at them.

"Okay, I'll push this dead worm out to the right. That'll block off the ones on that side for a few moments. Immediately I move, shoot the one staring at you—the big one on the left—in the eye. That blocks off that side, then we both leap out through the hole behind them and hope their necks can't extend too far outside the train."

He looked at her for confirmation that she understood.

She glared back at him in silence, his sodomy threat wailing in her brain like an ambulance siren. The fact that her anus still stung amplified the horror of the proposed rectal violation. *How dare you? Once we get out of this hell, I'll make you see hell, you rapist bastard, and I don't care if I get locked away for a million years afterwards. I'll—*

His hands occupied with the weight of the monster, Rachmiel kicked her. "Maxine, darling, answer me! Do you understand the plan?"

She shook her gun at him. "I heard you, you jerk. Let's do it. We're running out of time here."

He breathed easier when she swung the revolver to face the monsters in the corridor. "Okay, on my count of three. One, two . . ."

***

They burst into motion, taking the worm-creatures totally by surprise.

Rachmiel heaved the dead monster out into the corridor. The worm-creature directly in his path instantly ducked out of the way of his rush, then found itself barricaded behind him.

Maxine had fired on cue. Just like they'd planned, the creature she shot collapsed dead, partly blocking off the corridor's left arm. In addition, while falling, it became entangled with a pair trying to slither past it, both of which now thrashed about in a confused knot.

Around Rachmiel's feet were stripped skeletons. Apparently, like snakes, the worms regurgitated anything indigestible.

"Go!" he yelled at Maxine, standing on the corridor's forward side, the dead monster raised over his head like he was participating in a Chinese dragon dance.

Damn, he thought, as she rushed from their compartment, *I never imagined there were so many of them.* The first-class carriage literally boiled with the worm-creatures, the demonic annelids writhing over each other in frustrated hunger, all their maws bloody, their glowing red eyes staring at Rachmiel and Maxine.

How did this happen? he wondered, while with herculean effort bracing himself against the sudden pressure of the worms behind him on the one he carried, the monsters' weight threatening to force him down to the floor. *I mean: where did they all come from? And time is of the essence now—we have to get off this hell-train!*

Standing at the gaping corridor-side, Maxine stopped to look at him, her rage now tempered with worry. "Let's go, Rach!"

"You first! Leap the gap and I'll follow!" Then, looking past her, his eyes widened in horror. One of the entangled demon-worms had worked itself free of the fallen one blocking the corridor and was slithering forward over its body, its mouth opening to attack Maxine.

"Behind you! Shoot it!" he screamed at her.

***

Seeing the dread in her husband's eyes, Maxine Donovan spun around. Too late. The worm bit into her left shoulder, dug its teeth in deep. The pain was so intense that consciousness momentarily fled her. Then her mind was clear again, and she felt another set of teeth grab her buttocks, pulling her backward, over the dead worm, away from Rachmiel . . .

Away from *him*—her only love. The threatened separation hurt more than the teeth tearing into her. *Noooo, Rach, I'll never leave you. Not ever!*

"I love you, baby!" he screamed as she was dragged away from him, tears in his eyes.

"I love you too, baby," she moaned back as she bled more blood than she knew a body contained, as the pain took her down, down, down.

Fading fast, she raised her revolver and pointed it at Rachmiel. His eyes widened as he saw her aiming at him. Burdened under the giant worm, he was unable to dodge.

"I love you, darling! Forever and ever!" she shouted with feeling as she fired. She shot him till the gun clicked empty, all three shots hitting him in the chest and belly. She saw Rachmiel's pain and horror as his bullet wounds ran red, followed by his understanding (like satellites glittering in the night skies of his dark eyes) of *why* she'd shot him—

141

not because she was mad at him, or hated him (she realized now he'd only angered her to save her), but because she loved him.

Truly, desperately, madly, loved him.

She knew he knew she knew he'd be unable to live without her, and that she simply intended saving him that torment.

"No other woman will ever own you!" she gasped as a slobbering maw enclosed her feet, ripping away boots and skin. "You're mine, Rach—totally mine alone! *My* property! Mine! I love you! You know that, don't you? I love you, sweetheart!"

***

Overlooking the pain of his gunshot wounds, Rachmiel watched with horror and dread while Maxine (shouting endearments and blowing kisses after shooting him) was pulled off by the worm-creatures, their demonic faces rapt with glee over their catch.

Maxine reached the main throng of creatures. (It was horrible—he was unable to tear his eyes from witnessing her fate!) Amidst a bubble of violent slithering and screeches, Rachmiel Donovan saw his wife's body yanked apart into two, halves of her disappearing into two different worms. Still other worms ripped chunks of bloody flesh out of Maxine's halves as they slithered down those infernal throats.

Rachmiel felt like he'd just died. Blood foaming on his lips from a gunshot right lung, more blood streaming from holes that hurt like spears stuck through him, he somehow heaved the massive worm up off his shoulders, then leapt out through the hole onto the train platform.

He landed hard but kept rolling, ensuring he was well away from the train before he rested.

He stared back at the train—the erstwhile Berlin–Warszawa Express. Its lights now flashed erratically on and off like it had major electrical trouble. Through this faux-strobe effect he noted that all six coaches boiled with the demon-faced worms.

The train looked like God had used a divine can-opener on it. Blood dripped over the ripped-out carriage sides. Strips of uneaten intestine hung from onetime windows. From the second second-class carriage, a worm with eyes like cauldrons of crimson witch's brew vomited up a slimed-over human skeleton in Rachmiel's direction. He looked back to first class. The creatures in there stared hungrily out at him, but made no attempt to come closer.

I don't get it, he wondered. *How did a simple Saturday trip become this bloodbath? And where are we? Where is this unholy place?*

As though the demon creatures of the mountains were satisfied that he'd not survive—that *everyone* aboard the train could rightly be considered dead now—the train began moving again.

But . . .

Rachmiel leaned up and peered toward the platform's nearer end. *That's a brick wall! This is the end of the line! There's nowhere for it to go!*

Whoever drove the train clearly didn't think so, however. Or maybe s/he was simply insane now and wished to end it all. Or maybe one of the demon-worms had gotten into the control room . . .

Whatever the driver's reason, the train picked up speed at an impossible rate and smashed into the bricked-up station end.

There was a crash, then masonry flying everywhere as the wall shattered, then the train was through, speeding into . . .

Rachmiel gawked after it in shocked silence. *No, I'm just imagining this,* he fought to convince himself. *That isn't . . . and, no, the train isn't dissolving into liquid!*

He collapsed again. Maxine's loss now dropped on him like a bomb, violently wrenching his thoughts off the new oddity he'd just witnessed. Her death hurt Rachmiel worse than his bullet wounds. Incredible but true. *Thank God I won't survive this,* he thought, *She's right—I can't live without her.*

He lay there in a widening pool of blood, waiting to die.

Then he looked across the station rails to the opposite platform,

He winced. *This has to be a bad joke, right?*

The platform sign read: 'Lynch Place, 2nd Floor Station.'

He groaned loudly. *Lynch Place? Isis? This is your doing? You've conspired to mess up another of my relationships, murder another woman I love? Goddamn you, you stupid, eternally meddling bitch! You're responsible for Maxine's death?*

Rachmiel Donovan suddenly decided to put dying on hold. At least until he'd found and killed his elder sister.

Now enraged, he stumbled to his feet, and streaming blood, began searching for a door out of the train station.

CHAPTER 30

Lily & Nina

Lily pushed Nina's thighs up onto her breasts, then nuzzled her mouth into her girlfriend's crotch. She swung her head side-to-side like she was washing the vagina in its sweet juices. Nina gripped Lily's head in her thin fingers, moaning deliciously as the pleasure covered her like maple syrup coating a pancake.

Lily let her Nina's legs back down. Now, she pushed her thighs wide apart, regarding the glistening hole, its moisture clean and white; reveling in its beautiful smell of woman. She dipped her tongue into Nina's female fountain again and drank deep. Oh, how she wished her tongue was longer and thicker so it filled the proffered petunia-pink passage completely, an army occupying it with love.

***

While being made love to, Nina's mind vaguely replayed the day so far. It had been great. Isis Lynch had been a amiable host, even accepting a joint from Nina (though she'd balked at doing pills— "They clog the pores of my creativity.").

Lily and Nina had watched Isis paint: a portrait of a woman transforming into a lioness. Or maybe she was half of each—in the painting, the nude woman was transparent, with the great cat's body visible inside hers. Her head and shoulders were already fully changed into the lioness's; the rest of her body (and here Isis's immense skill was evident) seemed to quiver with the struggle to contain (or was it release?) the beast within. In the background, a group of red-robed figures knelt in prayer beside a lake over which pink elephants floated.

Isis hadn't been pleased with her work.

"The colors are wrong," she'd griped while touching up the woman-lioness's ears. "I need a purer bronze for the hair."

Only half listening, Nina had nodded. She'd been seated right opposite Isis to photograph her, her eyes focused direct on the painter's vagina. Isis, meanwhile, had painted unselfconsciously, seemingly unaware of how her sex split its folds when she bent and twisted while working.

"It looks perfectly fine to me," Lily had said. "Scary as hell, too."

Isis had paused, frowning as though offended, then giggled. "Please excuse me—I'm forgetting that neither of you is a painter." She'd begun blending colors on her easel. "It's so hard to explain the effect I'm going for. The tone needs to be vibrant, but not overly so. I need to show the lioness that lies below the surface of every woman, just waiting to claw her way out and devour those preying on her."

It was hard to think straight now with a tongue in her vagina, but Nina tried. Or rather, she didn't try—the pleasure triggered pleasant memories to occupy her mind. Pleasant thoughts indeed: Nina wondered how she'd ever managed to get good snaps of Isis—the woman so regal on her stool, a painter queen, brush and palette her scepters . . . the soft mature breasts above with their light-brown nipples, the blonde-furred pubis below, the spread thighs between which the petal-lipped orifice peered like a dark eye . . .

She'd quickly gotten wet between the legs, and just *knew* Lily had noticed her flushed face and determined the cause.

"Next time, stand *behind* the woman, honey," Lily had whispered, sneaking a kiss when Isis wasn't looking their way.

"That's easy for you to say—you've not taking her picture."

Lily had dropped her hand to Nina's buttocks and squeezed. "Don't worry, I'll cool your oven later."

Nina had been relieved when the painting/photo session was over and Isis slipped her robe back on. Any longer, and she'd have spontaneously combusted from sexual overheating.

They'd next had lunch, the gothic Olaf serving them grilled sole and white wine.

"He's a fantastic cook," Lily had approved.

Isis, her mouth full of fish, had grinned back. "It's how I manage to maintain my figure." She'd laughed. "And he's a great fisherman too. I once needed a monster carp for a project with my husband—we needed to dress John up as a merman—"

"What about that woman—the naked blonde we saw?" Nina had interrupted. "Olaf said she's a live model for you."

"Yeah," Lily had agreed. "We thought you *never* had visitors. Don't tell us the 'total recluse' (she made two-finger quotation mark gestures with each hand) thing is just a put-on?"

Their hostess had looked nonplussed for a moment, then had smiled tightly. "Oh, you mean Betty? She's one of the few people I trust. I've known her for . . . you could say forever. She comes and goes like the seasons." She'd swallowed some sole, sipped her wine, then smiled grimly. "Betty's a bit odd for sure—tramping everywhere naked as a cave girl all the time—but I've told her not to bother you."

"Oh, she's been no bother, Mrs. Lynch. She just looked so utterly weird."

Nina had sensed a slight chill in the conversation, but it had quickly passed, dissolved away in wine and anecdotal chatter, all three getting progressively more tipsy by the glass.

They'd finished their meal very good friends. "Oh, yes," Isis had jested, "please do come visiting again—in another twenty years."

They'd all laughed uproariously to that.

(Nina's vagina felt like a warm pool she was drowning in. *Oh, God! Lily's such an incredible lover! And she actually cares about me—I can read it in her eyes—she'll never hang me out to dry whatever my faults . . . and I've plenty, I know!* Her body melted like chocolate on Lily's tongue, dissolving in the liberating wet clitoral swirl.)

Olaf had served coffee.

"Now this is what I call coffee!"

"Delicious!"

"I feel like I'm in Brazil!"

Olaf had beamed at the compliments, his craggy brow wrinkling with pleasure.

And then Isis had left them alone.

With nothing else to do, they'd retreated downstairs to their room to pass the afternoon getting high and making sweet love.

***

Now, Nina groaned like she was dying, her thighs tensed against the hands pushing them apart. Her hands became fists against Lily's ears, her face tilted upward, her eyes squeezed tight, her nipples stiffened into hot stones.

She came like a flood, the slow-spreading maple syrup feeling thinning into a raging pink hormonal river that surged violently through her, shaking her body like flesh and bone were obstructions in its path.

"Yeeeeessss!" she screamed, trembling like she'd never stop, living like she was dying, the tongue on her clitoris the whole essence of her life.

Lily sucked her right thumb wet and pushed it up Nina's anus. Like a car blown up by a grenade, Nina's buttocks instantly lifted off the bed, then collapsed again. "Yes yes yes yes yes yes!" The word-stream thrummed from her lips like Spanish guitar notes, a sexual music that excited Lily, who, keeping her tongue sliding firmly over the engorged clitoris, worked her thumb in and out of Nina's rectum. The fecal smell of the reemerging digit added a dirty pleasure to their intercourse.

Lily's own vagina was aboil with sensation now, like ghostly lips were sucking her down there. She slipped her free hand down between her thighs, spread herself wide, slipped fingers in and out. The pleasure began to distract her, so she stopped and concentrated all her attention on Nina's vagina with its swollen lips like inflated flower petals, on the clitoris that looked about to burst.

"Close your eyes," she ordered Nina. "I've a surprise for you."

Nina did so, her body now helplessly buffeted by the waves of one orgasm into the next, sexual putty in Lily's hands. (*And I don't want to be any other place than here in this bed with you loving me, darling!*)

Oh, I do have a lovely surprise for you, Lily thought in amusement. Keeping her left hand fingers digging in and out of Nina's sex, she fiddled in Nina's purse for the little baggie of cocaine that always resided there. She retrieved a large pinch of the white powder and sprinkled it over Nina's clitoris and down into the moist opening.

"Ooh. What's that? It feels like raindrops."

Lily began licking the cocaine into Nina's sex.

The result was cataclysmic. Like an earthquake. Already in orgasm, Nina suddenly felt like she'd been murdered, staked like a vampire. Her heartbeat escalated, her eyes popped open.

"Stop—you're going to kill me!" she gasped.

In response, Lily laughed. "I'm just showing you the correct way to do drugs, darling." She got more coke from the baggie. She stuck her tongue in it then dug the white-coated organ into Nina's vagina. Licked her harder.

Nina began flopping up and down on the bed, seemingly unable to control her nerves as the coke elevated what was already an incredible experience to something that made her feel damned. (*No pleasure should be this awesome! No, it shouldn't! I'm . . . I'm . . . I'm . . .*)

And so it was. She had no words to describe where, who, or what she was in her drugged-out ecstasy. Her heart was racing now in excitement. Her muscles felt like strings, her tendons like razor blades of pleasure slicing her up, her breasts squirted nonexistent milk to feed the universe. *I'm . . . I'm . . . I'm . . .*

The only thing Nina was certain of, the only thing at all that mattered, was that Lily *loved her.* Loved her like none of her previous girlfriends ever had.

And Lily loved her on and on. Till all the cocaine in the baggie was gone and Nina was an exhausted wreck, totally incapable of doing anything more than stare at their room's white ceiling in sexed-out bliss. She only half-realized at one point that Lily was crawling up her body and kissing her, holding her tight and whispering tender words of sweet endearment to her.

***

Lily got out of bed and went to pee. Her mouth was numb from the coke, which also had her a bit wired. Her legs were trembly too from her own orgasm (she'd used the last of the cocaine to masturbate). At the bathroom door, she looked back at Nina—blue eyes open wide like she was having a seizure, massive nose stabbing the air, nipples still stiff as twigs—and tried to imagine what she was feeling. *Are you window-shopping in nirvana, darling?*

She blew Nina a kiss and entered the bathroom to do her business.

It's done, she enthused as her water drained from her. *We made it— we're made for good, big-time players now. Damn, some of the stories Isis told about people are just insane; I could practically already read the lawsuit notices . . .* She grinned broadly. *Unfortunately, dolls and dudes, she wasn't just mouthing off— I mean, I couldn't believe it myself till I saw that movie—prissy Baroness Diane Fielding, her eyes more glassy than Nina's are at the moment, actually taking a shit on an artist's palette, then picking up a paintbrush! Ha ha! I wonder what they'll think at UNICEF?*

She wiped, then stood up, chortling on recalling their editor's reaction to the selection of snaps they'd rush-emailed him. *Tricky Dick was practically salivating into the phone while congratulating us on our scoop. And his odd shortness of breath like he'd just run a mile? I'm sure he'd just finished wanking to the shots of Isis painting in her birthday suit. Ha ha!*

Lily felt real satisfaction over a job well done, an aspiration accomplished. *No matter what happens—Di Va is big time now . . . Okay, okay, they'll likely have to change the mag's name or the girls at the Brit DIVA mag will have apoplexy; not to mention we'll never be invited to anyone's parties anymore, but—*

Back standing in the bathroom doorway, once again staring lovingly at Nina, Lily was alerted by a loud sound on her left.

She turned. Halfway up its height, the wall opposite her (to the left of the dresser) was exploding.

Lily stared—surprise locking her body motionless—at the demolition: the drywall shattering and blowing across the room in bits as . . .

Is that a train?

It *was* a train. A bullet train miniaturized in perfect detail, like a little boy's toy. The foot-long engine, its rearmost coaches visibly rolling off the rails in the moody gray station behind the wall, floated into the room amidst the wallboard spray as if borne on clouds of air.

Then, once fully through the wall, the entire train—seven foot-long sections, each white with a thick blue stripe—hung in midair and began dissolving into a plasticky puddle.

Lily watched this odd happening in total confusion, her mind having no rational reference point for it. *It's heading for . . . hovering over . . . Nina!* was her first coherent thought. Another, unconscious observation of hers (which her mind instantly rejected), was that the little liquefying train was full of worms with demonic faces, several of which were vomiting up tiny human skeletons.

Clutching at mental straws to stay sane, the dimmest of hopes occurred to Lily: that this was yet another of John Lynch's illusions, just fun entertainment to give them a good scare; a practical joke. But somehow—and Lily had no idea why her conviction was absolute in this regard—she knew it wasn't. This, impossible as it looked, was the real deal: something utterly inexplicable happening before her very eyes.

She gaped at Nina. Her girlfriend still lay half-comatose on the bed, staring blankly at the white dissolution floating above her, making no attempt to get out of its way.

She thinks she's dreaming it! Lily realized. *That it's the drugs!* "It's not the pills, baby! Baby, get up!"

Then the white train with its demon annelid occupants finished dissolving and the white liquid mess fell on top of Nina, covering her all over, as completely as a sheet would a corpse on a dissecting table.

Lily screamed. On the bed, Nina and the whiteness writhed together like they were having sex. A white film spread taut over Nina's mouth; Lily saw she that was silently screaming. The white speared into Nina, tearing her body apart—smearing her meat, skin, and bones all over the bed in a coating of white paint . . .

Then—

Lily covered her mouth with startled fingers.

—The whiteness that had recently been a train began pulling the parts of Nina Kissing back together across the bed and rearranging her into a new composite form with itself.

Watching the odd happening, Lily just managed not to faint. She slumped to the floor, however, watching Nina's re-composition from the ground, her back against the bathroom door jamb. Her mouth was as dry as sun-parched bone, her heartbeat seemingly irregular from her confusion.

On the bed where she'd just loved her girlfriend, the strange dance of white liquid and flesh and bone continued.

Until it was suddenly over.

Lily stared dully at the horror that now faced her. *Oh, hell no!*

It was a *bird*. A huge white condor with massive feathered pinions and a huge beak. Bald as Stone Cold Steve Austin. The creature had Nina's blue eyes, though there was no humanity in them. Just primal avian hunger.

Lily regarded the bird. *Yep, it's Nina alright. That beak definitely came from her big nose.*

The condor launched itself off the bed at Lily. She rose from the floor in a rush, attaining her feet just as it reached her. The condor blocked her escape, planting its wings either side of her, effectively cutting off her retreat back into the bathroom.

Now terrified, Lily stared into the bird's eyes, seeking some kind of recognition, a memory of their past relationship.

"Nina, baby," she moaned in fright, "it's me, Lily, your girlfriend. Do you understand me, honey?"

The condor's reply was a loud squawk. Lily blocked her ears at the noise.

The condor struck, its attack a single undefendable bite at her chest. Before Lily even made sense of its actions, the bird had dug its massive beak into her left breast.

Pain flooded her as her skin and muscle tore and her ribs broke. Then she experienced a final burst of agony as the condor bit out her heart.

She stood upright, dying, watching the monstrous white bird swallow her heart with fierce jerks of its head and neck. Blood squirted from the hole in her chest and splattered the condor. *Damn you, Nina!* she thought as the world faded before her eyes, her brain going numb. *You cokehead cunt! I loved you with all my heart and you go and eat it? That's just so unfair!*

She collapsed dead.

The condor, its previously white beak now a bright red, regarded Lily's corpse for a minute and a half, like it was trying to remember where it had met her before. Then, after another ear-splitting squawk, the bird left her body and walked over to the hole in the wall through which the white train had entered the bedroom.

It left bloody footprints on the green carpet.

The condor peered out through the hole, regarding both the railroad tracks and the station platform beyond, then it set to work, ripping away the drywall to expand the hole. It worked quickly and efficiently, its beak and talons making short work of the wall.

Once the hole was large enough to admit its body, the condor crossed the room again to pick up Lily's corpse. Grasping her bloodied form firmly in its talons, it leapt out through the wall.

With powerful flaps of its mighty white wings, the condor flew off down the train station, down through the tunnel toward the light that ended it, seeking a place where it could relax and eat Lily's remains.

CHAPTER 31

Raven

Raven stared at DOG. Up close—fifty yards away—it seemed a physical impossibility. DOG's mountainous canine body was formed from a mixture of metals, colored plastics, huge pipes and cables . . . and televisions.

"Why is it covered with TVs?" she whispered to Fingers.

"Multimedia," he whispered back, pointing to a TV on their left, one set into DOG's left forepaw. The TV showed a scene of a condor sitting atop a demon-faced mountain. The massive white bird was ripping apart and eating a female corpse. A brunette, judging from her pubic hair. "It records lots of nonsense."

Raven winced as the condor crunched the dead woman's head like a nut. She looked away. "What does it need this stuff for? Transcendental CNN broadcasts?"

"Shush! You don't want to anger it."

With a soft whirring of gears and motors, DOG lowered its massive head to peer down at them. Raven gave a start—DOG's eyes were banks of television monitors: nine in each socket, arranged to project the illusion of a single oblong, the center TV its dark pupil. DOG's ears, each the size of ships, were coated with rows of satellite dishes and TV aerials. Its face seemed normal—hairy elephant-skin—but its whiskers were high-tension wires. Blue static crackled along and between them as it regarded its visitors.

It pointed a television-encrusted forepaw—immense riveted, bolted, and welded metal digits covered with fur like metal bamboo shoots—at them, then opened its mouth to speak. Its teeth were white columns, its purple tongue whale-sized and studded with huge flickering LEDs.

"I am DOG the upgraded deity," it said in a pleasant low-pitched human voice that made the ground tremor. "What is the matter, Fingers?"

Fingers indicated Raven. "Raven here has some trouble and needs your help."

DOG looked Raven over. "While it *has* been a while since anyone prayed to me, you don't look like someone with a problem worth my while to solve."

"How can you know that?" Raven asked it. "You haven't even heard what I want."

"You don't seem particularly desperate. Not like *him*, for instance— watch this."

Nine of the televisions in the forepaw DOG was pointing at them instantly flickered into a combined vision—of a screaming man being pulled apart, ripped limb-from-limb, by four lioness-headed women.

"His wives," DOG explained. "I'd have saved King Leopold if he'd just remembered to pray to me. But no, he was in too much pain to do so."

"Why does he have to remember? You could clearly see he was in trouble."

"A deity doesn't interfere in the affairs of mortals unless asked. People resent it when we do."

"They resent it even more when you don't help," Raven countered.

"Yes, being divine is a thankless occupation."

Onscreen, the four lioness-women finished killing King Leopold and began making a stew of him.

"I've seen enough," Raven said. "Turn it off. And, don't you have anything that isn't blood and murder to show?"

"The human world is blood and murder. But . . . my point is—you seem too calm to be really bothered by whatever is bothering you—"

Raven's eyes thinned to slits. She glared knives at the machine-dog deity. "You'd prefer I was raving and screaming like a loon? Half out of my mind with fear and worry?"

"Melodrama *is* more spiritually convincing, yes."

"What kind of—"

"Great DOG," Fingers interrupted Raven. "She *is* worth helping. The great John Lynch sent her to you."

"John Lynch from Pussy Transmission?" DOG peered reprovingly down at Raven, its attitude to her at once different. "Why didn't you say so at first?

"She's shy."

DOG grinned white teeth. "No need to be shy, girl. I'm a huge fan of Lynch's work. Some of his concepts are so far ahead of their time that . . ." It waved its building-sized metal forepaw. "I'll show you some of my collection of his work. Now don't be afraid, this is just playback of a recording."

"Afraid? Of wha—?

DOG and its desert had suddenly faded from around Raven. Instead, she now stood inside a hall with shiny metal walls. The hall was freezing; her breath condensed into mist before her face. More white mist spilled in from slits in the walls.

A quick look around revealed skinned animal carcasses hung on meat hooks above a wooden stage a short distance from her. People sat opposite the stage, staring raptly at the carcasses and those that tended them.

I'm in a meat packing plant's cold room, she realized. *But what on earth is going on in here?*

DOG's voice came to her like air. "This is one of John Lynch's masterworks," it said. "He calls it *Meat Symphony.*"

It took a moment for the implications to register. "I'm inside a video recording?"

"I am divine," came the miffed reply. "It is a trifling matter for me to do this. Fear not—my reconverting you back from digital to analog form again will not harm you in any way."

Raven resumed looking around, walking towards the sitting people. All were clearly upper crust. The women had perfect hair and makeup, mink coats and diamond rings. The men all looked like they'd stepped out of the pages of Forbes magazine. (Hats everywhere too, everyone wrapped up against the faux-Alaskan clime.)

Clearly, no one could see her, which she was grateful for. The seated gents and ladies all had snobbish airs to them, like they'd think themselves too good to address her if she was revealed as existent.

She reached the stage just as music filled the air. The sound was dissonant but oddly riveting, clearly the work of great intelligence, if not musicality.

The seated watchers began oohing and aahing, several women fanning themselves with their fingers despite the freezing cold.

Then Raven looked closer at the stage. *Wow!*

What first caught her attention was the man bent over the remains of a cow. The cow had no torso, was just a head connected by its spine to its rump and legs. It was propped up, so it looked like the man was still chopping it up . . .

Then she saw the four metal strings linking the dead animal's mouth to its udders. And how the man was slapping them with a consistent rhythm. And she now recognized the music stand facing him for what it was.

Oh, he's made a musical instrument from it!

She turned quickly from the man playing the cow-bass and examined the other 'musicians' on stage: A 'meat-guitarist' playing an instrument that was a strung and fretted cow's leg; two 'violinists' playing similar instruments; a pig-keyboard—black and white keys and electronics built into a dead hog's skinned back.

(Around the musicians, additional flayed carcasses—pigs, cows, deer, bunches of geese and rabbits—floated on hooks, moving back and forth in predetermined paths across the stage at the bequest of an overhead mechanism.)

A red-haired woman oversaw two xylophones built from bones. Another shook two tambourines—plucked chickens with bells attached.

The band's drummer beat on miscellaneous miked-up portions of cows and goats, using cleavers for drumsticks. The drums sounded like a butcher cutting up meat.

Finally, playing a flayed-lamb-keyboard hung from his neck on intestine straps so he could walk around and conduct the band, there was John Lynch—twenty years younger but easily recognizable—pounding blood-smeared keys built over the carcass's excavated ribs. He looked quite drunk.

Occasionally, John smiled at the audience, after which his eyes flicked to the rear of the hall, where a camera crew was recording everything.

And I'm currently standing inside that recording, Raven understood, shivering in the freezing cold.

The players all wore coats, scarves, and gloves to keep warm, and they played with the uttermost seriousness. The posh, equally well-wrapped audience watched with even more seriousness. The music was soft then loud, first brittle as a broken heart, then hard as a rapist's erection. At one point the dangling carcasses jerked in rhythm as if dancing to the beat.

Raven shuddered with insight: this wasn't a joke, this was serious ART.

She couldn't condemn it—she ate meat. She couldn't honestly view it as animal abuse either—all the beasts being used as musical instruments were long dead. But still, there was an existential cruelty to this scene that set her mind on edge—

One composition ended, another began. A man emerged playing bagpipes made from a whole piglet, the music tubes all stuck directly into the animal's stomach.

—I can't say why it's wrong, but it's honestly not right to do this . . . This is a spiritual outrage—way, way, way past John Waters level bad taste."

"DOG," she whispered desperately. "Take me out of this scene. I've seen enough."

"A nice pun," it replied. "But there's more yet to see. Oh, Pussy Transmission were such obscene geniuses. Why did they ever break up?"

Raven began thinking DOG itself wasn't the sanest of creatures. *But then dogs—normal ones anyway—are carnivores, maybe they like meat symphonies.*

To her relief, the scene instantly shifted. Now she was in a room (thankfully one at normal temperature), a small sunlit sculptor's studio.

On her right, a handsome if moody dark-haired teenager was building a sculpture of a woman . . . from eyes. The eyes, in different colors and sizes, filled a plastic bathtub, looking like frog spawn in their profusion.

"Rachmiel Donovan," DOG said in an admiring voice as the teenager picked a blue eye out of the tub, examined it (for defects?) then pinned it place in as part of the sculpture's right breast. "An absolute genius. Even now, no one can touch him."

"Those eyes are fake, right?

"No, he got them from the local slaughterhouse, some from the local morgue. They've been soaked in formol to preserve them."

Raven gulped. *Somehow, I'll keep my last meal down.*

Rachmiel worked obsessively. Like it had with the young John Lynch, *that* stood out about him—how totally serious he was about his art. Love him or hate him (and Raven had no idea where she fell), he clearly wasn't fooling around.

"Okay," DOG said, "you've seen enough here. Let's—"

"Hold on a minute!" Raven yelped as she began fading, pointing at the girl who'd just entered the room. "She looks familiar."

"Mary Sherman," DOG confirmed. "Rach's squeeze. He loved her so much. *Too* much, in my opinion."

Rachmiel looked up from his work, his moodiness dissolving like gas the moment he saw Mary. "Darling!" He rose to his feet and rushed to hold her. He kissed her passionately.

"She was fantastic for him," Dog said. "Pretty and vivacious. She made him happier than he'd ever been before."

"She seemed bothered about something when she came in," Raven said.

Rachmiel pulled back from Mary. "What's wrong, darling?"

She stared at him, her lips trembling, her face gripped in the middle of some intense emotion. Whether joy or sadness, it was impossible to determine.

"I-I-I . . ." She fell silent, just kept staring at him.

Something's definitely wrong with her," Raven said.

Rachmiel stared at Mary for a long while, his happiness lifting off his shoulders in stages as she kept staring mutely back. "Oh, no," he said finally, turning away, "you haven't come to say you want to break up with me, have you?

She rushed after him, wrapped her arms around him from behind. "No, Rach! It's not that at all!"

He turned round in her grasp to face her again. His smile had returned. "Then what is it, darling? Doesn't matter what it is—you know I love you."

Mary Sherman nodded, though her eyes were still unsure.

"Tell me, darling," he prompted in a gentle voice.

"Rach, I'm pregnant," she whispered. "Do you want it?"

He looked at her in confusion, then it seemed like a sun had fallen into his head, that was how bright his smile became. He grabbed Mary up off the floor and whirled her round and round and round, laughing loudly. "Pregnant! Fantastic! Do I *want* it? I've never heard a more silly question in my life! Of course I want it!"

His leg hit his sculpture, knocking the eye-woman over. He ignored the dislodged orbs rolling everywhere.

"Put me down if you want to be a father!" Mary squealed with joy. "You might dislodge the baby!"

"Let's leave them there in sunshine mode," DOG said in a depressed voice.

"You don't sound happy," Raven pointed out as the room dissolved and she once again stood facing the monolithic metal hound.

"It's a depressing tale. Rachmiel Donovan later had a nervous breakdown because of Mary. After that he never sculpted again. A total loss of one of art's most incredible talents."

"A breakdown? You mean she left him?"

"Forget it," DOG said with finality. "Recalling what happens always angers me. We just saw him at eighteen years old, just imagine what he'd have been doing today . . ."

Remembering the eye-woman sculpture, Raven considered that maybe it was best for everyone that Rachmiel had stopped making art. She however kept her opinion to herself.

DOG was still speaking: "I have that piece we just saw—*The Lady of A Million Perspectives*—in my collection. I cherish it deeply. Such genius. I also have several others—"

"I've honestly seen enough, thanks, considering also the meat concert."

"I understand. To the uninitiated, PT's work can be overwhelming at first." It laughed, humongous metal ears twitching. "That said, however, I'm not about showing you anything new."

She peered up at DOG suspiciously. "Huh?"

It laughed. "Haven't you heard that the best art imitates life, which in its own turn imitates art?"

"Yeah. So?"

"So Fingers here is also one of Rachmiel Donovan's creations."

Raven spun round to stare at Fingers, who sat beside her on a broken TV fallen out of DOG's side, and was clipping his penis's fingers' fingernails. "What?"

"It's true," Fingers said. "I'm one of Rachmiel's sculptures."

Raven stared dubiously at the finger-studded man, then back at DOG. "Uh uh. I'm not buying that. Prove it."

"You question my divinity?" DOG thundered, its voice vibrating the ground. Electricity sparked between its metal whiskers.

"The taste of cake is in the eating, the proof of God in his miracles.

"Quite true," DOG agreed in a calmer voice.

"So prove it."

"Show her, Fingers,"

Raven looked back at Fingers. The man pushed up his chin, causing his entire face to flip open sideways.

Raven gaped at the mass of wires and circuitry inside Fingers' head.

Next, Fingers pressed hard on his right eye socket. A DVD tray slid out of his forehead.

Fingers froze into immobility.

Raven walked over to Fingers and removed the DVD disc from the tray.

"DOG's Rachmiel Donovan finger-sculpture animation program," she read off. She replaced the disc in the tray, looked up at DOG again.

"My apologies. I'm unsure why I doubted you. Of course, it makes sense: Rachmiel Donovan built a woman from eyes, why not cover a man with fingers?" She frowned. "You could, however, just have pointed out that he's a robot."

DOG grinned columnar metal teeth at her. "You are impertinent, but I like you; a god needs the occasional sassy worshipper. Push the tray back into his head and let's talk."

***

"So, what does John want?" DOG asked when Fingers once again sat trimming his penis's fingernails.

"His legs back," Raven replied. "But it's more complicated than that."

A moving metal mountain, DOG sat upright, its parts whirring and creaking as it altered position. "How so? What happened to John's legs?"

Raven craned her neck back to keep DOG's face in view. "John's currently a merman. Half-human, with a massive fish tail from the waist down. His wife's a wit—"

"Isis Lynch? An utterly delightful woman," DOG enthused. "One of the most creative human souls ever designed. I'd utterly love to meet her someday." It looked searchingly at Raven. "John's a merman now? How'd that happen?"

Raven, now wondering if she'd ever get round to tabling her own request for help with DOG's endless conversational detours, glared at Fingers. Fingers shrugged back, mouthed 'humor it' at her.

"Never mind," Raven said. "John asks you to help him reattach his legs. They're currently hanging on his bedroom wall."

The eighteen TVs forming DOG's eyes simultaneously showed static for a moment, then reordered their visuals back to two sets of eight white screens surrounding a central black 'pupil.'

"Done," DOG said.

CHAPTER 32

Rachmiel

Standing motionless in a shadowed nook, silent as a scared mouse, it was with deep relief that Rachmiel watched the huge condor streak away down the station platform.

He'd been surprised as hell when it emerged from the hole in the station wall through which the train had earlier vanished. A true monster, the bird's wingspan extended almost wall-to-wall across the rail tracks. The condor's dead human burden, gripped tight in its claws, dripped blood over the station platform as it flew past, wingbeats thrumming the air.

Then the bird was gone, a white speck that might never have been except in his imaginings.

(Before the Condor's appearance, Rachmiel had considered entering the bedroom after the train. Then he'd changed his mind: *It shrunk; what if that happens to me too?*)

He resumed his motion along the platform towards where he figured the exits on his side must be. There was one open—bright light and brown steps—directly opposite, across the rails from him, but he'd ruled it out: *I won't make it over the tracks alive; the exertion will kill me.*

He was surprised that he wasn't already dead. His mouth and chin were both red with coughed-up blood, and each movement hurt like he was being shot all over again. But the thought of finally exacting some measure of revenge for Mary (and now also for Maxine) gave him sufficient strength to trudge on, leaving red-outlined shoeprints in his wake.

The first exit he reached was blocked off by a metal door apparently bolted from within. Wincing, he continued walking. Thirty yards ahead, a bright-semicircle on the concrete indicated the presence of an open exit.

Five steps on, he saw the rat. An insistent metallic scraping on his left alerted him to its presence.

Like the previous ones, it was big and black. It scurried along beside him, wheezing and panting because it was dragging a pair of bloodstained scissors behind it—running with its rear legs inside the tool's finger loops.

Rachmiel groaned. *Is there no end to this horror? I'm trying not to die here and yet this nonsense refuses to stop happening.*

As he'd expected, the rat turned to face him.

He jabbed an index finger at the animal just as it opened its mouth. "You dare say *anything*, and I'll cut you in two with your scissors."

The rat stared at him, wondering if he meant the threat.

"Just go!" Rachmiel spat at it. "I'm tempted to kill you now just to demonstrate my hatred of your pestilential species!"

The rat decided he was serious. It scampered away in the direction he was headed, puffing and wheezing as its rear legs dragged the scissors along.

Thank heavens, Rachmiel groaned, setting off after it. *I just hope it's not planning to climb those stairs as well.*

He returned his thoughts to how he'd go about finding his sister and killing her once he left this so-called 2nd Floor Station.

Hatred again streaming in him, he trudged toward the light ahead.

CHAPTER 33

Raven

"The gateway to 2nd Floor Station, where you'll catch the train to the fourth floor, will come into existence over there," DOG said, gesturing west across the landscape with a massive TV-studded paw. "I will shortly create it for you."

Fingers looked up from trimming his thigh-fingernails and nodded at Raven. "Should be only a short walk."

Raven smiled her gratitude. "Thank you, great DOG."

She was relieved. Her request for help hadn't triggered another trip into DOG's data banks to view more of PT's history. *Jake, darling, I'm coming! Dammit—I just hope I'm not too late! I've been in Absurdia for six hours now.*

DOG looked down at her, its eyes now both a gloomy gray color. "While I adore Isis Lynch's creations—her genius is incontestable— I'm no fan of her recent behavior. Character is essential—an artist must be more than what she or he creates. Trapping people in picture frames? That is totally unacceptable. I'll give you something to free the captives."

Raven suddenly found herself holding a white aerosol can.

"Stand by the door, point it into the room with the paintings, and spray into the air," DOG said. "Then wait outside for five minutes."

"John said the framing effect is irreversible."

"In some ways, not all."

It said no more.

Raven suddenly felt cold. DOG's left composite eye now showed an image of a black rat. The rodent sat by a wall, breathing heavily, its forelimbs wrapped around a pair of scissors.

She shuddered. *Those things look really sharp. And call it anthropomorphism if you like, but this creature looks morbidly expectant.*

Remembering the two rats she'd seen humping severed body parts, she grimaced at Fingers. *The females will consider him a sex-toy treasure trove.*

"The rats are back, mighty DOG," Fingers said with a look of disgust. "There's one in your eye." The robot resumed sweeping up a pile of nail clippings and packing them into a paper bag. A ruby-and-diamond ring slipped off a left-ankle finger. He retrieved the ring, replaced it on the waving digit.

"What?" DOG shook its massive head. The rat image instantly vanished from its eye. It frowned down at Raven. "The rodents keep disrupting my circuits."

She regarded DOG's mountainous plastic and metal bulk, with its television plating like mirror-scales and the hairlike clusters of radio antennae between them. Ten-feet-high ridges of blue electricity crackled along DOG's back, steam poured from its shoulder exhaust pipes. Its massive silver tail flicked across the heavens like the second-hand of a doomsday clock.

"The rats are *inside* you?" she asked, confused as to how a god could be infested by pests.

"Regrettably yes," DOG growled in an angry voice. "Nesting and breeding amidst my circuits. Tapping from my divine mind is how they became intelligent in the first place. I've tolerated them way too long—the wretched little squatters. Now they're just an increasing nuisance I must rid myself of."

It turned to Fingers. "I have created the 2nd Floor Station door. Escort Raven there. Then return to fumigate me."

Fingers nodded. "Yes, great DOG."

"Goodbye, Raven," DOG said. "Talking to you has been a refreshing change from talking to myself."

"Thanks for all your help."

She turned and walked away from DOG. Fingers caught up with her, matched his pace to hers. She admired the ornate gold ring on a white-nailed finger on his right bicep.

Fingers pointed to a white rectangle fifty yards distant. "There's the space-time door."

"Hold on a minute," Raven said, turning back towards DOG. "I've a question, great D—"

She gasped. DOG's right eye-TVs showed nine different representations of her—crossing a road, eating, sleeping, making love, buying a pair of jeans, having an abortion, laughing, crying, menstruating in the bathtub. The TVs in its left eye flicked also into videos of her—firing a rifle, walking a dog, riding a bicycle, trying on a pair of red high-heeled shoes, laughing while dining in a restaurant, reading a book, masturbating with a pink vibrator, carrying a friend's baby daughter.

She stared speechless at the videos of herself.

"You were going to ask me something?" DOG prompted.

She pointed at the screens. "You've been recording me?"

"No need to. I'm simply replaying you."

"What?" The images kept changing. She winced—one of them showed her getting drunk at a college party and puking all over Harlan Morrison, who she'd had the most intense crush ever on. Another showed . . . *Oh my God! Is that what I look like while receiving cunnilingus?* She also saw herself singing Karaoke, stealing a photo from a gallery, eating a hotdog, straining on the toilet with constipation, shrieking passionately at Jake, kissing Jake, getting money from an ATM, going down deep-throat on Jake, applying eyeshadow, boarding a yacht . . . her life went on . . . She stared at herself, felt sucked into each of the eighteen switching versions; relived herself . . .

DOG's voice fell on her, breaking the spell of herself. It was a magnificent sonorous sound, thunder that passed through earth and body instead of the heavens. "Raven, I am DOG the upgraded deity. Very little is hidden from me." It blinked her out of its eyes; its gaze turned neutral again. "The space-time door awaits you. What were you about asking me?"

She yanked her mind back into focus. "Yeah . . . em . . . er . . ." She pointed. "That door of yours . . . it doesn't open up close to Betty—I mean the naked psycho woman with the axe—does it?"

DOG rumbled like a set of divine exhaust pipes, the TVs plating its body switching through a multitude of gory serial killer scenes. "Ah yes, Betty Butcher—Elizabeth Genevieve Buchwald, rather."

"I'm not looking to get my head hacked off. John says she's unkillable."

DOG grinned. "Not true. There is a way to disable her."

Raven nodded grimly. "Shoot—I'm listening."

Five minutes later, armed to the teeth with fresh knowledge about Betty Butcher, Raven stepped through the solitary door in the wilderness—just a frame with nothing either side of it—into 2nd Floor Station.

CHAPTER 34

Rachmiel

Rachmiel paused at the open platform exit, at the start of brown ceramic steps rising up into the light. Bracing himself upright with bloodless fingers, he fought to get his strength back, to clear his mind and vision. At least one of his wounds had re-opened—blood was running down his left side. In addition, his right lung felt full of liquid; it was a struggle to breathe.

I've got to keep it together, he thought. *For Maxine; for Mary and my child . . . I'll kill—*

He hacked up a mouthful of blood. It splattered the rat with the scissors, which now crouched by the adjacent door jamb.

Blood running in its fur, the black rat glared angrily at him.

"Scram!" he growled at it, swinging his foot threateningly.

Knowing he was too weak to attack it, the rat smirked back. "You're gonna . . ."

Rachmiel stopped paying it any attention. Someone was coming down the steps.

He regarded the new arrival with surprise. *What's a naked blonde doing here with an axe? And why is she covered all over in blood? Did someone attack her too?*

"Die!" the rat said.

"Kill! Kill!" the naked blonde yelped gleefully on seeing Rachmiel.

He only realized she was hostile when she leapt down the remaining steps at him, axe raised poised over her shoulder.

Rachmiel spun out of her way, smacking his back painfully against the platform wall. He stood gasping, just managing to keep his legs under him, wondering what was going on.

The blonde landed like a cat. She straightened up and turned to smile coldly at Rachmiel.

"I'm gonna kill you, man!" she said, raising her axe.

Too weak to flee, Rachmiel glanced across the station. Another woman stood at the other open entrance, on the opposite platform across the train tracks.

The naked blonde swung her axe. Rachmiel watched death come for him, slowly lifting an arm to fend it off.

Death took Rachmiel Donovan.

Floating like an iron butterfly over Rachmiel's still-rising hand, the axe sliced cleanly through his neck, digging into the wall behind him. His severed head rolled across its blade, then fell to the floor. Blood bubbled up from his opened neck.

Betty Butcher stepped back. The corpse collapsed forward to the ground. She regarded the headless body with interest for a moment, then, with intense pleasure, she began hacking it to bits, reducing Rachmiel Donovan to a pile of raw meat.

She paused. *Something's missing!*

Looking around, she located Rachmiel's head from where it had rolled to and dropped it in amidst the pile of gore. Then she hacked up the head as well, the feeling better than orgasmic in her loins.

When she was done, the corpse was unrecognizable as once-human. The concrete floor under it was slashed up also, marred with bloody furrows. She felt great—strong, totally invigorated. It had been ages since she'd killed anyone and this had been just . . .

Hey? What's it looking for in there? Betty stared interestedly at the black rat, which (having abandoned its scissors) was now digging through the mess of flesh and clothing tatters.

At last, the rat emerged clutching a severed ear. Betty giggled with amusement, when, laying down amidst the shredded human remains, the rat began copulating with the human ear, huffing and puffing with its exertions.

Then she completely forgot the humping rat. She'd sighted the woman on the opposite platform.

CHAPTER 35

Raven & Betty

Raven watched with horror as, opposite her, Betty hacked the man to bits. "What the hell is wrong with you, girl?" she whispered to herself.

But she knew. DOG had phrased it this way: "Betty Butcher is incurably addicted to murder. To her, killing is like breathing."

Betty was slamming her axe so hard into the disintegrating corpse now that sparks flew where the blade smacked concrete. Gore spilled back over her shoulders in a red rain.

Her attention focused on Betty, Raven had just the barest impression of her surroundings. A quick glance around had already confirmed to her that she was in 'Lynch Place, 2nd Floor Station.'

The other thing she was conscious of was the auto-construction work going on to her right, where a hyper-realistic wall mural—a depiction of a bedroom—was being broken down to reveal an extension of the train station into a tunnel beyond it. It was odd—she could hear the sound of workmen demolishing the wall and unbricking the passageway, but there was no one there.

(The aerosol spray DOG had given Raven was clipped to her belt's grappler harness.)

On the opposite platform, Betty Butcher turned from staring at the diced corpse to staring at Raven.

Raven waved across at her. "Yeah, I'm back!"

She drew her gun. This was do-or-die time, she knew. Raven had no intention of going back, of pulling out of her quest to free Jake—so forward was the only way. *And if I have to drill the way forward through you, psycho chick, so be it—you'll be simply another casualty of love.*

Then Betty was rushing at her. "Kill! Finish unfinished business!!"

Watching Betty Butcher leaping across the tracks-space separating the station platforms, her axe whirling overhead like a helicopter's propellers, Raven had a moment of undiluted doubt. Flying through the air like that, a smile on her dead face, the oncoming blonde looked invincible, a naked blood-drenched barbarian superwoman. *Maybe I should try to find another way upstairs,* she thought desperately. *This could go really wrong. How the hell do I know DOG didn't lie to me?*

Then Betty landed on Raven's side of the station platform and was charging at her, and she had no time left for doubt. She leapt out of the onrushing woman's way, spinning behind her.

Betty smashed her axe into the wall, whirled around, and came at Raven again. She moved like a hunting leopardess, fast and furious.

Backing away at speed, Raven fired. Her first bullet missed Betty completely, zipping past her shoulder and zinging off the station wall.

Betty, seeing the gun, slowed her charge to a confident walk. "Kill . . . Kill . . . Kill . . . Kill . . . Kill . . . !"

The litany of death sought to drive Raven insane. "Screw you!" she screamed. She adjusted her aim and fired again.

Her second shot hit Betty in the left breast. Not pausing in her advance, Betty stared down at the wound, then laughed at Raven. "You poor, poor dope, won't you ever learn?"

She shifted her grip on her axe, holding it at shoulder height with its blade parallel to the floor like she was going to lop Raven's head off. Blood still dripped off the weapon's edges.

Raven stopped retreating. She stood her ground and fired. Her next three shots all hit Betty in the face, blowing out the back of her head. She sighed with relief when Betty dropped the axe and crumpled forward, falling flat on her face.

Dropping her now-empty gun and pulling out her switchblade, Raven leapt atop Betty Butcher. She had to do this quickly. Already, she could see the bullet-ripped chasm in the woman's exposed brain healing, the skull knitting; bloody blonde hair sealing shut over it.

Raven rolled Betty over on her back. She knelt over her shoulders, her feet pinning Betty's arms to her sides. Just as Betty's shut eyes flicked open again, Raven dug the tip of her knife deep into the raw seam of dead and living flesh ringing her face and began cutting along it.

In a flash, Betty realized what Raven was doing. "Noooo!" she screamed, the first expression of fear Raven had heard from her. She kicked and thrashed, fingers scrabbling for her axe, but it was too far from her reach. Raven, meanwhile, sat firm on her, her buttocks planted on Betty's pillowy breasts, her legs clamped tight by Betty's sides to restrain the woman's arms. She worked fast now, conscious of Betty's immense strength, capitalizing of her advantage of surprise before it ran out. She slammed Betty's shaking head back down to the concrete, held it there and kept slicing away.

"Noooo!" Betty's blue eyes now yawned wide as saucers.

"Oh, frigging yes!" Raven said in a cold voice, enjoying the woman's helpless terror. She'd now cut a deep line along the meat seam, from Betty's left temple down to her chin. Dropping the knife by Betty's head, she dug her fingers into the shrieking blonde's face and grimly ripped its skin off.

Everything came off. Not just the skin, but Betty's entire face, muscles, eyes, and all. Raven found herself holding a wet bleeding mass and staring down at an eyeless skull ringed with hair.

"NOOOOOOOOOOOOOOOOOOO!!!" the skull screamed, Betty's body simultaneously bucking beneath Raven.

Then skull and body both went limp.

Raven looked once at the mass of face she held in her hand, with its reproving turquoise gaze, then she flung it well away from her, out over the platform edge, down between the rails.

Then she collapsed sideways off Betty's body. She lay on the platform breathing heavily, watching with disbelief as Betty's body withered away to remain just a bloody skeleton.

Beside the skeleton, the axe vanished.

Raven finally sat up. She arranged her scattered black hair, retrieved her gun and knife, then waited for the train she was meant to catch.

A glance to her right showed her that the invisible workmen had finished unbricking the new train tunnel.

CHAPTER 36

Raven

Raven's anticipated train finally arrived at 2nd Floor Station. It was a modified streetcar—a single blue/white carriage with lots of wide windows. It rolled in from Raven's left, towards the new tunnel.

About time too, she griped on seeing it. Sitting on a platform bench watching Betty Butcher's skeleton had her all edgy. (As a plus, though, she'd used the interlude to reload her gun.) DOG had assured her that without a face, Betty would be out for the count, but Raven wasn't taking any chances. *There's simply too much weirdo nonsense going on for me to let down my guard.*

Also, though relieved that she and Jake would shortly exit this nightmare, she still couldn't shake off a sense of misgiving.

She rose from her bench, walked to the platform edge, and descended steps to a lower platform to board the streetcar.

Scratching an itch over her left nipple, she considered her feelings of impending catastrophe. It wasn't anything she could put her finger on, just a bad vibe that refused to go away.

She pushed her worries aside. *Nah, it's just seeing these bones and that chopped-up dead guy across the tracks.*

The blue/white streetcar slowed and stopped beside Raven. Its foremost door opened. She climbed aboard, then stared shocked at the driver. "Huh? You?"

Smiling broadly, John Lynch waved to her. "Thanks for relaying my request to DOG." The former merman now had his legs back, was dressed in full blue pajamas and hush puppies.

Her responsive smile was a perplexed, uneasy one. "Man, you're welcome; it was quite the experience."

He pointed out the door behind her. "Who's that?"

"Betty. DOG told me how to fix her—easy, just peel her face off."

172

John raised an eyebrow, then pointed across the tracks. "And the mess of meat over there was?"

"The last guy she killed." She pointed down the new tunnel. "Let's go, John. I'm sick of this creepy place."

He nodded, shut the door, and set the car moving along the rails again. "I was going to pick up Betty's skeleton for safekeeping, but I'll come back for it."

Raven sat next to him. "So, how come *you're* driving this thing?"

"Someone has to."

"Don't brush me off."

The streetcar was swallowed up into the dark of the tunnel, its headlights powerless to disperse the sudden night. The darkness felt like it was pushing its way into the vehicle, seeking to feed on the two travelers. Raven felt great dread, like they'd just entered the world's throat and were on their way to being digested in its bowels.

She stared pointedly at John Lynch, who gazed wide-eyed ahead into the black, his face as white with strain as hers. "I said—don't brush me off. I need an explanation for this—I'm tired of endlessly almost losing my mind with each new twist, and who knows how many more are yet to come."

He turned to look at her. "It's complicated, that's all. Do you like science?"

She shook her head. "I just like stuff to work. I like it even more if it's pink in color."

"I'll keep it simple then: Just consider this streetcar as an elevator, and me as its operator."

"Too simplistic."

"So's your cellphone. You have any idea how that works? So why bother about the rest?"

The blackness around them was brightening now, red light spilling in through slits in the walls.

"This is the part of the trip I hate," John said in a tense voice. "The walls have eyes."

Raven was about telling him not to change the topic when she saw what he meant. The slits from which red light spilled into the black tunnel were carved-out facial features like those of a jack-o-lantern. Only in this case, the faces were alive, the red slits writhing with malevolent expressions. Looks of anger, of intense agonies of torment, and of morbid lust extended ahead of them on both sides.

She gestured at the faces. "These look like the demon-mountains I saw in Absurdia."

"They can't hurt us," John said, "but they're depressing as hell to look at."

"Take your mind off them; finish your explanation."

He frowned, scratched his mustache. "That elevator analogy is really the best way I can explain it without a lot of scientific mumbo jumbo—"

"Don't give me that. The elevator explanation *is* mumbo jumbo."

"You're looking at it all wrong. Try viewing it this way—in Absurdia, objects regularly get assigned functions that, while feasible with a stretch of the imagination, would be ridiculous in real life. Imagine using monster trucks as taxis for instance . . ."

Raven let it go. *We're still in Absurdia?* Instead she said, "DOG's a huge fan of your work, you know."

He frowned, acknowledging her statement with a series of nods. "That makes sense, I guess. DOG is a scientific god, one formed by logical processes. My interest in art was, and still is, primarily scientific. You know—the applications of new technology. Demonstrating how multimedia can be used for art . . . turning science into art, if you will. Science for ART's sake."

She nodded. "You're quite the musician too—DOG showed me your *Meat Symphony.*"

"The instruments stank."

"Please go on."

"I espouse the principle of the media itself as art—real life as art. For too long the media was viewed as simply the means of dispersing the creation, but with modern technology, the packaging is now more relevant than its content. Indeed, it *now is* its content—how information is presented to the receiver is what makes it relevant in social context."

"You're essentially saying that *how* we're told a thing is now more important that what we're told?

"It's the modern truth—the machine is the message."

Raven whistled. "That's a mindful to digest, but I'm not arguing. You're the expert."

Around them as they sped on, the glow from the leering demon faces in the tunnel walls was now lightening to yellow.

"We're nearing the end of the trip," John said with relief.

"I've another question."

"Yeah?"

"If *you* can do this—won't your wife be expecting us?"

He laughed coldly. "No. Isis disdains science."

"What does *that* have to do with *this?*" Like he'd indicated, the light from the wall faces was now all white. The faces themselves had lost their demonic aspect. All now looked serene, innocent as choirboys. Raven almost expected their mouths to break into hallelujahs. "I'm just pointing it out like 'cos I hate surprises."

"Isis is a total, compulsive, artist. Like I just mentioned, I'm primarily a scientist who uses art as experimental data. Isis is an alchemist, I'm a chemist. Isis uses things, I know how to make them; she never really understands the results she gets. She's a magician, I'm a technician. Isis knows that there are doors in and out of Absurdia. I both know *where* they are and *why* they open, and also *how* to open them when necessary." He smiled at Raven. "So, no—my beautiful wife *won't* be expecting us."

Raven imagined she heard deep longing in his voice. "You miss her, do you? You still love her?"

He sighed. "After all she did to me? Shutting me away down there? Tormenting me by making me half fish? Yes, I do. It's stupid I know. Love is mad, blind, insane—it puts you completely in another's power, and all you can do then is pray desperately that they'll treat you well, because if they don't, you're screwed—leaving them is often much harder than remaining and taking their abuse. Even now, when I should rightly be thinking of murdering Isis, I'm instead thinking of grabbing her and kissing her, of making love with her . . ."

Raven grinned. *Like I intend doing to Jake.*

John's middle-aged face turned suddenly sad. "Anyhow, we'll see how it works out."

Raven tapped the aerosol can at her waist. "I'm forgetting to mention—DOG gave me this, said it'll free the people trapped in the paintings."

"It did?" John regarded the white can. "But . . . just a *spray?*" His brow creased in thought. "My experiments showed it was impossible, . . . but then DOG is a god, with access to higher technology—so . . ." He smiled. "That can of yours is twenty years overdue, I can't wait to free Mary—"

"Hold on a moment," Raven interrupted as a thought hit her. "One more thing: If your wife isn't tech-savvy enough to open the space-time doors—how'd Betty find her way down here?"

While the streetcar rolled out of the tunnel end into another station, John considered the question. "Not intentionally at any rate. She was likely just trying to walk down the stairs to the ground floor and got caught in the opening portal."

"That sounds too random. I mean—she killed someone."

He sighed, slowed the streetcar. "Accidents happen, Raven. Sometimes they're fatal."

CHAPTER 37

Isis

Isis Lynch sat in her rogue's gallery staring moodily at the massive ruined canvas propped on the easel beside her current work, *Vaginal Odor*.

All around her, the framed people watched helplessly, their projected emotions of hatred and despair (and lust—two of the men sported erections due to her nakedness) heavy on her.

Most times, while working, Isis reveled in this room's weird ambience, her captive audience a satisfactory replacement for the one she'd lost when Pussy Transmission had folded.

Now though, the accusatory, pleading eyes felt like spears piercing her, their owners' combined despair massive weights on her shoulders.

I'm really worried, she admitted to herself. *I'm worried because I've no idea what's going on. And that's unusual with me. I've been in control for so long, but now . . .*

Black light crackled around the edges of the canvas facing her. Isis winced. This was what had instantly alerted her the previous day that something was wrong with it—its flickering should normally be yellow in color. In addition, it should have been blank, not behaving like a digital picture frame. Then she'd looked at the ground below the man-sized canvas (which had both been mounted on a stout specially designed tripod and stood by an inner wall to keep it out of harm's way) and seen the little puddle of rat urine and deduced what had happened. Damn those rats!

She kept staring at the canvas, intrigued despite her fear of its implications, its dangers—attracted by its possibilities. *I've never ruined a 'capture' canvas before. It'll be interesting to experiment with it.*

Her brow wrinkled with her brooding. *First it showed a train, now a white bird—massive thing, looks like a condor . . . It's capturing things it wasn't designed to, isn't supposed to. Capturing them automatically, but capturing them from where? How am I supposed to determine that when the picture keeps changing? And with rat urine, just rat pee as the trigger? Ha ha ha! Oh, this'll definitely prove useful at some point. But what about the feeling of menace that seems to come from it? No, I'm just imagining that because of those mountains with angry eyes . . .*

And it's odd how the canvas is still active. And how—the paintbrush I flung at it vanished through it, as did those coins too, so . . . .

Unfortunately John isn't around to help me figure out the science angle . . .

Preparing capture canvases was routine for Isis. She always kept one up on an easel in waiting for the next art thief (or thieves) to turn up, somewhere to quickly 'store' said person(s). Because of the care required to handle them safely however, Isis only ever had one capture canvas at home at a time—she'd made this ruined one the day after she'd 'stored' Jake.

Ah yes! Jake!

Glad for the distraction from her picture puzzle, Isis turned to look at her latest, favorite captive, stuck in his Playgirl 'bunny' pose.

She laughed. Jake still had his erection from last night, stiff and throbbing, if anything more swollen than before. That was something she found odd—once stimulated, the trapped men simply couldn't subside until they'd ejaculated. Like the blood that flowed into their penises couldn't get out again.

So Jake—flattened Jake whose eyes were sad, sad, sad—had been hard as a rock since yesterday.

Isis got up and walked over to the portrait. "Ooh, darling," she cooed at him, stroking the turgid penis that stuck out proud—a purple soldier on parade. "Dear, dear me—you must be so uncomfortable now." She playfully cupped an ear at the mute portrait. "What was that, honey? Oh, you're pleading with me to relieve you?" She giggled. "Really, I should leave you like this . . . but no—your cock looks ready to explode and I don't want blood all over my clean floor now, do I?" She cupped her ear at the 'painting' again. "Oh, what was that, honey? I promised you anal last night?"

She smiled. "Okay, a promise is a debt. Let me get some lube."

Once she'd lubed them both up and was sliding Jake's manhood up her backside, Isis relaxed.

While having intercourse with the painting (braced with her hands on her knees), she busied her mind with non-sexual contemplation.

(Her not using her vagina on him was intentional: She wasn't aroused, and didn't wish to be at the moment. Besides, she didn't want the taste of semen in her mouth—then she'd have to brush her teeth to be rid of it. Meanwhile, relieving Jake by hand might mean arm strain and she intended painting in a short while. Anal was a good compromise.)

It's resolved then, she decided while crouching and rising on the stiff member probing her rectum. *I'll keep this damaged portrait for research and make another one in readiness for the next stupid intruder.*

Feeling Jake start ejaculating, she slid down fully on him, reaching hands back and gripping the painting's frame to prevent her knocking it over. As he spurted inside her (his mingled impressions of intense relief and intenser hatred breaking over her in waves), she returned to her thoughts: *Or, maybe I should make two new canvases, then catch one of the rats and get it to pee on one of them . . .* An odd thought struck her—she looked right, at the frozen Mary Sherman. *I wonder what effect rat urine would have on her? Hmmm . . .*

Jake wilted inside her and plopped out of her anus. A fall of semen accompanied his exit, sploshing the floor between her feet. She prevented more semen-fall by plugging herself with a finger and clenching her sphincter tight around it.

Stepping over the spilled come, she turned and hurried off past Jake to her bathroom to wash.

Despite not having had an orgasm she felt quite refreshed when she left the bathroom. Calm now she'd reached a decision. She brought some wipes back with her to clean up Jake and the floor.

One step into her rogue's gallery, Isis Lynch stopped. Paused in her doorway, she growled with rapidly escalating anger.

There was a black rat sitting on top of her new painting—her *Vaginal Odor.* (Isis had resolved her dissatisfaction over the portrayal's effectiveness by giving the woman bleeding into the fish's mouth two clitorises. Now she was entirely satisfied with it.)

"Get down off that painting!" she whispered hoarsely at the rat. "Don't you dare damage it. It's taken me three months to get right!"

"You're gonna die," the rat responded.

Isis looked around for something suitable to throw at it. *I can't use a knife—it might rip the canvas. Maybe a paintbrush? Hey, where the hell are my big scissors anyway? I'm certain Betty returned them to me after her face-trimming session.* She winced. *I'm gonna die? Oh, forget that—they always spew that nonsense! If this stupid little animal scratches my painting, I'll . . . I'll . . .*

"Get down off the painting," she repeated quietly.

Rather than comply, however, the rat began urinating on her masterwork. Isis's eyes widened with disbelief as it drenched *Vaginal Odor* with pee.

Totally enraged, she grabbed a knife off a desk and charged at the rat. "Stop pissing on my goddam painting, you goddam pest!"

Isis suddenly lost her footing. She was already falling helplessly towards the damaged black-flickering canvas showing the white condor before she realized what she'd slipped on—the residue of Jake's semen that she'd been coming to clean up.

She hit the canvas. All around her as she was sucked into it, she could sense clearly her prisoners laughing at her from their canvases.

CHAPTER 38

Raven & John

Except for the difference in name signs, 4th Floor station looked exactly the same as 2nd Floor station.

"Where's the tunnel lead?" Raven asked, pointing ahead into the darkened arch at the station's end.

"More stations," John replied distractedly.

"This building only has four floors."

"On this Earth, maybe. There are many others."

"Floors or Earths?"

"Both."

They disembarked from the streetcar and crossed the platform to an exit. John leading, they climbed the stairs.

Raven was now growing apprehensive of the coming showdown. She stared up at the love-stricken John Lynch—so desperate to be reunited with the woman who'd imprisoned him—then considered herself, equally desperate to free her boyfriend imprisoned by the same woman. "John, hold on a sec—what's to stop Isis from turning you back into a merman and locking you downstairs again?"

He paused at the top of the stairs, fingers on the handle of the closed door there. "The captive people were our bone of contention. Once you spray them free, we'll no longer have any real argument . . ." he forced a smile, "except for her anger that I let them all go." He frowned. "I'll get Isis out of the room before you do it, though, or they'll likely rip her to shreds."

Raven nodded.

John opened the door and they stepped out into a corridor.

"This way," he indicated. "Follow me."

They moved along quickly, heading for Isis Lynch's rooms.

***

Standing in the middle of Isis's rogue's gallery, Raven felt like she'd walked into a daylight nightmare. (Her gun hung limp and useless in her hand, which felt nerveless from the sheer depths of her horror.) The thirty-one trapped faces seemingly looked straight at her. Their horror and despair poured over her like a waterfall.

She saw Jake—*oh, my darling!*—posed naked, his penis protruding from the canvas. She ran over and touched his face, kissed his soft, frozen lips. His skin—raised a half-inch off the painted background— was warm and hairy, a blue vein throbbed in his forehead. His chest rose and fell almost imperceptibly.

Love for him flooded Raven, along with the eager desire to immediately free him and his fellow captives. But first (she knew) Isis *had* to be found and neutralized. It wouldn't do to have her ambush Raven and John during the freeing process.

John was currently looking for Isis amidst their suite's interconnecting rooms.

It hurt Raven to wait though. Dully, feeling psychically violated by the room's horrible vibe (and wondering how anyone could be so merciless to others) she looked around Isis's people-gallery. At its hopeless captives—all flattened on canvases, breathing, living in bas-relief.

Looking exactly as she had in the flashback of Rachmiel Donovan which DOG had shown her, Mary Sherman stood frozen by Jake's right.

Behind Mary hung an odd picture of a naked woman. *Odd* because the woman's face had been cut out—her head was just black hair framing a bloody hole in the canvas, a gap from which (now-dried) blood had dripped down over her body. With a shudder, Raven realized this was the woman whose face had been used to animate Betty Butcher.

Farther in, not instantly visible from the doorway, a canvas and easel had toppled over. The canvas had oddly flickering black edges. Curious, she walked towards it.

"Isis!" John's voice came loud from outside the living gallery, from a room filled with sculptures and gadgets. "Isis, honey, where are you?"

Raven stared hard at one of the captive portraits—a blue-eyed man with large nipples on each cheek like they were breasts. A monkey sitting on his shoulder was suckling from his right cheek-nipple. She realized that Isis had been magically altering her captives. Worried, she looked back at Jake again. *The witch didn't alter you too, darling, did she?*

She gripped her gun nervously. *And where the hell is she hiding? Show yourself, witch!*

She reached the fallen canvas with the strange edges—a wavering rectangle of dancing black flames. Then she noticed the pale gleaming streak leading from under Jake almost to the base of its collapsed tripod.

She knelt and examined the wet streak, noting the squishy toe-prints on the laminate wood floor. She quickly deduced their meaning. For a conclusive test, she ran a fingertip through the wetness, then sniffed it. *Oh, you were abusing Jake, you slut?*

Raven straightened up again. With a dull look at her frozen boyfriend, she walked over to the gallery door.

"She's in here!" she called to John through the adjoining room. "Or was, at any rate."

He came running over instantly. "Where?"

Raven led him inside, pointed out the toppled-over canvas. "I think she fell into it."

"Oh no!" John gasped, rushing over to it.

They both stared at the canvas—a painting of an endless meadow with a huge white bird soaring overhead.

Legs kicking feebly, tail twitching, a black rat's hindquarters projected from beneath the painting's left edge.

"It's empty," John said, choking back tears. "She must have fallen *through* it. And something's wrong with this canvas—its edges should be yellow, not black." He pointed. "The rat's not even dead yet—it must just have happened."

Raven nodded back at the distraught man. Personally, she was very pleased that Isis had met her nemesis—it prevented an ugly confrontation with the witch. She doubted very much that bullets would have been any use against magic like this.

She however felt immensely sorry for John Lynch. It was touching to see how much he loved his wife, even if . . . even if she was a very evil woman. Looking around the room at all the trapped people, feeling their hot, wet misery pour over her in torrents, Raven could reach no other conclusion about Isis Lynch but that she was EVIL.

"John," she said softly, "this room's traumatizing me—I'll have nightmares for years to come simply from being in here. Let's get this over with please. Free everyone?"

He nodded miserably.

Raven unclipped the aerosol can. After closing its farther door, she indicated that John come out of the gallery with her into the bedroom. There, standing in the bedroom doorway, she sprayed the gallery. She emptied the can into it then shut the door.

She sighed with relief. "Thank heavens, that's over."

John sat on the bed. She sat beside him.

"How long did DOG say to wait?"

"Five minutes."

They waited, watching the second-hand move round the wall clock. Tension built in them, a feeling of being on the verge of a climax.

"Something's wrong," John said finally. "We should be hearing the sound of people inside there."

Raven moved to open the door.

John placed a restraining hand on her arm. "Hold your gun ready in case they attack us. And wait a moment for me." He found another gun in a drawer. "Okay."

Raven opened the bedroom door and peered out. She looked back at John, her face confused. "It didn't work," she said in a brittle voice. "Everyone's still a painting."

She rushed into the gallery towards Jake.

Climax became anticlimax. Equally confused, John Lynch rushed after her. The room now smelt faintly of turpentine. "It *didn't* work? How could DOG make such a mistake?"

Raven examined her boyfriend's picture, then stared at John in alarm. "It's now flat—just like an actual painting!"

"Flat?" He quickly looked around at the other paintings in the room. "Oh my God, you're right! They've all been flattened. But why?" Then, suddenly, he understood. Sitting on a stool beside a painting of a woman and a fish that smelt of rat urine, he regarded Raven with calm, if miserable, eyes.

"You're missing something," he said.

"DOG lied to me!" Her voice was frantic. "It said—!"

"Look at their faces, all of them."

"What the hell for?" But she did look, starting with Jake. Now a real life-sized portrait of a Playgirl bunny (still with his penis exposed!), Jake was grinning, his eyes happy.

She looked around the room. All the other 'painted' people had similarly joyful expressions on their faces.

There was another change also: the gallery's former melancholic ambience was gone, totally vanished, replaced with a gaiety and happiness, the difference as clear as healing a wound. The happiness filled the room like it poured from concealed fountains in the walls.

The difference is like day and night, she pondered. *Even the air smells cleaner, as if someone planted flowers in*—

John interrupted her thoughts. "You see. DOG didn't lie—it *has* freed them all."

"But,"—her gaze became desperate—"where are they then? They're not still stuck in the canvases are they? I mean Jake . . ."

John shook his head. "No they aren't. There are an infinite number of worlds besides ours. Your boyfriend is over in one of them now." He smiled. "I always assumed it was impossible to extract a completely implanted person from a capture-frame. Thankfully, I was wrong. DOG found a way, only just not back into *our* space-time."

"And all these happy paintings?"

"Are just to let us know that they're all fine now." Then his brow furrowed. "Why is Mary carrying a baby?"

Raven turned toward the painting of Mary Sherman. It was true— in her portrait, Mary, now fuller-bosomed and grinning broadly, cradled a sleeping blue-swaddled infant.

Raven smiled. "She was pregnant with Rachmiel's child. DOG showed me."

John's eyes spread wide. "Oh, so *that's* why he was so mad with Isis!"

"What?"

He waved it off. "Ancient sibling conflict gone nuclear. Made the Cold War look like pro wrestling."

Raven sat on a bench facing him. She was utterly confused; nothing in the world had prepared her for this conclusion to matters. She was deeply upset that Jake was gone and she'd likely never see him again, but at the same time she was delighted that he'd not spend the rest of his life stuck motionless in a picture on a witch's wall.

"What do we do now?" she asked John.

He pointed to Jake and Mary's portraits. "You can have those two. Give Mary's to Jose Estrada—just don't tell him what happened."

"You're letting it go just like that?"

"Yeah, yeah. I'm happy she's happy now, but . . ." he shrugged, "keeping it will just be a source of bad memories for me—a constant reminder of how Pussy Transmission fell from fame to obscurity." He forced a grin. "Besides, if I don't let you take the painting to Jose, he'll keep sending people over to steal it anyway. And I don't have Isis's protective magic."

She nodded. "Thanks." She considered his solemn face. He was clearly even sadder than she was, doing his best not to weep, holding the pressure of his loss inside till he was alone and could free his tears and grieve undisturbed. "And you? What'll you do about Isis?"

John Lynch pointed over at the fallen canvas, which now showed a brown landscape with huge trees that had hanging people as fruit.

"Are those called Lynch trees?" Raven asked.

He winced. "Please don't."

She smiled contritely.

John sighed. "Isis? The way this blasted canvas keeps shifting images, there's no way to know where she actually fell into. Which means there's no way I can go searching for her." He gestured around the room at the happy paintings. "I'm all alone now with her legacy."

Then he smiled at Raven. "Feel free to come see me whenever you like."

She smiled back. "I will, thanks."

***

John called Olaf to help Raven move Jake and Mary's portraits downstairs. and then drive her back to her motel. (Raven and Jake's car was parked round the corner on Superior Street, but Jake had had the car keys, and John had no idea what Isis had done with his clothes.)

Once the gothic manservant arrived, John hugged Raven and left them to it. Raven understood—his grief was palpable.

The two life-sized canvases required careful handling. Olaf, for all his moth-ridden appearance (and pervasive smell of mothballs), was deceptively strong.

"When did *you* get in?" he asked Raven, as, portraits borne between them, they descended the stairs to the second floor landing. "*How* did you get in?"

"Yesterday. Magic."

The answers clearly satisfied Olaf. Raven next had a question of her own: "Say, what happened to your two guests—the female couple? They still around?"

Olaf looked confused. "What guests?"

His puzzlement was clearly faked. Raven looked him straight in the eye over the paintings and insisted: "The two women—blonde and brunette—who arrived in a shiny yellow car."

"Oh, you mean Misses Lily and Nina—the Dirty Vagina journalists." His weathered face creased up in a mysterious smile. "They're both still in the house . . . somewhere."

"Dirty Vagina? There's actually a magazine with that name?"

She was quiet while they got the paintings out of the house and secured them on the roof of Olaf's red Mercedes. The time looked to be about midmorning.

As they drove off, Raven looked back once. She wasn't surprised to see that Lynch Place's fourth floor now had windows again.

She grinned despite the immense sense of loss she felt. *Yeah, it's over alright—and this looks set to be a nice day, with the sun bright and warm and everything. Jake, baby, just be happy—have a good life—wherever you are.*

EPILOGUE

Isis

Isis Lynch fell and fell, so far and fast and furious, she thought she was destined for Hell.

She landed unhurt on brown sand. The knife she'd been about stabbing the urinating rat with spilled from her hand on her impact.

Cursing herself for her foolishness—*Drat it! I should have remembered Jake's semen was in the way!*—she got up. Brushing sand from her blonde hair and off her breasts, she tried to figure out where she was.

She grimaced. *Not the demon-faced mountains! Anywhere but there!*

The mountain range of scowling red faces lay ahead and to her right. She scowled back at them with instinctive dread. *The damn things look like they want to eat me!*

She calmed herself. *Okay, I'm in Absurdia now, I'm certain of it.*

Despite her horror, embarrassment (at making such a mistake), and her despair, Isis was immensely grateful that she'd not wound up stuck in the canvas like her captives—she recalled their laughter as she'd fallen into it. *I'd never have been able to stomach all those art thieves—the damn philistines—laughing at me forever.*

She turned for a complete view of her surroundings. *Okay, now I know where I am, I just need to find out how to get home again. John would know, only he's still locked—*

She heard the beating of wings overhead and spun quickly to face the sound.

The white bird! The massive white condor was speeding at her, its beak open to attack.

Hell no! Isis leapt out of the way of the swooping bird, but not quickly enough. Its HUGE left wing—*Wow, I never knew they grew to this size!*—slammed into her chest, knocking her off her feet and down onto her buttocks.

The condor didn't land. It rose skyward again and circled for a follow-up attack.

Isis sat up groggily. The condor's wing had flung her ten feet from where she'd been standing. Quickly, fighting to clear the cobwebs from her brain, she looked around for her knife.

She located it, a thin mirror on the sand ahead of her.

The white bird swooped again; Isis scrabbled desperately for her weapon.

The condor reached her before she reached the knife. Again, like it was toying with her, it knocked her off her feet, buffeting her away from the knife.

This time the bird landed.

Isis too, leapt up almost instantly, adrenalin-alert. Her heart pumped furiously in her chest. She formed her hands into claws. *Come on, you bastard! I ain't scared of you!* She'd have run, but there was nowhere around to flee to.

Squawking loudly, the bird advanced slowly on Isis. *Damn, it's so big!* She tried circling towards the knife, but it blocked her off.

It regarded Isis with piercing blue eyes. It leapt at her.

Isis tensed, certain she was about to die.

Then a loud gunshot rang out. Then another. Then a third blast. Giving a loud alarmed squawk, the condor abandoned its attack and rose skyward, blood trailing from wounds in its right wing.

Confused, Isis looked around to see who'd saved her. Then she stood staring at him in even more confusion.

No, I'm hallucinating! I'm not looking at a naked man covered head to toes with human fingers! Her eyes widened further. *He's even got fingers on his dick!*

Fingers cocked his shotgun again to eject the spent cartridge, then smiled at Isis. "Mrs. Lynch, I presume."

"Who . . . who are you?" Then her eyes widened with recognition. "Hey! You're one of Rach's sculptures! You're alive? How!?"

Fingers bowed. "Deacon Fingers at your service, Mrs. Lynch. I'm most grateful to your brother for making me."

She realized that he'd addressed her by name. "You know me too?"

Fingers gave a respectful bow. "You were a one time member of Pussy Transmission, Mrs. Lynch. DOG the upgraded deity is a great fan of your work. He sensed your arrival in his realm and sent me to fetch you." Fingers tapped his shotgun. "Good thing I arrived in time—that bird's a massive pain in the ass. But great DOG likes her for some reason."

Isis considered Fingers' explanation. "DOG?"

He pointed behind her. "Please turn around."

Isis turned and gasped. Gone were the huge horrible mountains with their hideous faces. Now in their place stood a monstrous dog, its metal and plastic body studded with television screens. Brobdingnagian pipes blew steam from its sides. It had immense radio antennae for hair. It was a mountain of machinery the size of a crush of skyscrapers.

Isis's confusion doubled—a three-story-high composite screen in DOG's left shoulder was playing video images of herself, John, and her brother Rachmiel as they'd all looked twenty years ago.

Fingers stepped forward to stand beside Isis. "This is DOG the upgraded deity. Treat it with great respect."

Isis nodded numbly.

Static electricity crackling between its metal whiskers, DOG turned its massive head to regard them both. Its eyes were rounded rectangles of flickering static with black TV dots at their focus.

"Hello and welcome, Isis Lynch," DOG rumbled like thunder, great delight evident in its voice. "How very nice of you to come visiting here. I've been dying to meet you for the longest time ever."

The End.

ABOUT THE AUTHOR

Wol-vriey is Nigerian, and quite tall.

He currently resides in a state of uneasy stalemate with his threatening-to-thin-beyond-redemption hair, and believes there actually are things that go bump in the night.

Wol-vriey recycles the ridiculous into reasonable reality for the reader.

His WEIRRRD philosophy?

WEIRRRD = Warp/Write Everything into Realistic Ridiculous Readable Distorted Dream Dimension Descriptions.

Wol-vriey blogs at:

http://oddityfarm.wordpress.com

WOL-VRIEY
BIZARRO AND TRANSGRESSIVE FICTION

BOSTON POSH (BUD MALONE #1)

In 2028 AD, the USA is a nation ravaged by hungry dragons and dinosaurs. In Boston, Massachusetts, private eye Bud Malone is hired to rescue a kidnapped heiress. But nothing is as it seems.

Malone works to unravel a tangled web involving Boston Chinatown, a 200-year-old woman with a 9-year-old body, white robots, a human-liver-eating psychopath, a golem, a porcelain dragon, and a snake goddess with a crush on him. There's also a woman obsessed with chicken sex. Then Malone meets Posh Lane, a gorgeous call girl who's desperate to quit her pimp.

Romantic sparks ignite between Posh and Malone, but Posh's past suddenly catches up with her in a BIG way. To save Posh, Malone agrees to run a quest for Earth's new rulers, the Forks. But, Malone has no idea that agreeing to the Fork's odd request will send him on the weirdest trip he's ever been on in his life.

BOSTON CORPSE (BUD MALONE #2)

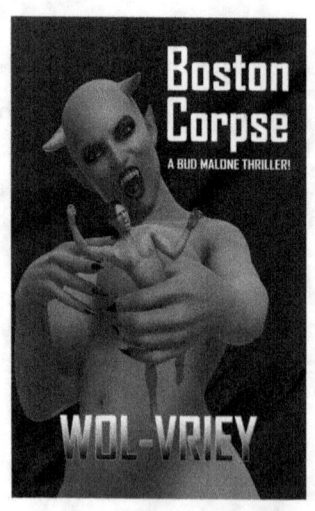

MAGIC CAN BE MURDER! - Drag queen Lucy Tang is back in Boston, and is hell-bent on settling her vindetta against casino owner Sookie Ling. And suddenly, Bud Malone, PI, has the case of his life to resolve.

When Boston's robot police force are baffled by a mind transfer case, they come to Malone for help. The one person who can likely help Malone out here is the witch Soledad Bathory. But Soledad seems to know a lot more than she's telling him. It's a case not made easier when Malone meets Soledad's beautiful cousin, Josephine 'Slave' Bailey. Slave has her own plans for Malone, most of which involve teaching him BDSM and making him her new Master.

Oh, and Rick Rogers owes Sookie Ling a whole lot of money, a gambling debt that's going to be literally Hell to pay!

BOSTON CORPSE - Not your average detective novel!

Burning Bulb
PUBLISHING

WOL-VRIEY
BIZARRO AND TRANSGRESSIVE FICTION

Dr. Orgasm

Wol-vriey

Communism = the political doctrine outlawing 'coming' (i.e. the female orgasm).

Courtney Taylor is young, intelligent, beautiful, and successful. She also has a boyfriend who loves her deeply.

The problem is, no matter what Courtney does, she can't climax during sex.

When Florence Rigid's communist forces destroy the city of Metaphor, Courtney and her friends Teresa, Highball, Miki, and Heather are cast into the midst of a quest to find the only person able to save the land of Innuendo—Dr. Carol Orgasm, wanted by the communists for developing the O-Pill, a wonder drug that grants women sexual ecstasy on demand.

The communists will do anything to get their hands on the O-Pill and prevent its reaching the millions of Innuendo's women.

But Courtney desperately wants that pill too. And so it's now a race between Courtney and the communists to find Dr. Orgasm first.

And Courtney has no choice but to win this race.

She must win it: For her own orgasm . . . and for the freedom of female sexuality everywhere.

Burning Bulb
PUBLISHING

WOL-VRIEY
BIZARRO AND TRANSGRESSIVE FICTION

VAGINA MUNDI

Rachel Risk is a professional thief with super-strong hair that can stretch like tentacles to manipulate objects. Ashley Status has both a digitally augmented brain, and 'muscle-purses' in her arms and legs in which she stores inflatable objects—cars, guns, rocket launchers, etc.

When Raye is framed as the fall girl in a jewel robbery, the pair flee Chicago's vengeful robot gangsters and take refuge in the Hotel Bizarre, where the gorgeous 'vagina singer,' Femina, is performing for a week.

But the Hotel Bizarre is even stranger than its name suggests, and very soon Raye and Ash are involved in an deadly adventure, a struggle for survival the likes of which they'd never imagined possible—with loads of deviant sex, drugs, music, and violence at every turn. And just what is the old woman in the skin desert really doing with all those cats glued to her walls?

VAGINA MUNDI—a Bizarro Hymn in praise of WOMAN!

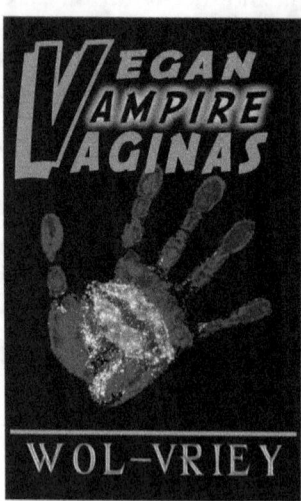

VEGAN VAMPIRE VAGINAS

The biggest bank heist in US history. And Tom Palmer can't remember pulling it off. And no, this isn't your standard case of amnesia. After a one-night-stand gone horribly wrong, Boston salesman Tom Palmer wakes up with a vagina implanted in his left hand. Then his day gets worse.

Tom is transported across space-time to a nightmare version of Boston, one where the Bizarro virus has transformed half the population into cannibals. Worst of all, Tom discovers that in this new Boston, he's the infamous gangster Pussypalm, wanted for robbing the Federal Reserve Bank of Boston a year ago. He also learns that the vagina in his hand is prophetic, i.e. it talks . . . after sex.

With 130 people left dead during his bank heist and six billion dollars missing, Tom knows he's living on borrowed time. It is in his best interests not to remember anything. Because once he does . . .

Burning Bulb
PUBLISHING

WOL-VRIEY
BIZARRO AND TRANSGRESSIVE FICTION

VEGAN ZOMBIE APOCALYPSE

In the post-apocalypse worlderness, zombies rule the earth. They're allergic to meat, and brains literally make them explode. Zombies now eat blood potatoes, parasitic tubers grown in the flesh of humancows corralled in maximum security farms. Two fugitives meet in the ancient ruins of Texas. The first is Soil 15-f, a womancow who's escaped her farm a week before she's due to be killed and her blood potato crop harvested. The second fugitive is Able Kane, former head necros food technician, now sentenced to death for heresy. But Soil is no ordinary humancow.

Unknown to herself, she's the vegan zombie agricultural revolution, and the zombies desperately want her back. And the necros equally desperately want Able Kane dead. He's fled with a forbidden discovery which will reshape the world for the worse if used. And Able is just hardheaded/misguided enough to use it.

MELANIE NEMESIS CATCHPOLE

In Springfield, Massachusetts, Melanie Catchpole is hired to fetch back a magic teddy bear worth millions of dollars from a warehouse across town. Problem is, the warehouse is down in Springfield's O-Zone-that totally weird sector of the city where Bizarro fell to Earth. The 'O' is a fairytale land, a place where dreams and nightmares literally live and breathe.

Worse still, the gingers—mutant cannibals—prowl the O. The gingers have already eaten everyone else Melanie's employers sent to get back the magic teddy bear.

Accompanied by the handsome but ruthless Doug Fisher (who she finds sexy but doesn't dare entrust her heart to), Melanie enters the O-Zone. Melanie and Doug are instantly caught up in an adventure they'd never have believed credible even if written as fiction . . . and Melanie's used to experiencing the very weird as the norm.

And now, additionally, there's a mystery to unravel: What does the dark, freezing-cold being called The Fixer want with Mary, the barkeep's daughter?

Burning Bulb
PUBLISHING

WOL-VRIEY
BIZARRO AND TRANSGRESSIVE FICTION

BIG TROUBLE IN LITTLE ASS

From Bizarro master storyteller Wol-vriey comes a truly weir western tale that will leave you awe-struck and on the edge of your seat...

In the town named Little Ass, tight-assed prostitute Rosa ove hears a gunslinger's plans to assassinate rancher Edison Ben nett. Once the badass Bennett learns of the plot, he ensure there'll be hell to pay for any attempt on his life!

Yes, it's going to take all of gunslinger Jude's shooting prowess his eclectic collection of strange firearms, a trusty horse that re quires an owners' manual, and the help of the lovely and in vigorating Nell (who's EXTREMELY odd when the going ge weird), to survive the Bizarro hell that Edison Bennett unleash es in order to hold onto the land that he'd stolen from Madan Zizi.

BIZARRO 101 (A BASIC PRIMER)

Welcome to the strange place:

A collection of 37 flash fiction stories designed to introduce one to the Bizarro/New Weird Genre.

Weird, dreamy, nightmarish, absurd, sad, surreal, humorous . . . th collection of tales is all this and more.

***

"This primer is the very essence of any and all styles and types of Bizar writing. Wol-vriey collects, distills, and bottles up these 37 tiny stories for yo sensory enjoyment. This is an absolute must-read for anyone new to the genr because it demonstrates the scope of what Bizarro is, and what it can be."
—Teresa Pollack, Bizarro commentator and blogge

Burning Bulb
PUBLISHING

OTHER GREAT TITLES FROM

Burning Bulb
PUBLISHING

WWW.BURNINGBULBPUBLISHING.COM

BELLY TIMBER

From the writers of Darkened Hills, Detour to Armageddon and Night of the Living Dead comes a novel unlike any other...

In the 1800's, ordinary people learned the secret of the Kala and undertook extraordinary measures to rid the earth of this evil. This is their story.

For John McCormick, life on the Indiana frontier held nothing but promise. His settlement along the White River would soon become the crossroads of America. Friends and family from back in Ohio and other points east were all making plans to see what all the fuss was about in the newly-formed city of Indianapolis. Yes, things were good. John had his general store and his friend George Pogue had his blacksmith business. Claims were being staked and relations with the native Indians were amicable. The town was growing and nothing could be better... or so he thought.

In Ohio, an evil was brewing. The Lecky Family, a group of ruthless Mongolian nomads, had made their way to America and were practicing their cannibalistic religion of Kala with reckless abandon. No one was safe, not even John McCormick's family.

Burning Bulb
PUBLISHING

NOVELIZATION BY
SOLON TSANGARAS & GARY LEE VINCENT

BOB GRAY'S ATTACK OF THE MELONHEADS

"Melonheads is what I love. Give me a body count and gore, but don't forget the laughs. Anytime that I can be reminded of what makes Horror great it is a good thing. Melonheads does that and is something we should all support. Consider it highly recommended."
—Screamsine.us

Fifty years ago, a doctor sought to cure a terrible disease. Hidden from the world, Doctor Malcolm Crowe toiled in the dead of night while the world was sleeping, creating a new breed of mutant—all in the name of science.

Yes, he thought he could cure the sick children. But he was wrong.

Today, the results of his cruel and unconventional experiments have manifested into an evil never before seen.

Now, in Kirtland, Ohio, the town's unsuspecting residents are about to encounter the full onslaught of this unimaginable terror.

Can something be done before it's too late?

Burning Bulb
PUBLISHING

EVERYTHING HERE IS A NIGHTMARE
Collected Works Vol 1.

"Pyles makes it look easy. His characters come instantly alive with the cocksure verve and swagger of rock stars."
> *- Daniel Knauf, creator of HBO's "Carnivale,"*
> *Executive Producer/Writer, ABC's "The Blacklist."*

The critically acclaimed author of Demons, Dolls and Milkshakes returns with fifteen tales of horror and suspense with Everything Here is a Nightmare.

From zombies in the old west, to a young boy tempted by the Devil. From vampires with romantic longing, to an abandoned lighthouse haunted by vengeful spirits. From a serial killer getting unholy justice, to a haunted English race car, Nelson W Pyles invites you to explore a landscape of fear, suspense and horror.

Take his hand and hold on tight. Remember that whatever you find here, whatever you see, no matter what you might think it could be... know this: Everything Here is a Nightmare.

Burning Bulb
PUBLISHING

ANTHOLOGIES
BIZARRO AND TRANSGRESSIVE FICTION

THE BIG BOOK OF BIZARRO SPECIAL KINDLE EDITIONS

OTHER AWESOME COLLECTIONS

 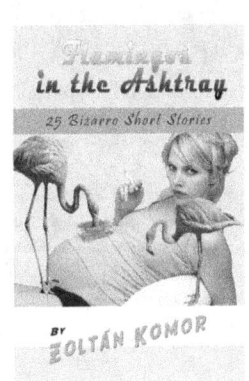 

Burning Bulb
PUBLISHING

ANTHOLOGIES
BIZARRO AND TRANSGRESSIVE FICTION

THE BIG BOOK OF BIZARRO

The Big Book of Bizarro brings together the peculiar prose of an international cast of the most grotesquely-gonzo, genre-grinding modern writers who ever put pen to paper (or mouse to pad), including:

NIGHT OF THE LIVING DEAD horror writers John Russo & George Kosana; HUSTLER MAGAZINE erotica contributors Eva Hore, Andrée Lachapelle, & J. Troy Seate and established Bizarro genre authors D. Harlan Wilson, William Pauley III, Wol-vriey, Laird Long, Richard Godwin and so many more!

From Alien abductions to Zombie sex, The Big Book of Bizarro contains OVER FIFTY STORIES of the most outrélandish transgressive fiction that you'll ever lay your capricious and curious hands upon!

WESTWARD HOES

Nine outlaw writers rode into town from obscurity to pen nine tantalizing tales of horror and fantasy, and leaving once they branded their own personal marks on the weird western genre and became living legends of the American Frontier experience.

Like drunken Indian scouts, the writers fervidly tracked down and captured the Western genre, tore off its fashionable veneer and ravished its exposed essence.

So belly up to the bar with your favorite soiled dove and enjoy perusing these thrilling tales of Old West debauchery, danger and desire; compiled by the publisher of The Big Book of Bizarro and featuring the bizarro novella *Big Trouble in Little Ass* by Wol-vriey.

Burning Bulb
PUBLISHING

DAVID J. FAIRHEAD

THE FALL

Hopelessness... How do you protect your loved ones when Hell itself opens its insidious mouth?

Horror... Nightmarish Creatures invade your world and there is nowhere to hide.

Blood... How long can you hold out before they come for you?

Pain... Where do you run to avoid being eaten alive by monsters with a voracious appetite for your flesh?

Screams... While you selfishly run for your own life.

Questions... Who is to blame? Where did they come from? How many people survived...and how does the human race find the means to fight back?

THE FALL OF TOMORROW is man's last tale of desperation told by those that are striving to salvage some hope against a ravenous bastion of evil beasts bent on ruling our world.

DWELLING IN THE DARK

From David J. Fairhead, author of the FALL OF TOMORROW, comes DWELLING IN THE DARK- A soulful anthology of creeping terror to keep you up in the small hours with horror set in the past, present and future. Overlapping bits of puzzle fitting each other, before and after The Fall of Tomorrow.

A place where three children facing a monstrous foe can only pray that their bloody summer would just come to an end. Go back to the 1960's- THE COMMUNE where overindulging hippies use a mage's diary to control the end of the world, only to see first-hand that their drug induced visions have horrific ramifications. Where a young boy's visit to a haunted house becomes a lesson in RESIDUAL morality. The story, DEEPER- plunges two brothers into a sinkhole only to find they were being hunted by an insidious creature from its depths. Visit the old west as hero Dekker Collins battles evil gunslingers in DEMONEYE.

And so much more...!

Burning Bulb
PUBLISHING

WWW.FAIRLYDARKPRODUCTIONS.COM

GARY LEE VINCENT'S
DARKENED
THE WEST VIRGINIA VAMPIRE SERIES

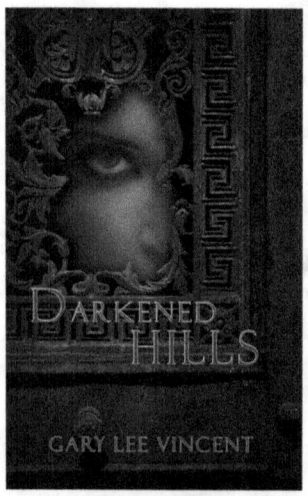

DARKENED HILLS

When evil descends on a small West Virginia town, who will survive?

Jonathan did not start out his life to become a rambler, it justworked out that way. William was a troubled youth with something to hide. Both were from Melas, a small town tucked away in the West Virginia hills... a town where disappearances are happening more and more frequently.

After the suicide of a wanted serial killer, the townsfolk thought the nightmare was over. But when a centuries-old vampire is discovered they find out the hard way it's just getting started. Dark secrets can only stay hidden for so long and when the devil comes to collect, there will be hell to pay. Can Jonathan and William find a way to stop the vampire before it's too late? Find out in *Darkened Hills!*

DARKENED HOLLOWS

In the heart-stopping sequel to the award-winning *Darkened Hills*, Jonathan and William must return to West Virginia to face possible criminal charges stemming from their last visit to the damned town of Melas, where both had narrowly escaped the clutches of a vampire seethe.

And as livestock start mysteriously getting murdered with all of their blood drained, worried farmers are searching for answers - leaving the local Sheriff and his deputy racing against time to learn the cause before a more violent crime is committed.

Burning Bulb
PUBLISHING

WWW.DARKENEDHILLS.COM

GARY LEE VINCENT'S
DARKENED
THE WEST VIRGINIA VAMPIRE SERIES

DARKENED WATERS

When the world goes to hell, the chosen must arise!

As Talman Cane orchestrates a flood of epic proportions in this third installment of the *Darkened* series the towns of Melas and Tarklin are caught completely off guard by the deluge. Hell-bent on finishing what they started, the evil brothers return to the lunatic asylum to take care of the witnesses and add to the ever-growing army of the undead.

Aided by Lucifer himself and the insane vampire demon Legion, the stage is set to channel all of the forces of hell to come forth. In an all-out race to survive, Jonathan, William, and Amanda soon discover they are up against impossible odds as Lucifer opens the Gateway to Hell, ushering in the zombie apocalypse and the End Times.

Find out who will survive this cosmic battle of the ages in *Darkened Waters*!

DARKENED SOULS

Melas and the Madison House are about to be rebuilt.
True evil is about to be reborne!

Young ex-priest and vampire-killer William is drawn back to the West Virginian town that almost killed him, where his vampire arch-enemy Victor Rothenstein still stalks the earth.

The town of Melas lies destroyed after the battle of the End of Days. But why is wealthy Jackie Nixon so eager to rebuild it using the bone dust of murdered souls?

Terrible evil has visited before, but the Gateway to Hell is about to be reopened in a horrific climax. And this time – it's personal.

WWW.DARKENEDHILLS.COM

Burning Bulb
PUBLISHING

WEST VIRGINIA-THEMED HUMORROROTICA

BY RICH BOTTLES JR.

HELLHOLE WEST VIRGINIA

From the heights of Mothman's perch high atop the Silver Bridge in Point Pleasant to the depths of Hellhole Cavern in Pendleton County, evil lurks within the shadows as the sun sets upon the haunted hills and hollows of West Virginia.

Bizarro author Rich Bottles Jr. blows the coffin lid off horror genre clichés with this tour de force cast of Eco-friendly vampires, beach-yearning zombies and sex-starved she-devils.

LUMBERJACKED

If you are easily offended or do not possess a truly depraved sense of humor, this story may not be the light summer reading fare you desire. As for the four feisty female freshmen stranded on top of West Virginia's third highest mountain, they have no choice but to experience the sick, twisted debauchery and perverted mayhem described deep inside the tight unbroken bindings of this horrific missive.

Lumberjacked takes the reader to a nightmarish world where character development and aesthetic integrity are prematurely cut short by the swinging axes of maniacal lumberjacks, who are hell bent on death and destruction in the remote forests of Appalachia. And at the climax, when paranoia crosses over to the paranormal, Lumberjacked makes Deliverance look like a family raft trip down the Lower Gauley.

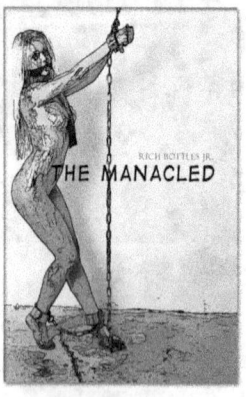

THE MANACLED

What happens when twin brothers lease out the former West Virginia State Penitentiary with the false purpose of filming a documentary on supernatural phenomena, but their true intention is to make a pornographic movie?

Chaos ensues as the disturbed spirits of murdered convicts, along with the reanimated dead from the neighboring Indian Burial Mound, take their vengeance on the unwary and undressed trespassers.

Zombies, ghosts, mobsters and porn collide in this bizarro tale from horror author Rich Bottles Jr.

Burning Bulb
PUBLISHING

ZAKARY MCGAHA
BIZARRO AND TRANSGRESSIVE FICTION

SEA OF MEDIUM-TO-HIGH PITCHED NOISES

The zombie apocalypse is changing; the world is coming to an odd demise; and a serial killer tries to change his ways and redeem himself before it all goes away. Now, Crabby has entered the world he left behind; the world of the undead. And things are changing. Everything will come to an end. In this new wave of the apocalypse, everything changes every five minutes. And death would be an absolute luxury. Psychological torment meets physical bloodletting in Sea of Medium-to-High Pitched Noises.

PARK MASTERS

Bad breakups, Bigfoot costumes, ghost bears, and more. Park Masters is a wacky, intelligent, quirky comedy about the power relationships have on people, good or bad. Also, it's just plain fun!

Burning Bulb
PUBLISHING

RISE OF THE DEAD
AN EARTH-SHATTERING ANTHOLOGY OF ZOMBIE TERROR

Featuring Stories By:
John A. Russo   Tyson Blue   E.L. Stice   Nelson W. Pyles
Andy Rausch   Stephen Spignesi   R.D. Riley   Zakary McGaha
David J. Fairhead   Gary Lee Vincent   David C. Hayes   Rachel Montgomery
Paul Victor Wargelin   David F. Walker   William Vitka
Rich Bottles Jr.   Douglas Brode

RISE OF THE DEAD - a collection of seventeen tales of unspeakable zombie terror. Featuring a foreword and short story by John A. Russo!

www.TheJohnRusso.com

Burning Bulb
PUBLISHING

THE MOST FRIGHTENING MOVIE EVER MADE IS NOW A NOVEL!

night OF THE LIVING DEAD

JOHN A. RUSSO

NIGHT OF THE LIVING DEAD

Why does Night of the Living Dead hit with such chilling impact?

Is it because everyday people in a commonplace house are suddenly the victims of a monstrous invasion? Or is it because the ghouls who surround the house with grasping claws were once ordinary people, too?

Decide for yourself as you read, and the horror grips you.

All the cannibalism, suspense and frenzy of the smash-hit move are here in the novel.

www.TheJohnRusso.com

Burning Bulb
PUBLISHING

THE BOOBY HATCH

With NIGHT OF THE LIVING DEAD, John Russo helped blaze a path in the horror genre that has never been equalled. In this hillarious erotic novel, he blazes a path through the wild, zany Sex Revolution of the 1970s.

Sweet, innocent Cherry Jankowski works for Joyful Novelties, where she tests sex toys ranging from the ridiculous to the sublime. But she can't find love or peace of mind and her efforts are hampered by a Peeping Tom, an exhibitionist, a cross-dressing boyfriend, a quack psychiatrist, and even her own product-testing partner, Marcello Fettucini, who can't get it up anymore and is scared of losing his job!

www.TheJohnRusso.com

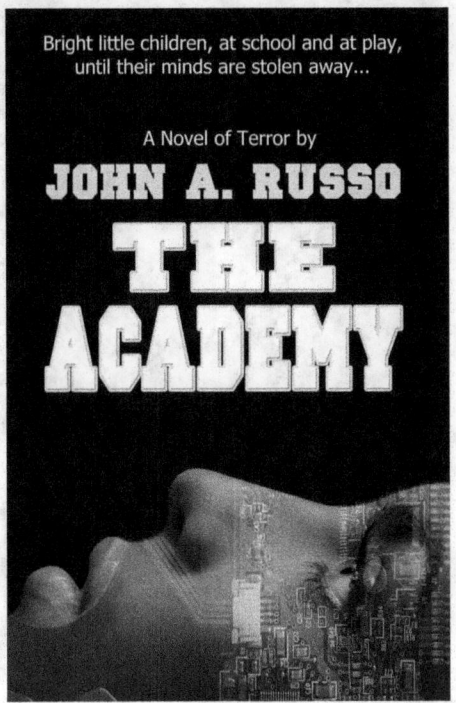

Bright little children, at school and at play,
until their minds are stolen away...

A Novel of Terror by

JOHN A. RUSSO

THE ACADEMY

THE ACADEMY

The Academy. It's every parent's dream, turning their little darlings into geniuses, superachievers, perfect little children.

And if there's a problem, the Academy fixes that too. It's a simple operation. Just a little device. Then a teeny pink scar on a tender little skull . . .

One boy knows the secret. Now he wants his mind back. But it's much, much too late. Too late for anything but the ugly feelings. The bad feelings. The messy sexy feelings. The knife-cold hatred, the murderous rage, for total, screaming, blood-drenching revenge . . .

www.TheJohnRusso.com

Burning Bulb
PUBLISHING

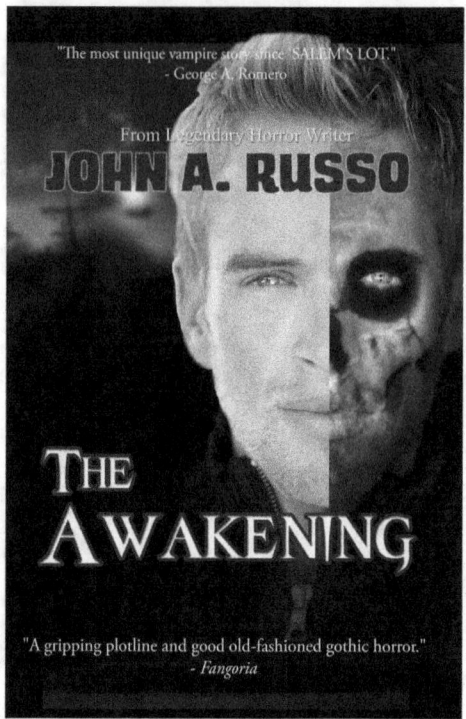

THE AWAKENING

For two hundred years, he has rested. Now he rises. Now he will be satisfied. Nothing can stop him. No one can resist him.

Benjamin Latham is young and handsome, his eighteenth-century mind wakened to a bizarre twentieth-century world. And there is the need deep within . . . an animal need, frightening, murderous, unholy . . . a vital need that must be fed.

And with his need comes a power over men and women to do his bidding, to quiet his dark craving . . .

Until the murders begin. And the inquiries. All suggesting the same hideous truth.

Now Benjamin must find a sanctuary: a lover, a partner, a friend. Someone who can share his darkness. Someone he can lead to . . . The Awakening.

www.TheJohnRusso.com

Burning Bulb
PUBLISHING

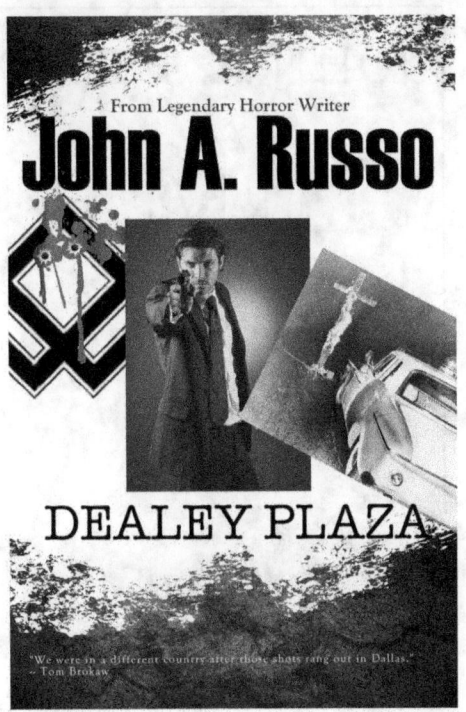

DEALEY PLAZA

From legendary horror and suspense writer JOHN RUSSO comes a harrowing tale where no one is safe!

Dealey Plaza is one of the most notorious places in America, and when youthful conspiracy buffs go there in 1964 to stage their own reenactment of the Kennedy Assassination, four of them are brutally murdered ~ the first victims of a hate-filled legacy that continues for four more decades.

The survivors of that long-ago Dallas trip, each of them now icons of the American way of life, are about to be honored ~ or killed.

Who will live and who will die? Will it be country-western star Lori McCoy? Her loving husband? Her scheming ex-husband? Or the case-hardened FBI agent and longtime friend who risks his life trying to protect them?

www.DealeyPlazaBook.com

Burning Bulb
PUBLISHING

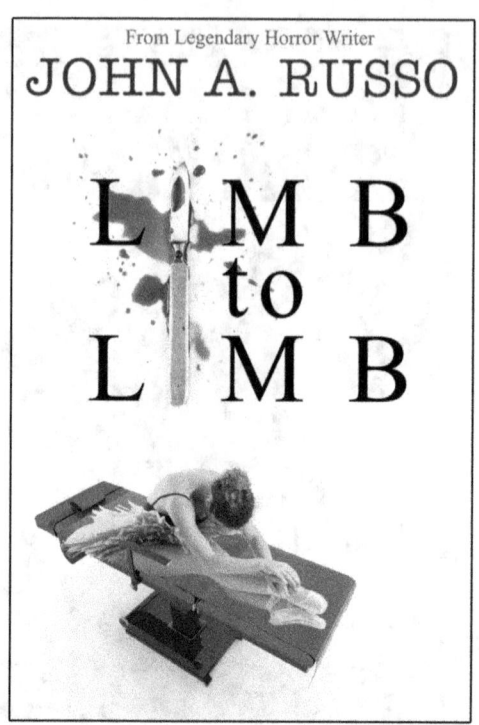

From Legendary Horror Writer

JOHN A. RUSSO

LIMB to LIMB

LIMB TO LIMB

SUCH A PRETTY GIRL . . .
Tiffany Blake was a beautiful long-limbed dancer with a glorious future and the backing of a rich benefactor. Then a monstrous accident severed her leg at the hip.

SUCH A COLD, CRUEL KNIFE . . .
And now her fellow dancers are disappearing without a trace. One by one they fall victim to a dark and deadly pattern of evil – caught by the bloody, brutal logic that would have them pay with their lovely bodies for the cruel fate of another . . .victims of the sadistic madman whose flashing knife will make them writhe a gruesome new dance.

www.TheJohnRusso.com

Burning Bulb
PUBLISHING

"A sense of infectious fun, straight from the author's pen."
-- Nightmare Library

From Legendary Horror Writer
JOHN A. RUSSO

LIVING THINGS

"Russo carries his talent for the horrific neatly over into the novel form."
West Coast Review of Books

LIVING THINGS

Beneath the shimmering Miami sun sprawls one of the Mafia's biggest empires, a glittering world of lavish beachfront mansions, neon-painted nightclubs, beautiful women, expensive cars—and absolute control over the state's billion-dollar drug trade. But, one by one, its ganglords and henchmen are falling prey to a new rival. His powers are fueled by monstrous ancient rituals; his hellish undead legions slaughter mobsters and innocent citizens alike, his unholylust for power is virtually unstoppable.

Now a burned-out ex-detective and a brilliant anthropologist must enter a gruesome, nightmare world to fight this master of malevolence and illusion. Their time is short, their weapons few, and they face an ultimate, terrifying choice - annihilation or the loss of their souls to the eternal torment of those who never die. . .

www.TheJohnRusso.com

Burning Bulb
PUBLISHING

ELVIS PRESLEY, CIA ASSASSIN BY ANDY RAUSCH

"I can guarantee you. Read this book and you'll never look at Elvis the same way again!"
~ Douglas Brode, author of ELVIS CINEMA AND POPULAR CULTURE

SOON TO BE A MAJOR MOTION PICTURE

In 1970, singer Elvis Presley secretly met with President Richard Nixon. This new comedic novel imagines that Presley became a Central Intelligence Agency operative, eventually moving up through the ranks to become a skilled assassin.

Presented in an oral history fashion, the book tells us about Presley's secret transformation by the people who knew him best.

Did he fake his death in 1977? Was Presley involved with the Watergate scandal? The Iran hostage crisis? Communicating with aliens?

Read this book to find out the answers to these and many more questions.

Burning Bulb
PUBLISHING

MAD WORLD BY ANDY RAUSCH

"*Mad World* is dark, twisted, no-holds-barred fun."
—Jason Starr, author of *Bust*, *Slide*, and *The Max*

EVERYONE'S PLAYING AN ANGLE IN THE CITY OF ANGELS

Mad World tells the stories of a black hitman who doubles as a university professor, a Catholic priest who longs to be a gangster, a would-be author from Kansas, a gay phone sex operator who claims he's straight, a group of rich twentysomethings playing a deadly game of life and death, a vicious Mafia boss, and a sleazy Hollywood movie director. As each of their stories intersect, the body count piles up and the action comes nonstop in this tense, white-knuckle thriller by first-time author Andy Rausch.

"A wild ride. If you like it gangster, *Mad World* delivers."
—Daniel Birch, author of *Get Some*

Burning Bulb
PUBLISHING

BLOODLETTING: A TALE OF REVENGE BY ANDY RAUSCH

"Relentless... Addictive... The kind of nightmare you don't want to wake up from."
—Heywood Gould, screenwriter of *Rolling Thunder*

He was just an average Joe. But when he finds his family held at gunpoint by merciless thugs, he's told he must murder a Mafia chieftain if he ever wishes to see his loved ones again.

Against all odds, Joe keeps his end of the bargain, but the criminals don't. Now at his wits end, Joe is pushed beyond his breaking point and forced to exact bloody revenge against those who've done him and his family wrong in this powerful and violent novella by author Andy Rausch (*Mad World*).

"Andy Rausch has a tight noir style that combines gritty, realistic drama with a cinematic flair that makes for a powerful, compelling (somewhat Stephen Kingesque), authentically visual reading experience."
—Stephen Spignesi, author of *Dialogues*

Burning Bulb
PUBLISHING

THE TAILSMAN

From the creators of *The Big Book of Bizarro* and *Westward Hoes* comes a new comic unlike anything you have ever seen!

He's hot on the trail, looking for some *tail*...

Sly Franko was a man of the West, a forger of the wild frontier. Like the Country Western song that would be written years after he died, the words, "Faster horses, younger women, and more money," seemed to be the anthem of this horn dog cowboy.

Franko would ride into town on a blazing saddle, find the closest saloon to wet the whistle, belly up to a good card game, and find him a hot-loving hussy to get his cowpoke on with.

However, Sly might have met his match when a visit to bathroom leads to terror and death. Can Sly and his poker buddies solve the mystery before more of the townsfolk are murdered? Find out in this exciting premier issue of *The Tailsman*!

WWW.BURNINGBULBCOMICS.COM

THE HAGS OF BLACK COUNTY

by Michelle Bowser

Ruled by a committee of Hags, and fueled by toothless rivalries, Black County lurks just far enough out of the way to be completely unnoticed by the rest of civilization. Its inhabitants have been mentally warped for generations and the land itself seems to have the power to drive anyone unlucky enough to visit into ridiculous hillbilly madness. When a construction Company needs to bury a pipeline through its ludicrous hills and valleys, a twisted charm goes to work and every aspect of already bizarre Black County life takes a gory turn for the hysterical. Take a preposterous trip along with its citizens, both native and new, through escapades such as the Hag parade, the grand opening of Madame Skunk's House of Ill Repute, the demolition derby riot and the rabid, zombie clown apocalypse.

THE ABANDONED SOUL

by Daniel Sellers

After spending most of his 20s in a drug and alcohol fueled daze, a young man finally hits rock bottom. Having used up his friends and their good graces, he ends up squatting in an abandoned house. Forcibly sobering he begins to realize that he is not alone in this abandoned house. Left with one last friend and a mountain of regrets, he must decide if this presence is a guilty conscience, or a malicious hunter.

WE WISH YOU A HAPPY KILLDAY

by Jason Heroux

"We Wish You a Happy Killday" is the story of an international b eloved holiday called "Killday" where one day a year everyone over the age of fifteen is permitted to register for a license allowing them to kill one other person. But this year Chad Ovenstock doesn't feel like killing anyone. His friends and family urge him to participate in the festivities, but he can't seem to get into the holiday spirit. On the day before Killday Chad comes in contact with Ambrose, an old friend who suffered a nervous breakdown and is now part of The One Ant Army, a mysterious cult dedicated to making the future disappear. When the holiday finally arrives Chad refuses to participate and tries to survive on his own, surrounded by constant gunfire, countless corpses, and the nagging suspicion that Ambrose may have secretly brainwashed him into becoming a member of The One Ant Army cult.

Burning Bulb
PUBLISHING

www.ingramcontent.com/pod-product-compliance
Lightning Source LLC
Chambersburg PA
CBHW061144170626
46809CB00003B/978